PALE WINGS
PROTECTING

Visit us at www.boldstrokesbooks.com

By the Author

Truth Behind The Mask

Playing Passion's Game

Dark Wings Descending

Pale Wings Protecting

PALE WINGS
PROTECTING

by

Lesley Davis

2013

PALE WINGS PROTECTING

ISBN 10: 1-60282-964-0
ISBN 13: 978-1-60282-964-0

This Trade Paperback Original Is Published By
Bold Strokes Books, Inc.
P.O. Box 249
Valley Falls, NY 12185

First Edition: October 2013

Credits
Editor: Cindy Cresap
Production Design: Susan Ramundo
Cover Design By Sheri (graphicartist2020@hotmail.com)

Acknowledgments

A huge thank you as always to Radclyffe for letting my imagination run wild and free at Bold Strokes. Your encouragement of my work is greatly appreciated.

For Cindy Cresap for her patience, still! I am really chuffed that with this fourth book I was able to hit you with a British-ism you didn't know! (It still got edited out though!) Thank you for all the hard work you do on every page I write.

To the brilliant Bold Strokes staff and writers who make me proud and honored to be part of such a fantastic team.

For Sheri, thank you for a truly beautiful piece of art that graces this book's cover. I'm in awe of your talent.

Thank you, Wayne Beckett, for your unceasing championing of me personally and of my work.

To Jane Morrison and Jacky Morrison Hart, your friendships will always mean the world to me.

For Pam Goodwin, a fellow gamer who understands the necessity to play but still encourages me to write first so she can read more! Just one more level then!

And with love always to Cindy Pfannenstiel, for your endless support in everything. xx

CHAPTER ONE

S pecial Agent Kent? Do you have a moment, please? I have something I need to run by you."

Blythe Kent looked up at her boss, Supervisory Special Agent Nathan Lake, who stood by the side of her desk. He looked so serious and somber that she felt a flash of unease. She sprang to her feet.

"Of course, sir." She followed him to his office, fielding curious looks from her colleagues and shrugging off their concerned faces. Instructed to close the door behind her, Blythe did so then stood at attention before Nathan's desk. She wracked her brain for what she could have possibly slipped up on without realizing it.

"Sit, please." Nathan waved her to a chair. "And don't look so worried; you've done nothing wrong. I just need to ask if you're willing to take part in an undercover assignment."

Blythe sat up straighter. "Undercover, sir?" She couldn't disguise the excitement in her voice.

He smiled slightly and held up a hand to forestall her eager questions. "You might want to hear me out first before you get your hopes up. It's not infiltrating a drug ring or anything that requires you to completely disappear off the radar. And I have specific reasons why I'm asking you to consider this assignment that you might take exception to."

Blythe settled in her seat. She tried not to get too apprehensive at the thought of being specifically singled out for an assignment. "Now I'm really intrigued."

"We have a detective flying in from Vermont tomorrow. She is looking to put together a team to investigate newborn baby kidnappings in Connecticut. Babies she believes are then being passed on to couples."

"They're stealing babies to order?"

"That's what Detective Chandler believes. She has proposed that we set up an undercover operation where two people go in posing as a couple looking to acquire a child."

"And you've picked me why?"

"You have the highest success rate of any agent in this building. Your profiling skills are excellent. You're a highly valued member of our team and would be perfect, in my opinion, for this assignment."

Blythe gave him a considering look. "Yet there's something you're not telling me."

"Firstly, the detective requires it to be a lesbian couple who pose for the adoption."

Blythe's eyes widened with surprise. "Wow. This has to be the first time my sexuality has actually counted for something here."

"You haven't been considered solely because of your sexuality. Even if you had a husband and three kids I'd still put you forward for the role. You're my most experienced agent. I want you to think this over, sleep on it tonight, and hear what she proposes tomorrow. If you think you can handle the assignment then we'll go ahead. This is Detective Chandler's investigation though. It's her baby, so to speak."

Lake's eyes drifted to look out his office window. "Between you and me, Blythe, you *are* the best woman for the job. Even if you weren't gay. For a start, I could hardly send Agent Reynolds on the job."

Blythe chuckled at the thought. "True, she's quite vocal in her lack of maternal instincts. She'd probably be happier handing them over to the kidnapper."

"Agent McBride has a family, and I really need someone who isn't going to mind taking maybe months away from their normal routine."

"*Months?*"

"You've got to establish a recognized presence in the area the detective believes these kidnappings are operating from. She's asked for our help in setting up a home for the couple and supplying new identities. Her department isn't equipped to do what we can do here, and that leads me to why she's come to us. The feds dealing with the

Connecticut FBI refused to let a detective from Vermont aide them. Even though the FBI there called her in especially."

"Was any reason given for the refusal?"

"Seems the new deputy assistant director doesn't play well with people who have *different* ideas from what he does."

"And just how different are Detective Chandler's ideas?"

"Her findings were dismissed because they didn't fit in with the profile and leads the officers working on the cases had worked up."

"So she's brought her findings to us instead?" Blythe gave Lake a skeptical look. "We're not part of these cases, sir. It doesn't make sense for her to try another agency to be heard when she's already been dismissed."

"She sought out *me*. I know her. I know her way of working and I know how damn good she is at finding lost kids."

"So she's come specifically to you to ask for help in going against another FBI team as well as the feds who don't want her assistance?" Blythe wasn't sure she liked the sound of that. "And you're seriously considering hearing her out? Sir, the DDU is still a relatively young division. We need the cooperation of other teams to run. Pitting us against our own FBI isn't going to do our reputation very good."

"Or *your* reputation if you are seen going against them," Lake said.

Blythe felt her skin prickle as the implication hit her. "I'm all for being flexible with the rules, sir. However, I try to follow the letter of the law because I want to do the best job I can *within* the law. I need to know I can count on the backup of my fellow lawmakers. Going against their decisions could leave me in a very precarious place in future cases."

Agent Lake nodded. "I know Detective Chandler well. I also know you. If she can prove to you that the direction the feds are leading the investigation is totally the wrong way then I think you'd want to be involved in finding the missing children."

"Well, of course I would, but..."

"Then just hear her out. If you don't think she has enough evidence to corroborate her theories then say so and the operation won't go ahead."

"You're hinging this on my decision?" Blythe balked at the idea.

"No, I'm justifying my choice in you as a part of this operation and in my total belief in her."

"What makes this detective so worthy of your trust that you'd go against the feds?"

"I worked with her father for years. And she found my brother," Lake stated softly. "When no one else could even say he was missing, she found him alive in a ditch miles away from home. I've seen her in action. If she says that the investigation into these missing children is being steered incorrectly, I'm more inclined to believe her than anyone else, no matter what their rank."

"That's serious praise, sir."

"And justified. I need you to listen to what she has to say, weigh your options, and consider the consequences."

"Find the children and possibly incur the wrath of the feds for doing so."

"We'll deal with that fallout if and when it happens. For now, the children are the main priority."

Blythe's head swam with the ramifications of what she was being asked to consider. "So should I agree with this proposal we move to Connecticut, play the happy couple, and then what?"

"Look to adopt a child. Detective Chandler has some leads as to where she believes the kidnappers are operating. She has hospitals and adoption agencies earmarked as possible targets. She'll explain all her findings in detail when she presents her case. She hopes that by masquerading as a couple who are desperate to have a child, it will bring out the kidnappers to make their move and they can be caught."

"Stealing babies is detestable. The birth of a child should be special. You don't use it as fodder to sell on the market to the most desperate bidder."

Agent Lake sat back in his chair and regarded her closely. "Do you think you could do this? Chandler is an exemplary detective. If she thinks she can stop these people then you can be sure she'll do her damnedest."

"So I get to play house in Connecticut if I agree. Well, at least it isn't too far away from New York." She looked at her hands conspicuously devoid of rings. "It's not like I have anything in my personal life that I need to put on hold. I have my job and my apartment. All I'll need to do is bring in my plants for Trace to look after and give her my keys so she can keep an eye on my place."

"You'll meet Chandler tomorrow then. I think you'll get along just fine."

"What's she like, sir?" Blythe was curious about the woman that Lake would risk their careers for.

"She's one of the good guys and more than a match for you."

Blythe smiled at his cryptic words. "I sincerely hope so, sir, because if I'm planning a family with this woman she'd better be worth it." She caught a hesitation in Lake's demeanor. "Is there something else?"

"No. It's just..." He shook his head. "I've known Detective Chandler for many years. She's outstanding in her field, but some people find her style of investigating...a little unorthodox. But she gets the job done with fantastic results. And don't think I haven't tried my hardest to get her on board here at the bureau. I've been trying to recruit her ever since she was solving her father's cases for him."

"She'd be an asset for the team," Blythe mused, now even more intrigued by the woman she was going to partner with, given Lake's obvious admiration.

"That's why I expect you to fully utilize her talents on this case. If anyone can find out who's behind these kidnappings, Daryl Chandler can."

❖

Detective Daryl Chandler thanked Agent Elliott for picking her up from the airport and driving her straight to the Deviant Data Unit's New York department. He merely nodded but still wouldn't hand over her luggage. Elliott was obviously determined not to let her out of his sight until he delivered her personally to the doors of the DDU. Daryl tried not to let amusement show at how he was struggling to balance both suitcases, but he'd seemed affronted when she'd reached for them herself. She decided not to bruise his agent ego any further. The flight had been pleasant, and Daryl had enjoyed the scenery as she'd been driven through the recognizable sights of downtown New York City. She was more than aware this wasn't a pleasure trip, for all the bright lights and tall buildings begging to be explored. She caught sight of a very impressive looking man heading her way. She recognized him and straightened her posture accordingly. Agent Elliott also snapped to attention.

"Thank you, Agent Elliott," Nathan Lake said, reaching for the suitcases and relieving him of his duty.

Daryl thanked him again and he gave her a small smile. "It was my pleasure, Detective. Good luck with your assignment."

Daryl shook Lake's hand and gave him a relieved grin. "SSA Lake, thank you for inviting me here."

"We're looking forward to going over your files and having you present your findings to us. Sounds like you've acquired a particularly nasty case."

"Child abduction is despicable," Daryl said. "But stealing newborn babies from their parents has to rank even lower."

"So how's your dad enjoying his retirement?"

"He loves every second he can spend out in the yard seeding and planting. He's taken to retirement better than I'd hoped, sir."

"Can't be easy after losing your mother," Lake said softly. "She was a good woman."

"Yes, she was, sir. She's still greatly missed. Thank you for the flowers you sent."

"I'm just sorry work kept me away from paying my respects to a remarkable lady."

Daryl followed after him into the main hub of the office. "Dad would be amazed by the force you have here."

"A bit different from what you're used to, Detective?"

"A lot more people for a start," Daryl said, swiftly scanning the room full of agents. "It's an amazing setup for your unit. And I was very grateful for the ride here. Some of the departments I've had to visit usually expect me to make my own way to their door."

"Common courtesy never hurts anyone."

"You do know that I can carry my own suitcases, right?" Daryl shifted her laptop bag on her shoulder more comfortably and wondered why it was men had to prove themselves.

"I know, but it's that common courtesy thing again rearing its ugly head." Lake led the way to his office. "I'll leave your bags here."

Daryl stared around the room in undisguised awe. "Nathan Lake, you did yourself proud."

Lake grinned at her. "Do you think your dad will ever forgive me for leaving his station and coming here for what he called a 'cushy job'?"

"I don't think Dad ever understands why someone would leave the street beat to join the FBI. He was supportive when I went for my detective badge, but I could see he just didn't get the appeal."

"He's old school. Times are changing, and technology is helping us find the bad guys. The word on the street doesn't always pay now."

Daryl nodded. "I agree." She ran her hand across the back of a highly padded chair. "So this is what you keep trying to tempt me away to?"

Lake guided her to the window. "Look at the view from up here. It's a huge area to police, and we're called out to anywhere in the country. The more hands we can gather on our side the better."

"My dad would kill you for corrupting his daughter if I defected to the Dark Side."

"He wouldn't kill *you* for being corrupted?"

"I'm his only child. I think you'd be top of his shit list and he'd just be disappointed in me for a while." She shrugged and gave Lake a slight smile. "He always comes around though."

"I still want you working here."

Daryl grinned at his earnest voice. She'd heard it so many times when Lake had called to see if she'd reconsider her detective status and try the FBI on for size. "I'm here now; let's see how it pans out."

CHAPTER TWO

From her seat in the conference room, Blythe could see through the large window out onto all the people at their desks. She turned her attention back to the file before her, flipping through the records of stolen children. Her innards twisted into knots at the thought of someone stealing a child from its parents. From the corner of her eye, she caught sight of Trace Wagner wheeling in to park her wheelchair beside her. Small and wire thin, Trace had been in the wheelchair as long as Blythe had known her. The loss of the use of her legs was the result of a car accident when she'd been a teenager. Blythe admired Trace's expertise with a computer and knew that Trace could run rings around anyone who was involved in tech.

"So are we just waiting on this detective's arrival and then the show can start?"

"Lake said she was coming in on the ten a.m. flight. She's being picked up by one of our agents and brought straight here." Blythe's attention went back to the file in her hand. "I think she's compiled one hell of a case here."

"While you've been looking over that file I've been checking into the woman who compiled it. From what I can glean from the cases she's been involved with, she's got an amazing success rate in locating lost kids."

"But?"

"But she's got a reputation of being a bit of a Spooky Mulder." Trace grimaced at Blythe's look. "I'm not kidding. The woman is classified as a little odd. We're not talking tarot cards or talking in tongues here, but she's renowned for pulling weird ass rabbits out of stalled cases hats."

"So she's good at investigating." Blythe wondered why she felt the need to stand up for someone she hadn't even met yet.

"It's more than that. She sees things others never even think to look for. She's either clairvoyant or has some other kind of crazy magic mojo working for her. I just thought you should be forewarned, *Scully.*"

"Thank you, I think." Blythe was beginning to wonder what the hell she was getting herself into with this investigation.

Trace straightened in her chair. "Oh my God. If *that* is the detective you've got to go play house with, then, honey," she drawled, "*Spooky* or not, you're going to be living the dream of every lesbian out there."

Blythe's head lifted to follow Trace's line of sight. Her eyes were drawn to the woman walking alongside Agent Lake.

"Well, would you look at that, *Stretch*? She's got to be even taller than you are."

"At least five feet eleven," Blythe guessed. Tall, broad shouldered, solidly built. Blythe's mind raced through all the details as if she were compiling a profile.

"Her hair is so blond it's almost white. Jesus, you two are going to complement each other so well. You with your dark hair and her with the blond. I bet with her skin tone she'll burn like a beacon when blushing…or aroused," Trace added slyly.

"It's work, Trace. We're not being set up on an interdepartmental date." Blythe was drawn to the woman's strong features. She was handsome but not overly masculine. A gentle smile curved her lips, and Blythe liked the way it lightened an otherwise serious face.

"Well, she out-butches me," Trace muttered.

"I'd say you have more tattoos," Blythe said. She studied the woman, taking in everything from her confident walk to the cut of her hair. The pale blond hair was pulled back from her face in a short ponytail.

"What are you thinking, Blythe?" Trace asked quietly.

Blythe tore her eyes away from the newcomer and glanced at Trace. "I'm thinking she's incredibly attractive and I really can't afford the distraction while we're working."

"But you've got to make nice with her. You're going to be playing the role of lovers. A little attraction wouldn't hurt to make the kissing go a little easier."

Blythe shivered at the delicious thought of kissing this woman. "Maybe I should just meet her first before I jump aboard."

"Perhaps you'll luck out and she has some goddamn awful accent that grates on your ears and sets your teeth on edge."

Blythe laughed with her.

"She is handsome though," Trace said. "I'm glad my Emma isn't here. She has a weakness for big, tall butch girls."

Blythe let out a shaky breath. *She's not the only one.*

Daryl had left her overcoat in Lake's office and was taking off her suit jacket as she followed him toward the conference room. *Damn suits make me feel like I'm going to a funeral.* She tugged at her shirt and hoped she still looked professional and presentable after her flight. Lake opened the door for her and she preceded him, heading to the top of the table to lay down her briefcase and begin rolling up her sleeves. She looked up to find two people already in the room blatantly staring at her. She flushed and saw the smaller one lean into the other to whisper something that sounded like *I told you.*

Her breath stilled somewhere in her chest when she caught the gaze of the other woman. She paused and stared back. *She is beautiful.* The woman had hair so black it shone with an unnatural blue, like the darkest night touched by the faint kiss of moonlight. It fell in wild curls that brushed at her shoulders. She was slender in build but curved in all the right places. Daryl tried not to be too obvious when her eyes lowered to the cleavage just glimpsed behind the confines of a severely tailored jacket and stark white blouse. Brown eyes the color of rich chocolate studied her with an unabashed intensity, and the smile that curved rich full lips made all thought of why Daryl was there slip from her mind. The stillness of the room was only broken when two other agents came walking in and closed the door behind them loudly.

"Okay, now we're all here. This is Detective Daryl Chandler from Vermont's PD. Daryl, these are Agents Tim Browning and Julian Caldow." Both gave Daryl firm handshakes.

Lake continued his introductions. "This is our technical analyst, Trace Wagner. Her team works to make sure we have all the information we need when we need it. She's also one of the brains behind the data units that our teams now employ."

Daryl smiled at her, recognizing another lesbian in the room. She cast only a cursory glance at Trace's wheelchair; she was far more intrigued by the woman seated in it.

"You're the one I sent all my data to," Daryl said.

Trace nodded, looking surprised that Daryl had remembered her. "I've set it all up for your presentation just like you requested."

"Thank you." Daryl wondered what policies at the DDU were being flaunted by all the tattoos Trace displayed on her bare arms. She decided she liked her; there was always room for a little rebelliousness in the world.

"And this is Special Agent Blythe Kent."

Daryl moved closer to shake Blythe's hand. The feel of her hand made Daryl's breath hitch in her chest. Blythe's hand was soft yet strong, her fingers long and tapered. Small calluses told of a woman who used a gun. Daryl liked the touch of the rough edges as they wrapped around her larger hand. She wondered if Blythe could feel the same worn areas on her own skin. She smiled at her. "Thank you for considering partnering with me on this assignment."

"It would be a fascinating case if it weren't so disturbing," Blythe said.

Daryl had to force herself to release Blythe's hand. She could still feel the lingering warmth when she closed her fingers to capture the touch inside her palm. She enjoyed Blythe's voice, rich in tone with just the hint of an accent that she couldn't quite place. It added a soft drawl to her words. Daryl knew her own clipped way of talking was considered harsh to some, but it gave her words an authoritative edge that she intended to use now to her advantage in the midst of the esteemed DDU. She cast Trace a look and held up a remote. At Trace's nod, Daryl switched on the screen to start her presentation. "Thank you all for agreeing to see me. Let me get straight to why I'm here. Two years ago, a young woman went to her local police department. She said her baby boy had been taken from her." Daryl moved to the head of the table but made sure everyone could see the screen. "Carol Malone was a single woman, struggling to make ends meet. The local PD couldn't find anything to go on, and the case went cold. Eventually, her case and the others I have here found their way to me, and I began looking into them. You'll no doubt come to hear that I have an affinity for cases involving children. I get requests to look into cases from anywhere and everywhere. New and cold cases."

Daryl continued on with barely a pause, not wanting to linger on those facts and invite unwanted questions. "I interviewed Carol, her family, and the folks where she lived. Her neighbors were firmly of the belief the father had come and taken the baby away. He had only been at the apartment a few times, but they'd all heard him shouting on one occasion that he'd take the child from her if she couldn't look after him right."

"Did anyone check up on him?" Browning asked.

"The police did initially and then I did. I found him living the white picket fenced dream with his wife and three kids and not being all that cooperative to talk while his wife was around. He didn't have the child, didn't want the child, and admitted he'd made a big deal of it with Carol to try, in his exact words, 'to get her the hell off his back.' He'd been trying to scare her into leaving him alone for child support payments. It worked. She stopped all contact with him for fear he'd take the child away like he threatened. Carol had lost her job just a few months into her pregnancy so life had started to get very hard. She was just a woman getting ready to raise a child with what limited resources she could muster on her own."

"Some guys don't deserve to procreate," Caldow said, scribbling something down on a pad.

Daryl brought up a picture of the little boy, barely a day old. "Knowing she was going to be a single parent, Carol had managed to get some help while she'd been at the hospital for her checkups. The maternity units run a support system for mothers to be, they call it Baby Aid. You get help for the first few months if you're struggling financially. It's a great scheme that really helps, and Carol thought it was the answer to her prayers. She got food tokens and money toward baby clothes and support from the ones who run the group. While she'd been there, one of the women had taken her under her wing. This Good Samaritan, one Mary Parks, snuck Carol extra tokens to help her out. After Carol gave birth, Mary was there again offering to baby-sit anytime to give her a break. Carol trusted her. She had no reason not to. Mary had asked if Carol had considered giving the child away. She'd asked numerous times before the child was born, but Carol just told her no, she wanted to keep the baby. The woman was kind; Carol never thought anything of it. She just figured she was playing devil's advocate, letting Carol know there were other options available."

Daryl brought up a picture of Carol's apartment and a picture of the baby's room. "This is where two-day-old Matthew Malone was snatched. Taken from his crib, from his bedroom, right next to the room his mother was sleeping in, and she never heard a sound."

"So maybe this Mary came right on inside and took him?" Blythe said. "You'd let a friend have a key to your place if they baby-sat your child."

"Carol gave me a description of Mary. She was medium height, blond hair, had dark tinted lenses in her glasses."

"Handy disguise," Lake said. "Did you check out all the staff at the hospital?"

Daryl nodded. "No one of that description worked there, and no one of that name was listed as a Baby Aid helper. I spent some time down there and was surprised by how many people wander the corridors of the maternity wing and no one pays any attention. If you look the part and act the part, you can blend in with all the bustle and no one would question your right to be there." Daryl brought up another picture. "Then something similar happened, just a few months after. Josie Jones, a single mother, was approached to see if she would consider giving her child up for adoption. Again, a Good Samaritan helped her settle in with the new baby and then, within a few days, the child was gone. Baby Heather Jones also disappeared from her own crib."

Daryl brought up a set of baby photos. "In total, there have been five kidnappings that I have been alerted to, spread out over the space of three years." She brought up the picture of each child taken. Daryl then switched to another set of photos. "There are two hospitals linked to the mothers giving birth there, two support stations, and the city has three legitimate adoption agencies. One of which has a nice record of adopting out to gay couples. The other two I still want to check into just in case there's another factor involved. The hospitals have to be checked out. I didn't have the manpower by myself, and the agencies won't divulge anything because of confidentiality. The trail runs colder than an arctic breeze whenever I try to follow it through conventional detecting. But I really feel this is where the investigation lies. Call it a hunch; you'll find I have a lot of them." She looked over at Blythe with a wry smile. "And that's when I came up with the idea to go in undercover to find out from the inside how these agencies work and what they might do to get a child for a couple that needs one so bad."

"It could be someone outside of the agencies running their own adoption ring." Browning cast a look at his partner. "Caldow and I had to bust up a child-selling ring before we were drafted to the DDU. Nasty business, babies to order."

"Glad for your experience, guys. I'm going to need it all. I have some thoughts about what might be happening here." She saw Blythe shift in her chair. "I know theories aren't facts, but I've put a great deal of time and effort into these kidnappings." She brought up a photo on the screen of a city block. "Welcome to suburbia. This is Cranston Heights, a strong community of the wealthy demographic who can afford anything and everything they desire. In this self-contained hub there are a huge amount of children, born to both straight couples and a healthy number of gay and lesbian couples."

"Utopia in Connecticut. Who'd ever believe it?" Trace muttered.

Daryl spared her a grin. "The Heights are perfectly situated in the geographic profile for this case. It's also perfectly placed for the hospitals and the agencies. Meanwhile, the children being snatched are on the edges of the ring and in the more lower class areas that skirt the more affluent Heights and surrounding wealth. But everything centers round the Heights."

CHAPTER THREE

Intuitive. That's what Daryl's mother had called her and had never allowed her to be afraid of what she could do and sense. Her father had been more apprehensive though, fearing his child had turned psychic overnight at the tender age of twelve. But Daryl saw no spirits of the dead, nor received messages from the great beyond. She just somehow instinctively knew where lost children were to be found. And it was only ever children; she couldn't use her ability to find anything or anyone else.

To her distress, the children weren't always found alive, but her mind could focus in and pinpoint on a map the exact area the children were. It had led her to solving child abduction cases from her father's desk when she was still in school. The other policemen merely looked on her ability as that of her being the daughter of a cop and following in her father's footsteps. They had known her from birth. Anything strange or unnatural about what she could do was never discussed. She was simply the sergeant's daughter, and she always found the missing children. Her father's men would have closed ranks around her to protect her had anyone said anything against her.

Soon, the cases of lost children always fell on Sergeant Chandler's desk, and he just set them aside for when Daryl came in from school and she could look them over. When the time came for her to begin her own police training, she was extremely cautious as to how much of her *talent* she revealed. She tried to temper her Intuitive state through the police academy and worked to find more tangible proof to add to what she instinctively knew. It made her a better recruit and, in time, an excellent detective.

She relied on both her policing skills and her Intuitive state to solve the mysteries. Daryl had never told anyone but her mother what exactly happened to her when she was forced to focus and the heavy weight of her *gift* pressed down on her. In that moment, she felt overwhelmed and almost crushed by something she could never explain. Her mother had said she was tasked with the weight of the world balanced on her shoulders. Daryl hadn't always seen it as the blessing her mother had considered it to be. It set her apart, made her different, and sometimes brought into question how serious she could be taken in her job. But Daryl used her talent to protect and serve. It was the code she lived her life by.

❖

The conference room was deathly silent after her announcement, then erupted into everyone asking questions at once. Lake put his hand up to quiet everybody down.

"Daryl, you never said anything about two in our phone call." His tone of voice was just a shade shy of accusatory.

Daryl knew he was aware that her picking Cranston Heights was not about just sticking a pin in a map; she *knew* they were there. What was infuriating Daryl was the fact she couldn't find all five of the children she had files on. At least, not *yet*. She'd told Lake she knew of one child's whereabouts. Now she was certain she could add to that number.

"I don't have any way of actually proving it unless I'm in the Heights and can gain access to the children themselves. If I go in as a cop, I'm going to blow whatever chances I have of finding the person behind the kidnappings. No amount of investigating has brought up anything further. We're hitting a blind spot there."

"How certain are you about the children?" Blythe asked.

Daryl brought up a set of photos of children playing at a daycare center. She pointed to a small child half hidden behind another. "I think this child is Heather Jones, but I really need a clearer shot for absolute proof." She brought up the next photo and pointed to the child in the center of the screen. "However, I believe this is Matthew Malone. When he was born, he had a very distinct birthmark on his head, one that would be hidden when his hair grew." She enlarged the photo. "Guess his new mommies like their little boy to look like a proper little boy and cut his hair to within an inch of its life." A dark-shaped birthmark was plainly visible in the child's hairline. She brought up a photograph of a baby with the same shaped mark. "This is a picture of Matthew Malone before he was taken. I'm sure you'll agree the marks are incredibly similar."

"That could just be a coincidence," Browning said. "But if it isn't, what about the other kids?"

"I have been conducting surveillance around these streets. When I was questioned by the neighborhood watch, I told them I was looking to buy property there for my wife and I to move into. I explained she was working and couldn't make the trip so I was scouting ahead for suitable locations to raise a child in a family friendly environment. Suddenly, I was granted access to the 'inner circle.' I got a guided tour of every facility available and I got to walk around taking photos without being stopped or questioned."

"Trustworthy, if a great deal foolish," Caldow said. "You could have been a pedophile picking out your next child."

"I've worked some undercover situations before. I know how to deflect questions. I projected money and power. It's the language this area recognizes. And I was driving a very elite car, courtesy of one of the young cops in my station who has more money than sense. While there, I didn't just take photos of the children's area. I was all over the Heights. It really is a fantastic place to live in. It's all but self-contained, the neighbors are friendly, and the whole area reeks of money."

"What was your cover story?" Blythe asked.

"I told them my wife and I were setting up our own IT based business from home. We'd decided to escape the rat race and settle down and have babies." She laughed at Blythe's amusement. "I know enough about IT to fudge my way through any questions, but they weren't interested in that. They were more interested in my being able to retire early. This area just screams wealth and prestige, and if you have it, they'll welcome you in with open arms. I believe if we can get our foot in the door there, so to speak, we can find out how so many of the lesbian and gay couples I saw have babies."

Caldow and Browning both laughed at that. "Good luck asking those kinds of questions. Though I guess, like anyone else, some folk are desperate to talk about their sex lives."

"I figure if Blythe and I go in as a couple asking questions about adoption, then those who have adopted will open up to us." Daryl clicked at her remote. "Word is the hospitals in this area will automatically put you in touch with adoption agencies if other methods of conceiving fail. Specifically, *babies* are mentioned. Those need to be checked out first to see if they'll direct us to a certain agency. I can't walk in as a single female looking to adopt. I'm of the belief these babies are being taken for couples only. Precisely, *gay* couples."

"There are a great many things I will do undercover, but getting examined for infertility isn't something I think I can suitably fake," Blythe said, her face coloring a very fetching shade that charmed Daryl more than she wanted to admit. She put her hands up to forestall Blythe's fears.

"I know a doctor who can work us up some very convincing medical files documenting our lack of fertility. Neither one of us will have to be examined by anyone. I want to solve this case, but I'm not going so deep undercover that we have to physically try to make a baby and fail in order to be accepted. I promise you, Blythe, your virtue is safe with me." Daryl couldn't resist smiling at her.

The agents in the room all laughed, and Blythe nodded her grateful thanks. Daryl caught Trace leaning over to whisper something in Blythe's ear that made her flush an even deeper red.

"You have the copies of all my files and the photographs in the folders on the table before you. I understand you need to talk this over and that the DDU is incredibly busy." Daryl wanted to make them realize how important this was. "These children aren't mine, but I've come to know the women who lost them. I know that in the grand scheme of things, missing children are a fact of life. But I believe I have a very good case here for the DDU to take on, and I'd love the opportunity to work it with you all. You'll no doubt hear that I've been sidelined by the feds from these cases, even though the Connecticut FBI called me in to consult. I believe they made the wrong choice and hope you'll help me rectify it. I'm available should anyone need to ask me anything. SSA Lake, thank you for letting me brief your agents. I appreciate your time." She held out her hand to Lake who took it firmly and held on to it.

"You're staying, right?"

"You carried in my suitcases, Nathan. I'll stay for as long as you need me to. I'm entirely at your disposal. I just need to find a hotel and rent a car."

"You can stay with me to save wasting your money on hotel bills," Blythe said over the underlying chatter of the others going through files and talking amongst themselves. "I have a spare room you can make use of. After all, you're going to need to save your money, Detective. If you intend to be my significant other, I'm going to expect wining and dining and showy displays of affection when we hit the Heights." She flashed Daryl a toothy grin to show she was teasing, but Daryl felt the slow burn from that first look ignite her blood.

"That's very kind of you. I appreciate that, Agent Kent, but I wouldn't want to put you to any trouble."

"It's no trouble at all. And you'd better get used to calling me Blythe." She tugged gently at Daryl's arm. "How about I show you where the cafeteria is so you can get something to eat after your journey and just relax for a while? On the way, I'll point out my desk and give you access to our Internet connection to allow you to check in on your own division back home. I know you detectives can't be away from your computers for long." Blythe turned to Lake. "I'll have food sent in here while we go over the files. Is that all right, sir?"

Lake nodded and regarded Daryl. "Go take the weight off your feet, Detective. Let's see if our resources can stretch to getting you two a house in the Heights to play happy family in."

❖

As she sat at Blythe's desk, Daryl's attention kept drifting from the laptop screen in front of her and over to the conference room windows. She tried not to be too obvious in her staring, but she couldn't tear her eyes away from Blythe Kent as she walked around the room. She gestured as she emphasized some point and Daryl found herself wondering what part of the case Blythe was so adamant about. *They couldn't have found me a prettier partner.* She looked around the room at some of the other women hard at work at their desks. She caught sight of one who looked very masculine in her black G-man suit. Daryl was glad she hadn't been chosen for this case. There'd have been a distinct imbalance of them trying to top the other. Daryl hid a smirk behind her hand as she thought about it. Not that she thought Blythe was going to be submissive in any way. She was an agent, after all. *But she's so much easier on the eye.*

Daryl pulled her attention away from the conference area and back to her screen with effort. *I didn't expect to be partnered with someone I found attractive.* She tried to focus on her e-mail. *I can be professional. I'm here strictly for the case and then I'm going back to my own station.* She surreptitiously looked around the room again, this time taking in the whole area. She watched the agents going about their tasks then swiveled in her chair back to the desk she was sitting at. *Special Agent Blythe Kent, how would you profile yourself, I wonder?* She took in the neatly kept desktop, the files laid out in order, the coffee cup with the department logo set aside just so.

Daryl paused for a moment. She craned her neck to look around at the desks surrounding her and noticed some had framed photos at their workstations. Blythe's desk was devoid of any such pictures. *No photos at work. Either you're very private or you don't have anyone to go home to.* She thought about her own desk, equally empty of a personal touch. *It's all about the job.*

❖

Blythe wasn't surprised to come out of the conference room and find Daryl in the company of one of the women in the office. She had a feeling Daryl drew women to her like bees to honey. What she was surprised to witness was the way Daryl was unobtrusively wheeling her chair back to put some space between herself and an obviously overbearing Agent Yvonne Tellman. Blythe altered her mental profile of Daryl. She didn't use her good looks to entice women to her. Blythe decided to go to her rescue.

"Detective Chandler, if you're ready?" She couldn't mistake the look of gratitude that flashed in Daryl's eyes. She bit back on a chuckle. Agent Tellman had struck out.

"Yes, ma'am." Daryl sprung from her seat and hurriedly began closing down her laptop. She gave a polite nod to Agent Tellman. "If you'll excuse me. It was a pleasure talking with you."

Blythe noticed that Agent Tellman didn't move out of Daryl's way at all. She gritted her teeth to stop herself from making a caustic comment on her blatant perusal of Daryl's body too. Instead, she said sweetly, "Daryl, I had your suitcases taken straight to my car to save you the bother. That way, we can just go home now and get you settled in." She chastised herself for being petty, but felt it was justified when she saw Tellman's predatory gaze.

Agent Tellman gave Blythe a coy look then slipped Daryl her card. When Tellman had walked far enough away out of earshot, Daryl asked, "What am I supposed to do with this?" She waved the card between her fingers. "I wasn't under the impression she was part of the team I'd be working with?"

"She isn't. I think she maybe meant for you to call her sometime."

Daryl looked the card over and then flipped it with deadly accuracy into the trash can under Blythe's desk. She then hastened to zip up her laptop case. Blythe was intrigued by Daryl's reaction.

"She not your type?"

Daryl shook her head and gathered her belongings. "She's married, to a *man*," Daryl bit out. "I don't appreciate being someone's side order of experimentation."

Blythe laughed. "That's a wonderful way of putting it. How do you know Tellman's married?"

Daryl gestured behind her. "She has a photo on her desk of them together. I saw it when I was looking around the office earlier."

She's very observant. "Ever thought about becoming a profiler, Detective?" She caught sight of Agent Tellman watching them closely so Blythe deliberately tucked her arm through Daryl's. "If I'm going to have to beat women off you with a stick during this assignment, I might as well get some practice in now." She steered an unresisting Daryl out of the office, more than aware of the warmth from Daryl's body permeating her own.

"Do you have someone, ma'am?" Daryl asked politely.

"No, I'm unattached, and I told you to call me Blythe. Or Bly; whichever you prefer." The shy smile she received was more than enough to nearly rock her back on her heels.

"I like Blythe. It suits you. It's a strong name but with a determined feminine touch." Daryl was still smiling slightly. "Please call me Daryl."

"Like the mermaid?"

"I'm no Daryl Hannah in looks, but my hair is blond enough I guess."

"I've never seen anyone with hair so pale." Blythe had to resist the urge to reach up and touch Daryl's hair to see if it was as soft as its shade.

"It's my father's fault. I got my coloring from him. I have paler than pale hair and skin so fair that a blush lets everyone know when I'm embarrassed." She shrugged. "It was the bane of my childhood. Still is, to be honest."

Blythe sympathized. Her own pale skin had caused her enough trouble at school, teamed with her coal black hair. "I'll try to keep the teasing down to a minimum to spare your blushes."

"I'll appreciate that." Daryl looked around at everyone packed into the elevator. "Is it always this busy at the DDU?"

"We're one of the larger units, so we have plenty of people in and out at all hours." Blythe tugged Daryl's arm when the elevator halted and guided her through the masses of people and out into the underground parking garage. "My car's parked not far from here."

"Your parking garage is bigger than my whole department," Daryl said.

"Are you suffering a hint of culture shock, Detective?"

Daryl looked chagrined. "I feel like a yokel gawking, but this is my first trip to New York and I'm in awe of everything."

"It's refreshing. It's easy to get blinkered by just how much we have around us that we take for granted." Blythe steered Daryl over to her Lexus. "What's it like where you live?"

Daryl shrugged. "Nothing as grand as this place. I never saw a reason to leave, though. My father ended up as chief of police in our town, and I followed in his footsteps."

"Until the detective badge called."

Daryl nodded. "I'd been fielding calls from the FBI for years but wasn't interested in moving away so I did the next best thing for my career. I took the detective's exam and got a smaller desk with a bigger case load." She flashed Blythe a self-depreciating grin. "There's not as much room in my station as your building has to offer."

"I bet your dad was proud."

"He was. And it meant I was still in his building so he could check up on me."

Blythe couldn't help herself; her eyes traveled from the top of Daryl's blond head to the tips of her shiny black boots. "To my eyes, you look mighty big enough to look after yourself, Detective."

"I am, but it's a dad thing, or so he tells me when I grumble."

"Do you live with your dad?"

"No, I have my own apartment."

"Anyone special to share it with?"

"Maybe one day if I'm lucky enough," Daryl said.

Blythe keyed off the alarm on her car and it chirped loudly in the enclosed garage. "Well, don't settle for being anyone's side order." She opened up the door and eased into the driver's seat. Once Daryl was seated, Blythe looked over at her. "You're definitely main course material."

Daryl chuckled. "Why, thank you, I think. Do you think your team will really be able to take my case on?"

"Do you think you can cope with me as your partner if they do?"

"Yes, ma'am," Daryl said and then cocked her head at Blythe's withering look. "*Blythe*."

Laughing, Blythe set her car in motion and pulled out of her space. "We're working on a profile for your kidnapper, and Lake is looking into the homes and apartments you listed as available. I can't believe you went to that much trouble for a case you've theoretically been kicked off."

"I'm thorough in my work. I was just frustrated by how far I could go before I had to realize this was a bigger case than I could handle on my own with no help from the feds. I need to catch this person before they take another child."

"Your research and attention to detail gave us an awful amount of work to go ahead with."

"I'm sorry this is going to cut into your personal life, but I really appreciate it if you do choose to work with me."

"The baby snatching needs to be stopped. I'm understandably concerned about the lack of cooperation with the other forces. But given your information and Lake's unswerving belief in you, I'm in for as long as it takes us to find the culprit and stop them." Blythe pulled out onto the busy main street. "So, do you like Chinese or Italian?"

"Excuse me?"

"I'm counting this as our first official 'date.' I can phone in an order for Chinese food or Italian. Which do you prefer?"

"I love noodles."

Enchanted by the way Daryl bit her lip after answering, Blythe nearly missed her first turn. She caught herself just in time and ignored the honk of a horn behind her. She handed Daryl her phone. "Press the top number. It's on speed dial. Just tell them it's for Blythe and they'll tell you what the specials are tonight. Pick whatever you want. It's my treat." She saw Daryl get ready to argue. "Hey, you're hooking up with a modern day woman. You can pay next time, and I warn you, I *will* order a richly decadent desert." Blythe drove them both to her home, for once knowing her apartment wouldn't feel as lonely a place to go back to.

CHAPTER FOUR

Daryl sat comfortably on the floor in front of a small coffee table that was covered in cartons of food. Between them, she and Blythe had eaten their way through nearly all of it and were lazily picking over the last remnants.

"Those noodles were the best I've had in ages." Daryl used her chopsticks to chase down what was left in the bottom of a carton.

Blythe sat behind her on the sofa and rested her hand on her stomach. "I love their food, and they always give me extra for some reason."

Daryl chuckled, remembering the people at the restaurant. She'd never seen so many workers come to the door to see Blythe leave. "I think that's because the son of the owner can't do enough for you." She searched in another box for anything left to pick at. "I saw the look on his face when you came out of that restaurant, Ms. FBI. I think he carries a torch for you." She speared the last bite of chicken. "I bet he'd offer to hold your chopsticks if you asked him nicely."

Blythe snorted behind her. "I can handle my own chopsticks, thank you very much."

Daryl grinned as she finally finished eating. She let out a satisfied sigh and stretched out her legs. "You have a great place here."

"I got it as soon as I was accepted at the Bureau. Sometimes I think it's too big for just one, but I love the view I get of the city."

"It is a fantastic sight." Daryl had already been at the window marveling at the sun setting over the buildings seen from Blythe's apartment. Her tenth floor view afforded a majestic panorama of tall buildings and endless lights. "Do you think the DDU can get us a house in the Heights? I mean, it's not like mortgages grow on trees."

Blythe cocked her head and favored Daryl with a sparkling gaze. "You'd be amazed at what the DDU can do."

"Your funding must be astronomical."

"Our funding is something I don't care to think about. I just do my job the best I can and apprehend the bad guys."

Daryl held up her beer bottle and they toasted to that.

"So," Blythe said, "do you think they'll get us an apartment or a house to live in?"

"I gave locations for both. I'm not sure."

"I'd prefer something with a yard."

Daryl blinked at her. "You like gardening?" She smiled when Blythe laughed at her. Blythe really did have a pretty laugh.

"No, but it would give us the extra something of having a yard so a child can play in it."

Daryl considered this. "There were some apartment buildings that seemed to be communities in their own right. They had a communal garden area and a playground all in one place. That would work too."

"We have to think like a family would. Where would we want our child to grow up? Can she run and play safely there? Is it near a good school?"

Daryl nodded, amazed at how much Blythe had already thought this through. "All I was thinking was to catch this person. I didn't even think past a rudimentary cover story other than we wanted a kid together."

"That's because you're a detective. You think only in terms of discover, gather evidence, and arrest. At the DDU, it's a little more… expansive. It's going to be all about creating the illusion others have to be taken in by. We have to be the couple we say we are— wealthy, independent, wanting a child so badly to seal our love. Being desperate, at any cost, to get one."

"Your agents are going to do the follow-up work at the hospital for the kidnapper, yes?"

"There are two investigations here. The kidnapper who takes the children is one, but then there's also the baby broker angle. The kidnapper is dealing out babies. Taking them and selling them.

Browning and Caldow will be checking into histories of the agencies in the Heights and seeing what the hospitals have to do with all this. I can't help but wonder if the kidnapper pre-orders babies. We were talking about this in our meeting. What if they pick specific mothers out because of their coloring?"

Daryl considered this. "Kind of like if one of the couple is a redhead, you pick a redheaded mother-to-be?"

"Exactly."

"That's a creepy thought. That's a premeditated and borderline stalker M.O."

"I think we should ask for a baby that resembles you," Blythe said. "Just imagine a baby with such spectacular coloring."

Daryl knew her face was burning like a beacon under Blythe's direct scrutiny. "Why not want one to resemble you? You're the dark to my light. Why wouldn't we want a child who would follow your midnight shades?"

Blythe smiled sweetly at her. "Midnight shades, eh? I usually get the Goth comments."

"Granted, your hair is black and you do have skin the color of fine porcelain. I don't doubt you could carry off the Gothic look incredibly well if you so desired, but I don't see that style on you."

"You're a charmer, Detective Kent. I can see I'm going to have my work cut out with you," Blythe murmured under her breath just loud enough for Daryl to hear. "I'd go for your coloring because it's so unusual. You're fair to the point of being almost white. That's got to be specific enough to catch their attention. Either of our colorings would though."

"Have you ever wanted kids for real?"

Blythe didn't answer right away. "I've never really considered them, to be honest. I knew very early on I was a lesbian, so I knew I wouldn't have children the old-fashioned way. I don't think I've ever found someone I wanted to share such a commitment with." She tilted her head slightly. "How about you?"

Daryl laughed. "I'm not exactly the maternal type, but I like other people's kids. I like holding them and handing them back. Besides, in this line of work you wonder if it's worth bringing kids into a world like we see. One full of monsters...but of the *human* variety."

"How are your bosses with you taking so much time off to organize this operation in another state?"

"They're just thankful that when word gets out that there's been a kidnapping ring operating for years right under everyone's noses, at least it wasn't in their state. Because these babies have been taken from single mothers who usually stay pretty low on the radar, and two of the mothers were prostitutes. Law enforcement in Connecticut has been sweeping it under the carpet so as not to cause panic. No one wants the mayor to have to announce that they have a baby snatcher in their fair city. I was called in to consult with the FBI, but once the feds got wind of that I was politely informed my type of investigating wasn't required at this time."

"And just what is your type of investigating?" The light in Blythe's eyes challenged Daryl to reveal all her secrets

"Apparently different to everyone else's. But no one brings these kind of cases to my door and then can honestly expect me to sit back and do nothing. Once I started to see a pattern forming in the abductions, I knew I couldn't wait for any more children to be taken. The five I had already were plenty to warrant an investigation."

"You're not looking to get promoted any time soon, then?"

"I can't play the team game they want me to. Not for the sake of these kids. Those women lost their babies. I don't care if they are hardworking single mothers or prostitutes working the streets, they don't deserve to have their babies snatched away from them." Daryl took a deep breath to dampen her growing ire. "A couple of the women were frightened to come forward. They didn't know who had taken their babies or if the police would even listen because of their jobs. When I began looking into it, the biggest rumor was an adoption agency was taking the kids to use for their clients. I have to hope that's the right assumption because contemplating the other uses some people have for children keeps me awake at night. But that's the direction the feds are taking. They don't see the Cranston Heights connection; they're following a trail that runs through each state instead."

Blythe rested her hand on top of Daryl's shoulder. "You've got the DDU behind you now. We chase only facts and leave the politics to the politicians."

"Something tells me Nathan doesn't stand for anyone interfering in his investigations. That's why I decided to come to him."

"No, SSA Lake is not a man to mess with. He's the best man to have guarding your back."

"I knew I had picked the right team to take this to. Maybe now I can start getting some concrete answers."

"And bring the guilty to trial."

"How long before we can take this assignment on the road?"

"You're awfully eager to set up home with me, Detective. I'll take that as a positive sign," Blythe teased her as she started to clean up the empty cartons.

Daryl jumped up to help. "The police work I can handle. I'm more uncertain about the domestic bliss part. I haven't exactly had much experience in that department." She caught Blythe's look. "But I promise I will treat you with the utmost respect."

"I have no doubt of that, Daryl, and you really need to stop worrying about my virtue in your hands." She flashed Daryl a sly grin. "So to speak." She stuffed the empty cartons into the trash can. "I can't say I have any more experience in that department either. And yet here we are wanting to have a baby together. Guess we just skipped the U-Haul altogether."

Daryl laughed and finished helping Blythe clean up. "I've never even gotten that far."

"You don't strike me as the player type."

"I'm not. I'm too job fixated to have the time to play the field." Daryl wondered what it was about Blythe that made her feel comfortable telling her anything she asked. "It's a lot to expect a woman to put up with the demands of my job. Sometimes it's easier to be alone."

Blythe nodded. "My traveling blows many a chance of a long-term relationship well out of the water. I can't count the times I've gotten text messages complaining about my missing a date when I'm on the plane heading out to the next case."

"Do you regret that?"

"I figure you can't regret what you've never had," Blythe said simply. "Or, at least, I never get the time to regret it."

Daryl just nodded. She wanted nothing less than what her mother and father had shared. His job had been police work, her mother was a teacher until her illness, but they had held their family together bound in love. Daryl wanted that for herself.

Blythe reached into the fridge and pulled out a bottle of wine. "Want to spend the night watching *Nikita* reruns?" She waved the bottle enticingly.

"You like espionage?" Daryl followed after her, picking up the two glasses Blythe waved her toward.

"Well, it doesn't hurt that the leading lady is beautiful as well as smart."

Daryl couldn't agree more, but her attention wasn't on the TV. She tried not to be too obvious staring at Blythe and instead her eye caught a photograph on one of the shelves. She leaned in closer to inspect it. "Who's the cat lady?" she asked, smiling in reaction to the comically exasperated look on the woman's face in the photo. An obviously rambunctious black kitten was perched on her shoulder with a paw placed squarely on the woman's cheek.

Blythe peered over Daryl's shoulder. "God, she'd be mad if she heard you call her that. That is my best friend with the cat I got her."

"You gave her a cat?"

Blythe picked up the photo and handed it to Daryl for closer inspection. "She's a detective in charge of the Chicago DDU now, but when she was a cop she seemed so…" Blythe hesitated, apparently searching for just the right word, "lonely, I guess. I wanted her to have a friendly face to come home to, and after a really bad case she was involved in, I decided a pet would fit the bill."

"She obviously didn't mind."

"Oh, she complained and fussed for a good hour about what in the hell she was supposed to do with some damn furball, but once the cat sat in her lap and purred, she was sold." Blythe pointed to the photo. "This is Trinity with *her* pet, Detective Rafe Douglas. Rafe and I went through the academy together. She is a sweetheart, underneath her strictly by the book way of policing."

"A stickler for the rules? I like her already."

"Everything is black or white with Rafe and the law is absolute." Blythe turned away and sat down.

Daryl put the picture back and joined her on the sofa. "What's wrong?"

"She was attacked recently by a suspect in a murder, and he almost killed her. Since then, when we've talked she seems different, knocked off center almost."

"A trauma will do that to a person. Sometimes something bad will make you question your purpose in the world. Losing my mother did it for me. Before she died, I was tied to my desk, passing paperwork back and forth. Then these cases came along, and I knew I had to act on it. Losing your mother, whatever age you do it, is the cruelest blow, and I knew I couldn't sit back and let this happen to these kids. So here I am, a year later, out of my comfort zone about to embark on an operation that I have instigated against the feds' wishes. It's a scary venture and I'm sorry for dragging you into it. But I need your team's help. Those children do too." She settled on the sofa next to Blythe as if it was something she did every night. Blythe filled her glass with wine. "So here's to us and this partnership."

"To our being successful partners in every sense of the word."

After finishing up a call with Trace who, much to Blythe's amusement, was on a fact-finding mission to see what Blythe had found out about Daryl already, Blythe settled down to sleep. She listened to the unfamiliar sounds of someone else moving around her house. She pictured Daryl's solid frame trying to fit into her small bathroom and had to grin. Her mind drifted as she tried to imagine what Daryl chose to sleep in, and she wasn't surprised when her breathing sped up at the thought of Daryl naked.

Groaning softly, Blythe put a hand on her stomach to quell the butterflies stirring. *Like this case isn't going to be difficult enough without me fantasizing about the woman I have to work with and pretend to be her lover.* She shivered as a thought struck her. *I'm going to have to kiss her.*

Her hand shifted a little lower, and her body twitched at the thought of their lips touching. "God," Blythe grumbled. "Just a few hours in her company and I'm all hot and bothered over her.

Some professional I am." Her ears strained to hear Daryl's footsteps padding across the landing leading to the spare bedroom. She hardly breathed as she listened to the soft shuffles from the room next to her own. The sound of the bed springs depressing finally let Blythe release a soft breath. She curled up on her side and screwed her eyes shut tight. *Please let us solve this case fast before I make an absolute fool of myself over her.*

CHAPTER FIVE

Daryl was up early the next morning, fixing coffee and poring over the morning newspaper. When Blythe came downstairs to join her, Daryl was already working her way through the cryptic crossword puzzle. She looked up and greeted Blythe. "Good morning. I hope you don't mind." She held up the newspaper. "I availed myself of your puzzle page."

"I never do them so knock yourself out."

Daryl had prepared enough coffee for both of them and watched as Blythe liberally laced hers with cream and sugar. "I like tackling a puzzle in a morning. It gets my brain cells working."

Blythe moved to see what Daryl was doing. "Oh my God, it's way too early to be attempting cryptic clues."

"But they're the best sort."

"Don't you get enough of solving things at work?" Blythe drank deeply from her mug and let out an appreciative moan. "God, this is good coffee."

Daryl's body tingled at the sound Blythe released. Daryl wondered if that sound would be anything like Blythe sounded in more intimate surroundings. She forced herself to act normal and not give in to the urge to lick away the slight remains of cream that clung to Blythe's lips. "I've always been fascinated by puzzles. I like the ones you have to work out mentally more than the ones you work by hand. I still can't figure out a Rubik's cube."

"I'll make sure we have a newspaper delivered to our assigned home so you have a crossword regularly to start your day."

"That's awfully nice of you."

"I figure if I'm asking for cable TV, the least we can do for you is supply you with a newspaper."

"This assignment is a whole lot bigger than I probably imagined, yes?"

"I think it's safe to say that this isn't going to be an easy assignment where we just go in, find the bad guy, and move on to the next case. We've got to create a whole relationship between us and make it wholly believable. The people of the Heights have to believe we're a couple with no hidden agenda or secrets to hide. Then we have to sell that same story to the adoption agencies because we have to be convincing that, more than anything in the world, we want a child together."

"Is there anything you want that much?" Daryl asked.

"Contentment," Blythe said. "I think I'd like to be happy with all aspects of my life. So how about you, Detective? What's your heart's desire?"

"I want these kidnappings solved."

"But what about *you*?"

Daryl hesitated, not really sure how to answer. "I don't think I've ever seen myself outside of my job, to be honest. I'm the daughter of a cop whose only dream in life was to follow in her father's footsteps."

"Well, you have to convince people that you want to be a mommy with me so I think we need to see more of who Daryl is without the badge."

"I knew I should have delegated this job."

"And miss out on all the fun we're going to have?" Blythe patted her on the shoulder. "No way, sweetheart. You and I are going to be partners in every sense of its definition for this assignment."

Daryl's head snapped up at the endearment that so easily rolled from Blythe's tongue. She fought against the blush she knew was coloring her cheeks.

"Do you mind being called sweetheart?" Blythe moved around the kitchen gathering up fruit while Daryl sat watching her. "Or would you prefer *lover*? Or there's *honey*?"

The words captured Daryl's imagination as she listened to each one spoken in Blythe's rich tones.

"Daryl?"

Daryl jerked and felt foolish at her attention visibly wandering as she met Blythe's concerned look. "I'll answer to anything you call me," she said.

Blythe shot her a warm smile. "Really? Well then, I'll have to try them all on you until we find one that fits you just right. Not everyone is a *honeypie.*"

Daryl knew she was staring as Blythe continued to putter around the kitchen. *Oh God, I think this investigation might be more than I can handle. I'll end up demoted back to a beat cop busting careless drivers. I haven't been anyone's honey for a long time. How can I convince people I'm worthy of being someone's lover when I'm not sure of it myself?*

"Stuck on a clue there?" Blythe asked, glancing over her shoulder at Daryl.

"I'm realizing things aren't as simple as I'd imagined."

"You're not talking about your crossword, are you?"

Daryl wasn't surprised by how astute Blythe could be. "Am I going to regret being partnered with a very proficient profiler? Does this mean I'm going to have no secrets whatsoever around you?"

Blythe laughed softly. "Profiling is just one part of my job. If I can't work out all your secrets with that skill, I'll just employ one of the other investigative talents I possess to wheedle it out of you instead."

I don't stand a chance.

Blythe took pity on her. "Are you ready to face the team again to see what we have planned?"

"I'm eager to see how the DDU works."

"We're becoming a formidable team."

"Then I'm even more grateful to have you on my side."

❖

Four days into the setting up of the undercover investigation, Daryl was feeling more and more at home at the DDU. Every day, she'd been driven in by Blythe, had taken a seat at a desk marked out specifically for her, and had dealt with her own work until called to join the agents in their conference room to discuss her case. Trace wheeled over to where Blythe and Daryl sat looking over files. She jingled a set of keys at them.

"Ladies, we're going on a little field trip to see a friend of mine."

"The last time you pulled that stunt, Trace, I found myself in a tattoo parlor. It took all my powers of persuasion and finally drawing my weapon and badge to stop your friend Razor from tattooing my ass," Blythe said.

Daryl's eyebrows rose, and she had to forcibly not let her eyes fall to check out that particular piece of Blythe's anatomy. "You have a tattoo?"

"No, I don't, but it's no thanks to this one here." Blythe pointed toward a grinning Trace. "I thought we were just going out for a few drinks and maybe pizza. Apparently, Trace had a different girl's night out experience in mind."

"You needed to loosen up, Agent," Trace said, unrepentant.

Blythe purposely turned away from her and back to the file in her hand. "I'm certain I could have done that without having love birds etched on my butt cheek."

Daryl fought to hide a smile behind her hand and tried in vain not to let her mind wander to what lay beneath the tailored dark pants Blythe wore so well.

Trace put the keys down on the desk noisily. "Alas, this isn't a request from me for a road trip to broaden your horizons, Blythe. This is the big boss sending you two to seal your partnership."

Daryl frowned at her. "I beg your pardon?"

"You're going to need photos taken. You can't set up a happy lesbian home without having photos of the happy couple dotted around the place showing off your couple-dom." Trace pushed the keys toward Blythe. "Besides, you're supposed to be married. You're going to need at least one wedding picture as proof. I am not Photoshopping you."

"Oh God," Daryl muttered under her breath. Blythe heard her.

"What's wrong?"

"I never even thought of having to need proof we were together. I just figured our being together would be evidence enough." Daryl began to worry she hadn't thought any of the details through enough. What else had she missed?

"A picture tells a thousand words, Detective. My friend has everything you're going to need at her studio. She'll make certain you look suitably ceremonious."

Blythe cocked her head at Trace. "Do I get a wedding dress?"

Trace nodded. "And we'll find a suitable penguin suit for the fair detective here."

"Oh God," Daryl moaned again and caught Blythe eyeing her. "My mother always dreamed I'd find the right girl and settle down. She would have loved to plan a wedding. Somehow, I don't think this is quite what she would have had in mind."

Trace grinned. "Well, today you two get to put on your happiest smiles because you're going to be married. On an eight-by-ten glossy at least." She pushed away from the table. "And then we have to go shopping for wedding bands so you look suitably shackled."

Oh God, help me now.

Daryl wasn't comfortable not wearing her gun at her side. She was even less happy with the fact her sidearm was in the possession of Trace while she got changed. Sharon the photographer had brought out clothing for Daryl and Blythe and directed them into changing rooms to get ready. She'd overheard Blythe being taken off for something to do with makeup so she'd been hiding behind the curtain of her cubicle hoping she wouldn't get the same call. The full-length mirror caught Daryl's attention, and she stared at herself in the dark gray suit that had been chosen for her. A pale blue shirt brought a splash of color along with her patterned tie. She hardly recognized herself.

"You have to come out of there some time, Chandler," Trace called.

"I'm not being made up to look like someone I'm not," Daryl said.

"They're just going to make you lose the tight ass ponytail. You're not being subjected to the pampering Blythe is going through."

Daryl tugged her hair free from its tie and quickly combed it out. It fell just shy of her shoulders. Reluctantly, she finally stepped out of the cubicle.

Trace's eyes widened and she let out a low whistle. "Look at you all duded up. You're looking mighty fine there, Detective. Or should I say Mrs. Kent?" The sly words made Daryl's head snap up.

"Am I changing my name?"

Trace fingered her armrests innocently. "I figured you to be the old-fashioned type and would expect our Blythe to become Mrs. Chandler instead."

Blythe's voice came from behind them. "It could be hyphenated and we could be Mrs. Chandler-Kent."

Daryl's breath arrested somewhere in her chest when she saw Blythe. She stared in awe at just how beautiful she looked in her wedding finery. The dress was an ornately patterned affair with a low neckline that revealed more than Blythe's work suits ever could. Her dark hair fell upon her shoulders and her eyes looked even more striking with the expertly applied makeup. A smile curled lips darkened with a wine red lipstick.

"You look very handsome, Daryl," Blythe said softly, her eyes sweeping over Daryl from head to toe.

"And you look breathtaking." Daryl hoped her voice didn't break and make her sound as adolescent as she felt.

"At least your shoes go with what you're wearing. My black work boots apparently ruined the look of this dress." She raised a foot now wearing a white high-heeled shoe. "We need to get this over with; these shoes are not my size. I want to smile in our wedding photos and not be grimacing in pain."

A woman appeared and singled Daryl out. "I was coming to do something with your hair."

Daryl shook her head. "I've combed it down. It's sorted."

The woman let out a small sigh. "At least you got rid of the unflattering ponytail. You're supposed to be getting married after all, not looking like you have a court appearance."

I think I'd rather go to court. Daryl fidgeted with her tie nervously. A warm hand stilled hers over the thin material. Blythe's fingers trailed up the tie and positioned it just right at Daryl's collar.

Daryl's eyes fell to Blythe's ample curves. "You're rocking some major cleavage in that wedding gown," she said softly.

Blythe laughed and ineffectually tried to pull up the top of her dress. "It's the cut of the dress. It forces everything up front and center."

Daryl couldn't argue with that, but the photographer walked in and broke the moment before she could say anything more. Daryl took a step back and tried to breathe normally.

Sharon cast a critical eye over them both. She singled out Daryl. "You're extremely pale. I'd prefer makeup on you to brighten your skin."

"I don't wear makeup," Daryl argued. "And if I were getting married for real, I still wouldn't wear it."

"Butches," Sharon grumbled, fixing a lens on her expensive looking camera. "They all think a beauty regime is to apply ChapStick." She waved for everyone to follow her.

Daryl felt Blythe step in close to her side. A hand slipped into hers and squeezed gently.

"Let's get married, Detective."

Daryl dutifully followed her lead.

❖

Blythe wondered how many more times they had to strike the same pose and tilt their heads this way and that before the perfect picture was captured. The intimacy of the photos had Blythe leaning in close to Daryl, and she was enjoying how seriously Daryl was taking all the fuss and unwanted attention. The look of concentration on Daryl's face made Blythe want to kiss her senseless.

"And now I need you to kiss."

Blythe couldn't believe she'd heard her own thoughts spoken out loud from the photographer. She caught sight of the surprise on Daryl's face before she hastily covered her emotion with a more professional front. Blythe was unsure how to respond to the look written all over Daryl's face. Part of it was trepidation, but she could also see desire. She smiled inwardly at that, enjoying the fact that Daryl obviously found her attractive.

"We're going to end up kissing sometime, Detective," Blythe said softly. "We're going to be married. Married couples usually kiss." The way Daryl caught her bottom lip between her teeth made Blythe want to run her tongue over her lip to smooth away any hurt. She took the opportunity handed to her. She softly ran the tip of her tongue across Daryl's lower lip. When Daryl gasped in surprise, Blythe kissed her. The feel of Daryl's lips beneath her own drew Blythe in further to explore. What started out as a gentle pressure became more urgent, and when Daryl kissed her back, Blythe knew she was lost. Daryl's lips were firm yet tender, and for every kiss Blythe instigated Daryl returned it in equal measure. Her hands rose to capture Daryl's face and just hold her. Daryl's own hands moved to Blythe's waist, her fingers pulling her closer until their bodies touched. Blythe's whole body ignited at the gentle caress of Daryl's lips and the soft nipping of her teeth on Blythe's full lower lip. Daryl's tongue soothed over the sting, which only served to make Blythe desperate for more. She pressed her chest closer to Daryl's and felt Daryl moan into her mouth.

"You can stop now. I've got more than enough," Sharon said dryly.

Barely registering the fact someone had spoken, Blythe had no intention of pulling back from the heat of Daryl's kiss. She let out a moan as Daryl's tongue began to seek out her own once more.

A piercing whistle startled them both apart as if they'd been doused with cold water. Trace lowered her fingers from her lips. "Time out, guys. Sharon only takes photos of the wedding, *not* the honeymoon. And you two look like you're in need of getting a room!"

Daryl's face was aflame. She kept her head averted while she struggled for breath. Blythe rested their foreheads together, keeping Daryl's face in her hold as she stroked the heated cheeks gently.

"I guess that's one area we don't have to worry about fooling anyone," Daryl said for Blythe's ears alone.

Blythe had to agree. This case was going to be a difficult enough assignment without the added pressure of Blythe not being able to keep her hands off Daryl. But Daryl kissed like a dream, and Blythe was sorely tempted to savor her lips just one more time. Sharon's voice broke the mood, and Blythe released an annoyed grumble.

"If you ladies will go get changed into the casual clothing, we'll take some general snapshots." She picked up another camera and began getting it ready.

Daryl started to loosen her tie, and Blythe had to steel herself from reaching out to tug on the material and use it to pull Daryl close again. Daryl chose that moment to look up and must have caught the predatory look on Blythe's face. She grinned.

"What are the DDU's interdepartmental guidelines for fraternization, Agent Kent?"

Blythe smiled back. "We're going to be recognized as married in a week or so. They can't say a word."

"And here I was thinking this was going to be all about the case." She undid the top buttons of her shirt and began shrugging out of the jacket.

"Oh, Detective Chandler, you're on the DDU's turf now. You'll find nothing is ever as it seems."

Trace broke into their hushed conversation. "Will you two quit with the flirting so you can go get outside and get your photos taken? And, Blythe, wash off your wedding makeup. Sharon said you can be more natural for these shots. She did try to tell you herself, but you two were too busy giving each other the eye."

"Thank goodness," Blythe said, deliberately ignoring the last part of Trace's comment. "I wouldn't want to wear this dark a shade of lipstick all the time."

"You don't have to worry about that. Most of it's been kissed off anyway," Trace said.

Daryl ducked into the changing cubicle. Blythe laughed and rested her hands on Trace's wheelchair and leaned in. "You're just jealous."

"Because you got to lock lips with Detective Angel Hair? I only wish I'd had enough brain cells firing while you two were burning up the atmosphere with your smoldering kisses. I should have whipped out my cell phone and recorded it."

"The film wouldn't have done the actuality justice." Blythe slipped away into her cubicle. She caught sight of her full-length reflection in the mirror and paused for a moment before taking the dress off. It's just an assignment, she told her reflection sternly, but that didn't stop her from touching her lips as she recalled their kissing. *It's just an assignment with a woman whose first kiss turned me on in an instant. So much for professionalism. All I can think of is when I can kiss her again.*

CHAPTER SIX

"Having second thoughts already?" Daryl asked from the kitchen as she prepared their evening meal. She'd informed Blythe she could make a fairly decent spaghetti bolognaise and was just setting out the plates on the table when she'd caught Blythe playing with the shiny gold wedding band she had recently placed on her finger.

Blythe looked up. "No, I just can't get used to having something there and what it means. Even if it doesn't mean the same to us that it will for those who see its significance."

Daryl spared a look at her identical ring. She was pleased that Blythe had picked out a simple plain band for them both. Daryl wasn't drawn to ostentatious trappings. She was a plain and simple woman. She looked at her watch; it had been a present from her parents when she'd graduated from the police academy. She could have afforded to replace it many times over by now, but it still kept excellent time and had meaning to her.

"Your meal is ready," Daryl said and headed back into the kitchen to dish it out.

"I could get used to this treatment," Blythe said as she chose a wine to accompany their food.

Daryl set a full plate before Blythe's seat. "You might want to reserve judgment until you've tasted it."

"I'm sure it's wonderful. It smells divine." Blythe poured them each a glass of wine. "Are you reasonably set for what next week has in store for us?"

"Which part? Going from confirmed bachelorhood to wonderfully wedded bliss? Or doing all that while trying to gain a foot in the door among Cranston Heights' powerful and elite?"

Blythe moaned aloud in appreciation at her first mouthful of Daryl's cooking. "Oh my God, you have to cook this for me every night! It's amazing!" Blythe swallowed another mouthful of her food. "I mean the whole undercover deception part. Where we get to investigate but can't be seen to be investigating, all the while keeping up the appearance that you and I are a couple."

"It does seem to be a dangerous juggling act," Daryl said. "I've never gone undercover like this before. This should prove to be an interesting investigation in many ways."

"The hardest part is getting you to stop being such a cop." Blythe grinned at Daryl's affronted face. "Oh, you are too such a cop!"

"I can't help it. It's who I am."

"No, it's *what* you are. Your job defines you but doesn't make you who you are. You're going to have to be Daryl Chandler, wife to Blythe, whom you happen to love more than anything on this planet and want to make babies with. It's not like filling in a report, ticking a few boxes, and you're done. You've got to play the role, make people believe it."

"Our kissing is dangerous. It makes me forget what I'm supposed to be doing," Daryl blurted out. She was glad to see Blythe hesitate.

"We obviously like each other," Blythe said softly.

"It feels more than like." Daryl couldn't take her eyes from Blythe's face.

"I know." Blythe's voice came out on a whisper.

"So what do we do about that?"

"I don't honestly know. I've never had to worry about being attracted to someone I had to go undercover with. I have enough trouble finding someone interesting enough in my meager personal life."

"You think I'm interesting?"

Blythe slipped her hand across the table and touched Daryl's sleeve. "I think you're more than interesting."

"But you don't really know me. I could be harboring some deep dark secret." Daryl wondered if Blythe could ever imagine how true those words were.

"Sometimes it's the darkness in people that helps us celebrate the light."

"That doesn't sound like a very profiler-ish thing to say. You deal with the dark side of people every day. It's not pretty."

Blythe's eyes cut through to Daryl's very soul it seemed. "I don't see a darkness in you. All I see is a bright, shimmering light."

Daryl shifted uncomfortably under her intense stare. "That's you being dazzled by the overhead lighting glancing off my all too pale hair."

Blythe laughed and the tension at the table eased. Daryl searched desperately for something to change the subject that hung heavily in the air. Blythe beat her to it.

"So, care to tell me what your secret is?"

"Secret?" Daryl asked, knowing what was coming but hoping like crazy she could wrangle a way out of it.

"You have the most scarily accurate solve rate to your cases. I'm wondering what your secret is to that."

Daryl tried to shrug it off. "Just lucky I guess."

"You're not seriously expecting me to swallow that, are you, Detective? Your lucky streak, if used in another situation, would amass you a fortune so that you could hang up your badge and retire to Florida."

"I think the local casinos are safe from me. My luck doesn't run to cards or slot machines."

"Then what is it, Daryl? I've read your files, gone over cases you had a hand in from before you even set foot in the academy. You very rarely miss a target you're aiming for."

"You did delve deep, didn't you?" Daryl should have known that Blythe would be the one to research her. She understood why. They were going to have to trust each other in a very intimate operation. She just wished Blythe wasn't so conscientious in her job. "Those early cases were my dad's. I was just learning the ropes on them."

"I'm a profiler, Detective, and have interrogated more people than I care to count. Don't try your stalling tactics with me. You have the uncanny knack for finding missing children, one way or another."

Daryl couldn't help but grimace. "It's the 'other' part when I don't do so well. All the investigating in the world doesn't always bring back children to their families alive."

"But you bring them closure. Sometimes that's the best thing in those circumstances."

Daryl nodded diffidently, not really believing that.

"Are you psychic?" Blythe pressed.

"Not that I'm aware of." Daryl laid down her fork and looked across the table. She saw nothing in Blythe's eyes that told her she couldn't trust her. "You know that feeling you get deep in your gut when you know something fits the case you're working on?" Blythe nodded. "I have that magnified by about a hundred times stronger. I don't know exactly what I do or why I can do it. But I do know that I can look at certain cases and know instinctively where to start. Then it all boils down to good old-fashioned investigation work and a lot of knocking on doors."

"So it's not *just* luck."

"It's something out of my control but helps me do my job."

Blythe took a long sip of her wine. "Whatever it is it obviously works. So I don't have to worry about you going into a trance and contacting ghosts of cases past?"

"No, Blythe, I won't be consulting on this case with anyone from the dead."

"Pity. I wouldn't mind finding out where my aunt Joan left that necklace she always promised me." She lifted her head from her meal and gave Daryl a wink. "Just kidding."

Daryl knew she was in trouble when that sly fluttering of Blythe's lashes made her stomach tighten in arousal. She wracked her brain for something to move the conversation away from her so-called talents.

"Would you do something for me?" she asked.

"Certainly."

Daryl began fidgeting. "Could you recommend some shops for me where I can get clothing more suitable for a Web designer? Because all I have in my suitcases are apparently going to be blatant cop clothes."

Blythe's laughter lifted Daryl's spirits. "I would love to go shopping with you. If you promise not to drag your heels or grumble as I help dress you for this assignment, then I'll even take you out for dessert."

"It would have to be my treat seeing as you're the one going out of her way."

"We'll talk about your not being able to let a lady pay her way while we shop. This is going to be fun!"

"I was thinking maybe just getting a couple of T-shirts," Daryl's voice ground to a halt when Blythe fixed her with a searing look that dried up whatever she was going to utter next. "How about I just leave it up to you?" she offered weakly.

"See? You're thinking like a proper partner already. It pays to always let your wife have her way. It's easier in the long run, and besides, she is always right."

"There are some things they just don't cover at the academy," Daryl muttered around a mouthful of her food.

"Welcome to the magical world of undercover enlightenment."

❖

The conference room table of the DDU was littered with files and documents.

"Are you even reading what I'm putting before you?" Lake asked as he hovered over Daryl's shoulder replacing sheet after sheet that Daryl was signing her name on.

"I trust you, Nathan. If you've just had me sign my life's savings over to you, then you're the one in for the shock, not me."

"Had I known you'd just put your signature on any piece of paper, I'd have had the office draft up a transfer notice and had you tied to the DDU until retirement."

"You've had me sign a document for my supposed buying of the property Blythe and I will live in. You've got me insured with the DDU just in case something goes wrong. You'd had me sign a car rental deal for a flashy vehicle that I would never be comfortable getting behind the wheel of, but we need it for appearance's sake."

"You have been paying attention," Lake muttered and let out a small sigh. "I still wish you'd reconsider joining me here. We could use someone with your talents on our team."

Daryl liked the fact he didn't emphasize the word talents with the inflection she knew he could have. "Who knows, Nathan? Maybe one day. Let me see what it's like working with the team on a case before you have a parking garage space with my name on it and a seat and mug laid out."

"You would have to supply your own mug," he said while slipping another piece of paper in front of her.

"A credit card? I don't need a credit card." Daryl pushed the paper aside.

"This is a company card. You won't be using your own money to finance this operation. We'll cover everything."

Daryl looked back over her shoulder at him. "Where was this last night when I had Blythe dragging me through every store to find the perfect shirt I could wear if we had company over?"

Blythe looked up from where she was cosigning everything. "I kept the receipts. We can just add them to expenses so you'll be reimbursed. Tell him how handsome that lavender one makes you look. It not only compliments your hair coloring but really makes your muscles stand out."

Daryl stared across the table at her but didn't dare turn to look at Lake who she heard chuckle behind her.

Blythe waved the credit card sheet. "How much are we talking here? Groceries every week or a three-week cruise once this case is solved?"

Lake took the paperwork from her. "Items necessary to perform your undercover status. That does not include cars, second homes, or pets."

Blythe burst out laughing along with Lake. Daryl looked between them, mystified. Once she'd calmed down, Blythe explained their amusement. "We had an undercover operation in the Bureau where the agent involved put on his expense payment a *pet project*. When the auditors were checking the receipts after the case had been cleared, it came to light that the pet project was the guy buying himself a furry suit so he could dress up as a panda on the weekends at a fetish club!"

Daryl caught sight of Lake still shaking silently with laughter. "I think it's safe to assume I won't be using the credit card for that kind of expense."

"Glad to hear it," Blythe said. "I'm allergic to fur."

Lake snorted and gathered up his papers. "We have secured a home for you. A removal team made up of our DDU members will deliver your furniture along with all the technical equipment we need that will be hidden in your office. They will set up everything. You just need to pretend to coordinate the move. I've arranged for cell phones and IDs for your new identities. You keep your names, but no one will be able to link either of you to law enforcement. Trace has already prepared your IT documentation and you have"—he spared Trace a look as she wheeled into the room right on time—"what did you call them?"

"Geek sheets. That way, if anyone quizzes you on your work you can blind them with enough technical jargon they won't dare ask again. I did a sweep of the neighborhood you'll be living in. No one works in website design, so that's your job descriptions." She reached into a pannier bag hooked on the side of her chair and held out a box to Daryl. "These are your business cards. Should you meet someone who needs your designer skills, I'll be on hand to do all the necessary tinkering. I'll give you a list of my costs and design specifications and you can pass them off as your own. You won't have to lift a finger; I'll do all the work and will just walk you through the features." She grinned. "But the money is mine."

"Trace," Lake said with a scowl.

"Nothing is for free, SSA Lake," Trace said. "A girl's got to make a living. My expertise in Web design is not what the DDU pays me for, so it's only fair that I should receive the dollars should anyone test out Blythe's and Daryl's cover stories."

"God, I hope no one asks," Daryl muttered. "I just want to do my real job of finding those children and getting the kidnapper put away. I want to put such a tight stranglehold on Cranston Heights that the kidnapper never takes another child again."

"I won't ask if you're sure about this. I know you too well," Lake said for Daryl's ears alone.

"We have to stop this now before something terrible happens." Daryl had the very unsettling feeling that the number of the abductions was only going to escalate. She couldn't explain how she knew what she did. She had long since learned to just trust the feelings when it came to her work. She knew her mother had been so proud of what she could do. Being a very spiritual lady, Mary Chandler had attributed Daryl's gift to that of a higher power pointing her in the right direction. Daryl didn't always agree with her mother's beliefs, but she never forgot what her mother had said.

You've been marked as a protector, someone who can help those who can't help themselves. You're special, Daryl, because you're a protector of the innocents.

Daryl recognized each missing child whose picture was pinned on the board in the conference room. She knew the mothers and the devastation they were suffering every day their child was not in their arms. She stood before the board. The map of Cranston Heights seemed to vibrate before her eyes, and she blinked rapidly as it flashed in a strobe-like effect.

"Daryl?" Lake's voice was soft beside her.

Daryl focused in on a point on the map. Then her line of vision was drawn to the children. Matthew Malone, Heather Jones, Calum Bridges, Francis Weeks, and the last child Daryl had started to investigate, Tanya Pope. Daryl believed Tanya to have been the first child stolen, three long years ago. "Calum's there too," she whispered, relieved to have another child confirmed. She'd wondered at the situation concerning these abductions. Usually, her talent led her straight to the missing without delay, but this case had been like trawling through molasses. Information had been patchy, and clues had been slow in arriving to her. She wondered what she was being made to wait for. The flashing stopped, and Daryl was able to release a breath. *Message received.* She felt the tightness in her chest lighten and her shoulders lift as the weight removed its almost crushing pressure. Lake was staring at her intently.

"I'll do everything I can to keep this investigation on a need to know basis and keep the Connecticut FBI out of the loop for now," Lake said. "But be careful not to cross paths with the investigation they have ongoing. We don't need that kind of exposure."

"If this blows up in our faces and I'm wrong, you need to pull Blythe out and keep her career unblemished. I know she has some misgivings about the direction I'm leading us into. I don't want her losing her credibility for working alongside me."

"You've never been wrong yet," Lake pointed out.

"The feds seem to think this time I am. Unfortunately, I'm liable to drag you all down with me if they prove to be correct."

"Then prove them wrong and bring those children home." Lake placed his hand on her shoulder and squeezed. "You brought Luke back home to us when we thought we'd lost him for good. You can do this."

"Then I guess I'd better go pack up my suitcases and get ready to start married life," Daryl said.

"You ready for that?" he asked with a small smile.

"I have to be. I step off that plane committed. In more ways than one."

Chapter Seven

Daryl had experienced mixed feelings leaving the comfort of Blythe's home. It also felt strange knowing that the other members of the DDU were staying behind in New York so as not to alert the local police that an investigation was going on under their noses. Daryl wondered if Blythe felt a little cut adrift from her usual partners. The plane journey had been uneventful, and Daryl had used the time to reread her files, going over them with Blythe and committing each child's features to memory. Not that she had any worry about not recognizing them, even as their features changed, as all baby faces do, Daryl would know them; she would recognize each of them instinctively. She'd told Blythe that and was relieved that she hadn't questioned her assured tone.

Daryl brought her eyes up from the printed pages she all but knew by heart. She took in her surroundings, recognizing where they were from her own surveillance of the area. Blythe was driving them to their new home.

"Any new insight?" Blythe asked.

Daryl sighed. "No, nothing at all."

"Then put the files away for now seeing as nothing new is going to magically appear on the sheets. You need to shed your detective persona and get ready to be a new homeowner."

Daryl shoved the paperwork back in her briefcase and snapped the lock closed. "How'd they get us a place so fast?"

"The sellers were ones who lost out in the recession. They were looking for a quick sell and we could offer them that. They vacated the place over a month ago so the DDU snapped it up."

"Fantastic timing for us, but not so great for the previous owners."

"It will be a happy home for us, sweetheart." Blythe flashed Daryl a brilliant smile.

Not for the first time, Daryl wished part of this setup was real. The way Blythe called her affectionate names, teased her gently, and just as easily listened intently when Daryl spoke made Daryl *feel*. Just being with Blythe made everything feel right. She'd never connected with someone so swiftly. Part of that terrified her. The other half knew they were going to be able to pass as a normal loving couple. Daryl just wished they had met without the kidnappings looming over them.

"Daryl, you need to be wearing your happy face for me," Blythe said sweetly. "You're thinking way too deeply over there in the passenger seat."

Daryl rubbed her hand over her face and forced her mind to focus on the task ahead. "Sorry," she muttered. "Don't you feel like you've been thrown in at the deep end and have forgotten how to swim?"

"Sure, but it's just a job like everything we do. Only we're partnered up in a house and we've got to go about getting our information indirectly. Sadly, it's not as simple as just interrogating every woman with a baby who crosses our path. We've got to fit in, get to know people before we can start asking the big questions."

"Oh God," Daryl moaned, "I suck at small talk!"

"You'll do fine, I'm sure. And if you really do suck, I'll just tell everyone you're the strong, silent type, and I'll do all the talking." Blythe pulled into the street where their new home was situated. The moving vans were already there and boxes were being taken into the house. "Looks like all the hard work is being done for us." She pulled in the driveway and turned the engine off. She shifted in her seat and her eyes warned Daryl that something was going to happen. Blythe reached over and captured Daryl's face.

"We've got company," she whispered before kissing Daryl softly.

The unexpected kiss set Daryl alight, and she couldn't stop the groan that escaped under Blythe's lips. She pulled Blythe closer, thankful for the car's small interior. She let her fingers spear through Blythe's hair, holding her in place as she began to return the kiss in earnest. She was rudely jerked out of their kiss by someone tapping on the car window. She stared into Blythe's eyes and was pleased to see they were as dazed as her own.

"Time to meet the neighbors," Daryl uttered under her breath and turned to roll down the window. A smiling woman stood beside the car brandishing a plate of baked goods.

"Hi there, you two. Welcome to the neighborhood." She stepped back as Daryl got out of the car. Her eyes traveled ever upward as Daryl's height was revealed. "Oh my, didn't they breed them big where you came from." She laughed and held out a hand, which Daryl politely shook. "I'm Mia Connelly and I live right next door to you." She turned to Blythe who had walked around the car to greet her. "Well, aren't you two a matched set!"

Blythe took her hand and introduced them both. "It's very kind of you to come greet us."

"I've been hanging out on the porch all day waiting for you. The guys said you'd be here soon so when I saw your car pull up, I knew I could come say hello. It's going to be so good having someone live in this place again."

"We appreciate your kindness." Daryl was distracted by a man trying to carry too many things at once. "Please excuse me for a moment. If he breaks my monitor I'll kill him!" She hastened away to help, leaving Blythe to deal with their obviously nice but nosy neighbor. She removed several packing boxes from the harried man and registered his surprise. Her voice deliberately low, Daryl said, "Thanks for moving us in, but please, let me help. Otherwise, I've got to make nice with Betty Crocker over there."

He grinned and cocked his head for Daryl to follow him. He led her through the hallway toward the back of the house. "This is what you're going to be interested in, Detective Chandler." He spoke her rank quietly as he ushered her behind a closed door. Inside, two women were setting up what would be the command center for the operation in their house.

"You're linked to the DDU's main computer from here, a direct line to God herself," one of the women said from behind a desk as she plugged in endless cords.

Daryl laughed at her description. "You mean Trace?"

"The one and only. She's going to walk you through all this setup herself once you're settled and we've got you all secure."

Daryl was in awe of the technology spread out before her. "So much for me expecting a laptop and simple Wi-Fi connection."

"Welcome to the DDU, Detective. Things run a little different for their operations." The woman got up from the floor and patted Daryl's arm. "Good luck with finding the children, ma'am."

"Thank you."

The man who'd directed Daryl in popped his head back around the door. "You might want to go rescue your partner. I think the local neighborhood watch is making her twitchy for her concealed gun!"

Daryl went to get Blythe. She stayed in the front doorway and leaned against the jamb. "Love, we're going to need you in here please. You know I don't have a clue where everything goes."

Given the excuse to extricate herself from Mia, Blythe hastened to Daryl's side, the plate of cookies in her hand. "You are an angel," Blythe breathed, "but I've found our font of all neighborhood goings on."

Daryl picked up a cookie and chewed. "A lead sitting right on our doorstep. Not bad for our first five minutes in our new home. And she bakes too. We'd best keep on her good side."

Blythe put the plate down and tugged at Daryl's hand. "Want to explore our new place?"

"Let's check it out." For a moment, the severity of the case faded as Daryl trailed after Blythe as they dodged the DDU's own who were bringing in furniture and building them a home.

The master bedroom housed a very large bed, a TV monitor on the wall, and enough closet space to seemingly fit the whole of Daryl's apartment inside. She gaped at the luxury money afforded. Blythe halted before the bed and Daryl noticed what had been done. Their suitcases had been brought in and laid together in the same room.

"There's that small room just across the hallway. I'll sleep in there," Daryl said. "It's done up like a spare bedroom anyway, and it's more than adequate for me."

"You're leaving me to the luxurious comfort this king-sized bed no doubt boasts?" Blythe sat on the mattress and patted the space beside her, inviting Daryl to sit.

Daryl did so and had to admit the room was lovely. "The guest room will suit me fine. We'll keep most of my belongings in here just in case we have someone who wants to sneak a peek inside our lives."

Blythe let out a dramatic sigh. "We haven't even spent a night together under our new roof and we're already sleeping in separate beds."

Daryl smiled. She caught Blythe's chin in her hand. "You are a tease, Mrs. Chandler-Kent."

"It's one of the many reasons why you married me," Blythe replied. "Maybe we'd better go supervise the downstairs crew before one of them comes up here to see if we're already undercover." She winked and bounced a little on the bed.

Daryl groaned. "You're also incorrigible." She stood and reached out a hand to help Blythe to her feet.

Blythe bumped her shoulder. "And that's another reason why you married me. That and my undeniable beauty."

Daryl couldn't argue with that. She felt herself fall just a little more under Blythe's spell.

❖

Seated on her new couch, Daryl relished the silence that had finally descended once everyone had cleared out of the house and left her and Blythe alone. She was still taking everything in. She was in their new living room, now all fully furnished and looking homey. Above the fireplace hung a beautifully framed picture of her and Blythe taken just days before but looking like they'd been together forever. The surreal quality of it all wasn't lost on Daryl, and she kept waiting for something to happen to drag her back to earth with a resounding bump.

"You look a little stunned," Blythe said as she handed Daryl a glass of wine.

"I can't believe how fast all this has happened. It wasn't a moment ago I was presenting my case to the DDU, and now we're undercover and living in a house I could never dream of affording."

"Our personal conference room in our office is all set up. Lake said he'd contact us at seven p.m. But now it's all up to you and me. The good old solid police work starts here."

Daryl took a small sip from her wine. "How soon can we start talking to the neighbors?"

"We've been invited to a 'getting to know you' barbeque this weekend. Is that soon enough for you?"

"Christ, someone works fast."

"It's all courtesy of your friendly neighborhood baking guru, Mia." Blythe took a drink from her glass and sat opposite Daryl. "I made your bed up."

"You didn't have to do that. I could have done it."

"I know, but it made me feel better seeing as I'm getting the better end of the deal and having the master bedroom with en suite bathroom. Your bathroom is two doors down from your bedroom."

Daryl shrugged. "It's just a room where I'll sleep. But thank you for doing that for me."

"We need to go grocery shopping tomorrow. The bits and pieces we picked up today on the way here won't last us until the weekend, and I'd like to have some food in our fridges so we don't starve."

Daryl remained quiet for a moment, her mind whirling.

"What are you thinking?" Blythe asked softly.

"How domesticated all this is." She gestured toward the photo on the wall and the others strategically placed on view. "One day, I'm single; the next, I'm married and moved into a dream home. I feel a little overwhelmed by it all." *And by how much I like it.*

"How did you see the operation working?"

"I thought it would be less…intimate." She cringed at her own words. "But all this…" She waved a hand to encompass the room. "This is beyond what I imagined."

"Then are you ready for a hard dose of reality?" Blythe checked her watch. "It's time to report in."

❖

The office set up for their faux business was a techie's dream. Blythe skillfully connected them to the DDU's New York base for a face-to-face conference call. Lake sat before the computer screen. Daryl could see the other two male members of the team sitting behind him.

"How are you settling in?" Lake asked.

"We've already been met by the neighborhood watch, a Mia Connelly," Blythe told him and Browning began tapping her name into a computer. Caldow leaned over his shoulder reading off the screen.

"She's clean," he reported.

"She's nosy," Daryl said, "but that may work in our favor."

"We've already been invited to meet all the neighbors this weekend at a barbeque so we can start putting out our story of wanting to adopt among the ones that have already been down that route," Blythe added.

"That will be a perfect opportunity," Lake said.

Caldow leaned into view. "So how's married life treating you so far?"

Daryl laughed. "It's hectic. Even though we had the help of the Bureau's finest moving us in, it was still stressful. At least I know where my suitcases are so I can have at hand anything I need that was packed in those." She paused for a moment. "It's going to be strange at the barbeque. *We're* the ones who are going to be scrutinized and questioned. I just hope our new neighbors don't realize we're doing the exact same thing back."

"I'll expect updates when you have them. For now, we'll step back and let you get on with it and just inform you when we find anything on our end. We're gathering hospital employee records at the moment and having to cut through some red tape to do it. It might take us a day or two to bang some bureaucratic heads together."

Daryl stared at Lake then looked at Blythe, surprised that they wouldn't have to report to the DDU every day. Lake chuckled.

"You're newlyweds. I thought you'd appreciate our stepping back and giving you some space."

Daryl knew her fair skin was broadcasting her embarrassment for all to see. Blythe just laughed beside her.

"We'll be in touch if anything develops. I have a feeling our neighbors aren't going to be the shy, retiring types. They smell new blood; they'll start circling soon."

"Just stick to your story and you'll be fine," Lake said. "Someone in that area is skilled enough to take children without anyone seeing them and then transplanting them in plain view with new identities. Be cautious, and let's wrap this case up tightly to bring those children home."

CHAPTER EIGHT

Daryl laid out a clean shirt from the ones Blythe had picked out for her on their shopping expedition. She liked the pale blue piped with black pinstripes, and teamed up with jeans, she hoped it would be considered suitable attire to meet and greet their new neighbors. She slipped her feet into a brand new pair of Nikes and couldn't remember the last time she'd worn casual shoes. She and Blythe had spent the morning grocery shopping again. Living with someone and not existing on a diet of pre-packed sandwiches or a candy bar at the police station made Daryl realize just how out of touch she'd gotten with the three meals a day routine.

Daryl didn't expect to enjoy the shopping quite as much as she had, but in Blythe's company it had been entertaining. Blythe had an infectious sense of humor that charmed Daryl, and she found herself relaxing more and more in her presence. She took all the gentle teasing in good part and found herself wishing that if she could ever settle down, it would be with someone like Blythe. With a sigh, Daryl put her shirt on. A tap on her bedroom door caught her as she was buttoning it up.

"Are you ready to face the horde of nosy neighbors?" Blythe asked through the door.

Daryl opened it to find Blythe wearing a bright red patterned summer dress that complemented both her figure and her dark coloring. Blythe caught her looking, even though she'd tried not to be too obvious.

"Will I do?"

Daryl just nodded, not trusting her voice.

Blythe tugged gently on Daryl's shirt collar. "You're looking mighty fine yourself. Very Yuppie. Have you got our story straight?"

Daryl nodded again. Their cover story was so ingrained in her brain she almost believed it herself. "I'm more than ready to get this investigation started."

"Then it's time to put your social game face on, sweetheart. Be sure to leave your badge behind," Blythe teased her. "Don't make me frisk you to make sure it's not hidden somewhere on your person."

"I feel naked without it," Daryl grumbled but patted her pockets to prove she wasn't carrying her shield.

"Just bring your investigative skills and your patience because we're the new folk on the block. We're going to be grilled as much as the meat on the barbeque."

❖

The spacious backyard of their hosts was bustling with people and children running around with high, excited voices. Mia Connelly spotted them right away.

"Blythe, Daryl, come meet everyone!" Mia waved them over and Blythe led the way, Daryl's hand in her own partly for appearances, but mostly because Blythe didn't want to be left to the jackals alone. She put on her brightest smile and strode forward.

"Niki, these are our new neighbors that moved into the Meyer home."

Niki was a short brunette, stocky in build, and sporting a sleeve tattoo Blythe knew Trace would have been all over. She shook Blythe's hand but was eyeing Daryl. She out butches you, short stuff, Blythe thought, amused when Niki straightened her shoulders and puffed out her chest to make herself look bigger. She shook Daryl's hand with a stern look.

"Niki, thank you for inviting us to your home. Did you build that barbeque pit yourself?"

Blythe looked over at the big fancy barbeque Daryl was referring to that was obviously used to some heavy-duty cooking.

"I did indeed."

"Man, that's so cool," Daryl said. "I wouldn't have known where to start."

Niki slugged Daryl on her arm. "Come check it out. Let me show you my baby."

Daryl flashed a smile at Blythe and kissed her on the forehead. "Back in a bit, babe."

Mia sidled in closer to Blythe and bumped her with a hip. "There was a time I was the only baby Niki got that excited over. But a three-tier grill and cooking tongs stole her heart. Your Daryl will be roped into helping now. Niki loves showing off her pride and joy." She waved over two women who were hovering nearby. "Jenn, Gina, meet Blythe. Her partner is that gorgeous hunk of blondness over there with my Niki."

Blythe laughed as the two women fanned themselves as they checked Daryl out.

"Where'd you find her, Blythe? She's beyond gorgeous," Gina asked breathlessly as her eyes swept over Daryl from head to toe.

Blythe enjoyed the opportunity to stare at Daryl herself. "Isn't she though?" she replied with a playful smile. "We met in New York." Their back story rolled from Blythe's lips as she told of their courtship, each romantic moment devised by the DDU.

"So you're settling down here?" Jenn asked.

Blythe nodded. "We decided we'd love a family very early on, but things haven't exactly gone according to plan for us in that area." Blythe paused as if overcome by emotion. She looked away to brush at her eye then back at the women who clung to her every word. "But we're looking into adoption because we want a child so much."

"You should talk to Claire and Liz. They'd been trying to adopt for years before they moved here. They registered at all the agencies, and now they are mommies," Mia confided. "I bet they'd have tons of advice to share with you."

Blythe smiled and squeezed Mia's arm in gratitude. "That would be fantastic. We'd love any assistance we can get. You'll have to point them out to us."

"They're over there with their little boy." Gina pointed to a couple indulgently watching the antics of a young child toddling around. His unsteady gait wasn't helped by the fact he was trying to run. One of his mothers scooped him up and kissed him all over his face. His high-pitched laughter rang through the air.

"You moved to Cranston Heights for that kind of life, Blythe?" Mia asked, watching Blythe's face as she stared at the happy family.

Blythe nodded, easily caught up in the role she was playing. "Maybe a little blond-haired child, someone Daryl can spoil to pieces and rock to sleep at nights."

"She could rock me to sleep any night," Jenn sighed and fluttered her eyelashes outrageously at Blythe.

Blythe just laughed at her, recognizing the teasing of a well-practiced flirty femme. "Honey, believe me, she rocks my world. She's just so full of love a child would be lucky to have her, just like I am."

Daryl was secretly amazed by how much there was to know about a barbeque setup and just how much Niki could talk about it. Daryl figured if she could listen in court to testimonies that were tedious works of fiction as people lied under oath, then she could listen to BBQ Betty spouting lyrical about how much steak she could char. One minute, Daryl was nodding and feigning fascination, the next, she was in motion, sprinting across the yard. She all but swooped in to scoop up a small child who was just seconds away from tumbling headfirst into the fish pool. She blinked dazedly as she looked down into the face of the small boy in her arms. Wide-eyed, he stared up at her then he gave her the most beautiful smile. In the suddenly unnatural silence, sound returned with a deafening boom, and Daryl was startled back to reality by the loud screams of a woman.

"Oh my God! Oh my God! Justin!" She and another woman ran over to Daryl, their faces ashen and equally terrified.

"He's okay," Daryl said softly, handing over the now squirming child to his frantic mothers. The one began running her hands all over his little limbs to make sure he was all in one piece. The other stood twisting her hands together in knots.

"I only looked away for a second," one said, her voice shaking in her fear.

"He's okay." Daryl barely had a chance to repeat before she found herself hugged between both women in their relief and gratitude.

"Niki, put the damn cover on that pool right this second!" Mia ordered angrily. "You were supposed to do that earlier today."

Niki hastened to do as she was bid. "I forgot," she grumbled to no one in particular.

Daryl tried to extricate herself from the sobbing parents. She was relieved when Blythe appeared beside her and slipped in to put an arm around her waist once the parents had stepped back to fuss over their son.

"Are you all right?" Blythe asked, fixing Daryl with such a curious look that Daryl cocked an eyebrow at her in question. "Daryl, you just seemed to sprout wings and fly down the yard to rescue him. I've never seen anything like it."

Daryl looked around and only then realized how far away the barbeque pit was from where the pool lay.

"She's an angel," one of the mothers said, hugging her son close, not caring that he was struggling to be let down again.

Daryl shook her head. "It was nothing really. Just so long as he's safe. Sorry if I startled him."

The shorter mother gave Daryl a considering look. "Usually, if a stranger holds him he screams blue murder. He never murmured with you. He obviously knew he was safe with you."

"She loves kids," Blythe said, leaning into Daryl and resting her cheek on Daryl's shoulder. "Hopefully, she can use that speed to corral our own kids when we're blessed."

Everyone crowded in around them, and only then did Daryl feel the unusual weight slip from her shoulders and leave her feeling lighter. She barely heard any of the excited conversations around her. All she could feel was Blythe's hand gripped tightly in her own as she stayed pressed firmly into her side. All she could see was little Justin flapping his arms about as if trying to fly. The pressure on her shoulders returned, her sight shifted, and Justin's face came into sharp focus. Daryl barely suppressed her sharp intake of breath.

Well, hello, Matthew Malone, we meet at last.

❖

The rest of the afternoon passed mercifully uneventfully. The food was plentiful, the beer was cold, and Blythe believed she'd been introduced to enough people to fill an entire football stadium. She sat beside Daryl and was amused to see that Justin kept looking over in their direction, flashing Daryl winning smiles.

"I think you've got a little admirer." She leaned close to whisper into Daryl's ear to make sure she was heard over the chatter and the music that was now being played. To everyone's eyes, it looked like she was nuzzling her lover's ear.

Daryl looked up from her plate at the child and he beamed even wider. She chuckled quietly but didn't say anything.

"Is he trying to fly?" Blythe asked, watching the toddler flitter about like a demented butterfly.

Daryl shrugged beside her. "He probably thinks he's Superman or some kind of weird fairy. Who knows what goes on in a little kid's head?"

"Maybe he's alluding to the fact you flew in to save him from falling in the pool. Daryl, I swear I've never seen anything like it. One minute, you were with Niki, the next, you were at the pool edge with him in your arms stopping him from falling in."

Daryl looked at her. "Really? Can't say I remember it much. It all happened so fast."

"Did you see him heading to the pool? Is that how you got to him first?"

"I can't remember. Good thing I did though. He could have been facedown with the fishes and none of us would have known with all the commotion here."

Blythe nudged her gently. "Protect and serve, eh?"

"Something like that, I guess."

"Claire and Liz are saying you're their son's guardian angel."

Daryl's laughter was swift. "I'm no angel."

Blythe moved closer. "Glad to hear it," she said and was delighted by the reddening of Daryl's cheeks. She couldn't stop the shiver that raced through her when Daryl leaned in closer still and made a show of pushing back Blythe's hair from her ear to place a kiss there. She also whispered in her ear.

"The kid I saved is Matthew Malone." She drew back and went back to picking food off her plate.

Desperately trying not to be obvious, Blythe sought out the child again until she found him now in Liz's arms. "You're certain?"

"As sure as I know I could eat more of these." Daryl waved a neatly stripped bone in Blythe's direction.

Blythe let her eyes wander around the yard and at the people gathered to party. Her gaze returned to Justin/Matthew who was leaning heavily on his mother's shoulder, obviously tired now and ready to take a nap. She recalled what Daryl had said to her. *When I find my kids, I'll recognize each of them.* Blythe had no reason to doubt her. She watched Liz rock her son to sleep, Claire behind her, both watching over him.

Just how do we tell them that he's not their child to keep?

Her inner turmoil was cut short by Mia loudly tapping a fork against the side of her beer bottle to get everyone's attention.

"On behalf of all of us here, I'd like to welcome our new neighbors, Blythe and Daryl, to the neighborhood." She smiled over at them. "I hope you find what you're looking for here and that you have happiness above all." She raised her bottle. "To Blythe and Daryl, Cranston Heights' new residents."

Everyone drank to the toast, but Mia wasn't finished. "And here's to Cranston Heights; our own slice of heaven on earth."

Chapter Nine

Ashley Scott slid her newly acquired key into the lock and opened the front door to her lover's home. Our home now, she thought with a smile. The welcoming call from the cat in residence made her smile widen.

"Hi, honey, I'm home," Ashley crooned as the black cat bounded down the hallway, chattering the whole way. The animal began twining around Ashley's legs, rubbing against her and purring up a storm. "So where's your other mommy, eh, Trinity?" Ashley asked, picking up the fussing cat and petting her. She carried Trinity into the kitchen where she dutifully prepared some fresh food for the animal whose vocalizations were getting louder. The sound of the front door opening made Ashley pause. Trinity head butted her to remind her to complete the task she was working on before becoming distracted by another human.

"Ashley?" Rafe called out from the hallway. "I pulled up just as you were opening the front door. How's that for perfect timing?" Rafe wandered into the kitchen and waited patiently while Trinity was suitably catered to. Once the cat bowl was on the floor, Ashley was swept up into Rafe's arms and kissed thoroughly. Ashley clung to Rafe, delighting in her passion. Not even when Rafe pulled back for air did Ashley loosen her hold. She kept her close, relishing Rafe's warmth and the feel of her body pressed hard against her own.

"I've missed you all day," Ashley told her, tracing Rafe's angular features with her palm then running her fingertips through hair that was finally growing back. The bruises on Rafe's face had long faded, but the ordeal Rafe had suffered, at the hands of a drugged up assailant with demonic strength, had left their mark inside and out. Her shaved head was slowly losing its stubble and getting some length back, though it still did little to hide the scars that marked Rafe's healing skull. "You're home early for a change." Ashley leaned up to kiss Rafe's lips in a welcome of her own. "Not that I'm complaining."

"Dean kicked me out of the office. I'm on call if anything comes in tonight." Rafe rocked Ashley gently in her arms. "But for now I'm all yours. Feel like having takeout?"

Ashley chuckled. "You're such a cop. If your food doesn't come in a carton or in a pizza box then you think it's not worth eating."

"Hey! I resent that insinuation. I can cook just fine," Rafe argued without much heat.

"Frosted flakes don't count, sweetheart," Ashley said as she slipped her hand to Rafe's belt and unhooked her cell phone. She speed-dialed a restaurant and gave their regular order then replaced the phone and patted Rafe's side. "It will be here in less than half an hour." She pulled back deliberately so she wouldn't be distracted by the spark of intention she could see glistening in Rafe's eyes. "We don't have time, Detective, for what you're envisioning in that sexy brain of yours."

"We can do fast now." Rafe leaned forward to nuzzle at a particularly sensitive spot behind Ashley's ear. "Then we could take it slower after."

Ashley moaned at the sensations that threatened to derail her thought processes. She struggled weakly in Rafe's grasp as she tried to recall what it was she had to discuss with her. Finally, before she could weaken any more, Ashley stuck her hands on Rafe's chest and pushed her back a little. Startled by the unexpected push, Rafe rocked back on her heels.

"What's wrong, Ash?" she asked.

"I need to speak to you before you cloud my brain with sexy endorphins that leave me wanting your body all over mine and nothing between us but kisses and searching hands."

Rafe leaned back against the kitchen counter and smiled cockily at her. "Then by all means talk, because I like that picture you've just painted for me, and I'd like to get back to it while my motor is still running."

Ashley took a deep breath that straightaway altered Rafe's mood. "What's wrong?" Rafe's voice changed to her serious cop voice and Ashley wanted to cuddle in close to soothe her.

"Calm down, tiger, nothing big, bad, and demonic is making their appearance known tonight." She paused then added, "That I'm aware of anyway. I just wanted to check something with you. Have you heard from Blythe at all?"

"Blythe? No, not recently. The last time I was in contact with her was reporting we'd caught the killer she'd helped profile for me. She's undercover on something now so I'm not expecting to be able to chat with her."

"She's in Connecticut, right?"

Rafe went very still. "You know she is. I told you that." Her eyes widened. "Why? What have you heard about her?"

"I haven't heard anything about her, so calm your fears, sweetheart. There have been some stirrings in the ether and some mutterings reaching ears."

"Mutterings from the angelic or demonic grapevine you have access to?"

"Via the good guys. There seems to be something hinky going on in that area and I recalled you saying Blythe was there."

"*Hinky?*"

"It's a technical term." Ashley grinned at her, reaching for Rafe's hand and making sure they were touching again. "Word is there might be a demon there, but whatever it is, it's staying off the angelic radar."

Rafe huffed. "You know, for all-seeing, all-knowing entities they need a better system to keep track of the demonic forces that are roaming over Earth."

Ashley nodded in agreement. "Still, something is pinging and drawing attention to an area there, and it made me think of Blythe."

"Do you think there's a connection between that and the case Blythe is working on? She's investigating babies being snatched. Do demons steal children?"

"It's rare. They usually covet more shiny objects. But if there's money to be made..." Ashley thought back to a previous case that she'd worked on, the breaking up of a large pedophile ring. Oddly enough, Blythe had been in on that investigation, though they had never formally been introduced. Ashley remembered the FBI team going into the house where the children had been hoarded by men for their unsavory dealings. Ashley had gone alone after her prey. She had tracked down the demon running the distribution of the videos taken of the abuse. He'd been banished to hell for his involvement and for daring to come topside. His punishment was nothing compared to what the children had been subjected to in the basement of the house they'd been found in.

"Is it a coincidence that there are rumblings of a demon where Blythe is when I know you've worked on a case with her before?"

"It probably isn't even in the same area where she is. It's most likely just a scavenger demon, a lower class scrounger doing nothing more than feeding from Dumpsters."

"Can I warn her?"

"Warn her of what, sweetheart? Can you really see yourself placing that call? *Hi, Blythe, heard there might be some demon activity where you're living.* It's not like giving people a heads-up to look out for tornadoes, Rafe. You'll only worry her that you got more than your bell rung when you were attacked."

Rafe tugged Ashley close. "Oh, I got more than that and you damn well know it. I got my own personal front seat into watching hell walk on earth."

"You got me too," Ashley reminded her.

"You are the only good thing that came out of any of it."

"That and the fact you can talk to angels face-to-face."

"One angel; your angel. I'm still not sure he trusts me completely."

"He gave you the Spear of Light to incapacitate demons. How more trusting is that? And he never materializes in our bedroom. I'd say he has more than enough respect for you."

"I guess," Rafe muttered. "Are you sure I can't find a way to let Blythe know she needs to be careful? I can be subtle."

Ashley let out a sudden burst of laughter then hastily kissed Rafe to take away the sting. "Yes, you can be subtle. You are oh so subtle as an avenger armed with your Spear of Light when you banish demons back to hell."

"I do have a flair for that; you have to admit I do."

Rafe had come a long way in such a short time, from rabid disbeliever to dedicated banisher of the demon hordes. "Yes, you do, and it's very sexy watching you in demon banishing mode. But I don't think there's much call for that in Connecticut this time. So put away your demon hunting go-bag for now, and I'll apprise you if and when I get any more information. I might not even be called in."

Rafe wrapped her arms about Ashley and pulled her close. "Good. I mean, we've only just started to live together and sleeping together every night and I'd hate it if you had to go."

Ashley smiled against Rafe's breast. "I'd be coming back, Rafe. I'd be called in to assess the situation, probably deal with it, then I'd be high-tailing it back home." She felt Rafe's arms tighten.

"I like how you say that."

"Home?"

"Home meaning here with me."

"And Trinity," Ashley added mischievously.

"You spoil that cat," Rafe grumbled.

"I like to spoil you more." Ashley brought her head up and her eyes focused on Rafe's lips. She licked her own in anticipation at the look that flared in Rafe's dark eyes.

Rafe lowered her head with intention but was interrupted by the sound of the doorbell ringing. "Damn, they're fast. Food first, then you can spoil me all you like."

Ashley set the table for them while Rafe paid the man at the door. Only when they were halfway through eating did Ashley ask a question that had been playing on her mind.

"How open do you think Blythe would be to being told that there are more things walking this soil than she could have imagined?"

"She hunts monsters for a living. How do I think she'd take to being told that there really *are* monsters out there? Demonic ones with horns and eyes that burn with the sulfuric fires of hell?" Rafe shrugged. "I haven't a clue. She'd probably profile *you* as certifiable if you told her."

"I seem to recall you did the same."

"Then I got to know you and the crazy world you live in. Now I *know* you're certifiable."

Ashley reached across the table and took a big piece of meat from Rafe's plate and took a healthy bite from it in retaliation.

"Hey! At least we're now crazy together," Rafe said, smiling sweetly across the table until Ashley relented and gave her what was left of the meat back.

"It's probably nothing to do with her at all," Ashley said. "I mean, really, what are the chances of her being the key element involved in demon activity?"

"Slim to zero I'd hope?" Rafe answered around a mouthful of rice.

"Exactly."

"But you'll let me know if anything else comes from the grapevine?"

"You can count on it. We make a good team when we investigate together."

"So can I come to Connecticut with you?"

"You'd take time off work to accompany me?"

"I have plenty of time accruing. We could class it as a vacation."

"Vacations are supposed to be relaxing."

"I'll relax knowing there's one less demon out of the picture thanks to you."

Ashley sent her own heartfelt prayer of gratitude up for the circumstances that had brought Rafe to her. No one else had a partner who understood and supported her daily work quite so much as Rafe did.

"You're my everything; do you know that?"

"Yeah, yeah, but I know you love that damned cat more." Rafe picked out a choice piece of food from her plate and put it on Ashley's without a word then went back to eating her supper.

Ashley found the act so sweet but didn't say anything. She'd make certain Rafe knew exactly where her heart lay once they'd finished their meal.

❖

Daryl dusted off a few stray leaves from the park bench and gestured for Blythe to take a seat. They sat close together, Blythe's arm stretched out behind Daryl, her body leaning against her. From that position she had a clear view of the Three Little Ducks Daycare Center they had been observing for the past four days.

"It would be so much easier if we could just march in there and ask to see their attendance sheets," Blythe said.

Daryl hummed her agreement as she flicked through the photographs she had stored on her phone. She brought up the baby picture she had of Heather Jones and then the not so clear shot she had taken herself when last in the area.

"We're going to be screwed if her mother has taken her out of the class here."

Daryl rested her head on Blythe's for a moment. "I have the utmost confidence that Heather's new mommy has a routine she sticks to and that little girl is in there." *She has to be, I just know she's here.*

"Your confidence is inspiring, if not a little strange," Blythe drawled, shooting Daryl a look over her shoulder.

"If I had a dollar for every time I've heard that," Daryl muttered as she flipped through her messages. She reread a mail sent by the DDU and frowned. "Not sure how I'm supposed to be able to get DNA samples from kids I can't legally touch."

"Then you had better hope your instincts lead you in a way that we can legitimately prove these children are not who everyone thinks they are."

Daryl sighed. It always came down to the part of the investigation that could be written down and read without the stigma of her *intuition* being attached. It wasn't enough she could focus in and find where the children were; she always needed evidence. Evidence she had no clue how she was supposed to retrieve.

Blythe shifted at Daryl's side. "Don't worry about that for now. Let's just enjoy the sunshine and the beauty of the park while we sit and wait to watch lots of little toddlers pitter-pat out of the Center like ants on a sugar high."

"With Heather Jones among them."

"And if she is?"

"Then we follow her home and gather another address for Trace to research. Hopefully, that will prove I was totally justified in dragging you all into this investigation with me." Daryl watched as a steady stream of parents started to gather at the gates. "Two confirmed sightings will stand stronger than just one in my case."

"Then there's three children to go."

"Yes, and I'm not leaving without them all." She felt Blythe eyes on her and met her intense gaze with her own. "No child gets left behind."

"I understand that. It must be gratifying to return a lost child home."

Daryl smiled at the wistful sound of Blythe's voice. Daryl's pride at her job was always tinged with the shadow of regret. "It is. Sadly, not all the children I find are alive."

At Daryl's tone, Blythe shifted closer. She brushed her fingers over Daryl's knuckles and then placed her hand on Daryl's thigh. She squeezed her gently in reassurance.

"Don't get me wrong, any find is a result. But that doesn't stop me from hating the fact that I can be too late to truly help."

"You can't be everywhere at once, Daryl."

"I know. But sometimes I wish I could be in the right place at the right time a lot more." She lifted her head up at the sound of the school bell ringing. "School's out. Let's see if Heather is among them."

She began searching the faces of the little children that spilled out of the building. The sound of their high-pitched voices carried in the air. A familiar weight pressed down on her shoulders. *Finally.* Her sight focused in on a tiny child dressed in a bright pink T-shirt. She was skipping around a woman who was laughing at her exuberance. Once the pressure was removed, Daryl lifted up her phone and snapped off a volley of pictures.

"You've found her?" Blythe sat up straighter.

Daryl showed her an image she'd captured. She rose and reached to help Blythe to her feet. "Care to take a stroll?"

They followed Heather at a respectable distance, easily mixing in among the mass of toddlers and their harried parents. Heather and her mother headed toward a car and Daryl tugged at Blythe's hand to slow their pace to give the woman ample time to get Heather fastened in her car seat. Before the door closed, Heather's pacifier fell out onto the road. When the car pulled away, Daryl wandered over to the curb and knelt to fiddle with her shoelace. Unobtrusively, she picked up the pacifier and palmed it. She and Blythe hastened across the road and circled back toward the park. Once away from the crowd, Blythe opened her handbag and drew out a small brown bag that Daryl dropped their evidence into.

"It's a good thing you came prepared."

"Force of habit," Blythe admitted.

"And you try so hard to get the cop out of me." Daryl was so giddy at their good luck that she was hard-pressed not to gather Blythe up in her arms and kiss her. It must have shown on her face because Blythe's eyes flared. Daryl knew she was fighting a losing battle trying to stifle her feelings toward Blythe. She forced herself to just take Blythe's hand and tug her forward. "We need to contact the courier Lake set up for us just in case this eventuality occurred."

"Ah yes, the DDU's version of FedEx."

Daryl made a face. "Please, don't mention fed," she joked, delighted when Blythe laughed.

"I'd say you've just proved how wrong they were to dismiss you."

"Here's hoping that pacifier validates everything I believe so you can believe it too."

Blythe cuddled into Daryl's side. "Oh, honey, I've never doubted you from the start."

It did Daryl's heart good to hear the quiet sincerity in Blythe's voice.

"I can't say I truly understand you or what exactly it is you do, but I can appreciate an air of mystery in a woman!" Blythe bumped Daryl's shoulder and favored her with such a wicked smile that it brought a rush of blood to Daryl's cheeks.

Daryl could only hope Blythe wouldn't live to regret those words.

Chapter Ten

D aryl stood before the huge closet and just stared at the clothing hanging there. *What do you wear when going to an adoption agency for the first time?* She reached for one shirt, discarded it, and then reached for another.

Blythe walked in looking very chic in her dark skirt and soft cream blouse. She chuckled at Daryl's harried demeanor.

"This is the one occasion you can wear your cop clothes, Daryl." She pulled out a plain blue shirt, holding it up against Daryl's chest, then picked out a pair of dark blue chinos to match. "There you go. Smart yet casual. We want to show we can be serious and professional in this endeavor, but we're also young and vibrant."

"I don't feel very vibrant. I feel queasy and more than likely to puke." Daryl accepted the clothes gratefully. She was glad she had one less thing to worry about. Blythe patted her on the shoulder.

"You'll do fine. And if they see you clinging to my hand with a death grip, they'll just think you're nervous and very sweet."

"Sweet?"

"Yes, sweet, Daryl Chandler. It's not a bad thing. Now go get dressed. We have our first command performance to go to."

Daryl let herself be shooed out of the master bedroom to go get changed in her own. She divested herself of her jeans and T-shirt and put on the more familiar clothing. Daryl hesitated in tying her hair back, instead leaving it loose. No sense in getting too comfortable in what felt like her usual clothes. She looked at herself in the mirror as she finished fastening up the buttons to her shirt. Her hand went to her belt to touch the badge that usually hung there. Force of habit made her reach for it. She was so used to touching it for good luck before she left the house.

I've got to stop that automatic reflex. I'm Daryl Chandler, Web designer. I live with my wife Blythe in our way too expensive home with more rooms than we'll ever use. I drive an ostentatious car and wave at the neighbors every day as I go for my run around the neighborhood. I've been here three weeks, and so far all I've done was save a kidnapped child from drowning and helped a clueless computer-phobe not to wipe her entire hard drive clean while playing Farmville on her PC. I'm finally about to try to get an adoption agency to believe that I want the gay American dream—to add a child to our happily ever after. She stared at herself in the eye. *And I'm worried if I have the right pants on to do this.* She rubbed at her face briskly then shook herself. *You can do this. You can play the role, make them believe it.* She saw her wedding band and twisted it gently on her finger. *Face it, this kind of life, with someone as beautiful and smart as Blythe? Who wouldn't want it all?*

The medical information that Daryl's contact had made up for her and Blythe was clinical and sobering in its details. She watched as it was being pored over by a middle-aged man in a rumpled suit and bifocals. Every so often, he'd look over his glasses at them then back at the documents. Daryl knew none of what was written there was true, but there was still a part of her that felt it was an invasion of their privacy, having this man reading about their supposed inability to carry a child of their own. Daryl had a feeling that undercover work might not be a good choice for her again; she took it to heart too much. She didn't like the way this Thomas Grace kept eyeing Blythe either.

She willed herself not to fidget and let her eyes instead take in the office they sat in. The walls were lined with awards and legal documents. She wondered at the lack of photos of children anywhere. She also wondered how Blythe could be sitting next to her in what she was sure was as uncomfortable a seat as she was stuck in and remain looking so relaxed. Daryl watched as Grace picked up their financial records and wasn't surprised to see a small smile creep onto his face. It was there for a brief second, but she caught it. Daryl didn't jump when Blythe's hand slipped over her own. She knew Blythe had also seen that telltale pleasure at their supposed combined wealth.

"I believe I have all the information I need for now," Grace said, collecting all their paperwork together and pressing a buzzer to call forth his secretary. "Photocopy these." The young woman slipped out as silently as she had entered. "I'll just need to run some background checks, verify some details, and then we can set up a home visit so we can ascertain if your home is suitable for a child." He grinned as he looked up at them both. "But you live in Cranston Heights. I really can't see there being any problem, but we have to be seen to go through the formalities." He walked them to the door. "You can get your paperwork back from Anne-Marie when she's finished taking copies for your file. I'll be in touch. I have all your numbers."

I know you do, and you have our monthly earnings engraved in a special place on your heart. Daryl's head was full of all the information they'd received. She felt like she'd just stood on the stand and been judged and tried by a jury without mercy. Judging not whether she could be a fit parent for a child, but could she afford the material upkeep of a dependant that would need college tuition fees and designer labels on everything. She thought about her own upbringing and was thankful her parents had brought her up to value the simple pleasures of life and not be weighed down by the material things. She'd grown up surrounded by love, and even though both parents had worked, she had never felt neglected. Especially as she'd spent so much time at her father's side in the police station. She followed Blythe to the secretary's desk and waited while the girl quickly ran their documents through the photocopier. Thankful to be leaving, Daryl escorted Blythe out of the agency and away from the obsequious little man who held their parenting hopes in his damp little hands.

Blythe slipped her arm around Daryl's and hastened their departure. She shuddered once they were far enough away from the agency's building. "Please tell me you found him as creepy as I did?" Blythe said, wiping her hand on her skirt as if trying to remove his handshake.

"Mr. Thomas Grace was indeed a strange little man. But does he fit your profile?"

"My profile points to someone with an agenda that isn't dollar oriented as much as he seems to be."

"We really need to talk with Liz and Claire, find out how they got Matthew."

"Justin," Blythe corrected her. "He's Justin to them."

Daryl sighed. "I know. It's just so damn hard when I know who he really is."

"I'll see if I can invite them over for a meal or something. Do the big pretence of wanting to ask them about their experiences with the agencies. Maybe they'll tell us who they got Justin through. Anything they say might save us time and energy and stop us from having to shake hands with any more sleazy baby brokers."

"Did you see the way his secretary acted around him? She made sure she didn't come into contact with him and never looked at him. I wonder what the story is there."

"Maybe he's got wandering damp hands. I checked out her nameplate on the desk. I'll have Trace look into an Anne-Marie Stokes. I didn't see many more people in the office. Looks like Grace's Adoption Agency is a one-man show." She started the car up and pulled out into traffic. "I'll also have her check if we've got Thomas Grace in our database. I can't help think that Ms. Timid's reaction to him means he has something devious going on in that office. Hopefully, we might be able to find prior proof of that."

Daryl leaned back against the headrest and closed her eyes. "God, how do people deal with all the legalities that are set in place to hinder more than help them get a child?" Her head was still spinning from the reams of information imparted to them and the endless stream of questions they had had to answer.

"You'll jump through fire if your need is strong enough."

"And that little maggot back there knows it too. I swear I saw dollar signs flash in his eyes and a loud *ka-ching* noise when we walked into his office."

"Do you think the two other agencies we have to see will be equally as distasteful and as badly decorated as this one was?"

Daryl laughed, recalling the severely out of date wallpaper that had decorated the office walls. "I'm hoping that at the next one we're due to visit alarm bells start ringing so we know who to start investigating."

"I didn't hear alarms bells with this guy, even though he made me uncomfortable in his presence. I hope the guys back at the DDU can dig up something on his record, if he has one. Tomorrow's appointment is with Criton and Welch Adoptions. They're the only one of the three with religious affiliations."

Daryl groaned. "That can't be good. Especially when we walk in."

"That's what we need to see. Are they pious and self-righteous in the office but then offer us a child out of office hours that they steal from ungodly folk?"

"Suffer not the little children, eh?" Daryl said. She wished something had tugged at her Intuitive state where these agencies were concerned. Her cop instincts told her one of them was involved because of how the children had been placed. The children Daryl had found were all in good homes with wealthy parents. Wealthy *gay* parents. Someone had to have the knowledge that these people wanted a child; a child hadn't been taken for it just to be given away or left on the street. These abductions were meticulously planned and the recipients were as specific as the mothers whose children were taken.

"Can we stop somewhere to get ice cream?" Daryl asked. She was in desperate need of something sweet to get rid of the nasty taste in her mouth after their first visit to an agency.

"Sure." Blythe sounded a little surprised but switched lanes to take them to the nearest Dairy Queen. "You okay, Daryl?"

"I just feel the need for ice cream." *Maybe the cold treat will calm the raging fire of uncertainty in my soul. I need to solve these cases, but it's taking too much time. It's driving me crazy that I have held one of the missing children in my own hands and can't hand him back to the mother who is frantic for him to be returned. Why is my Intuitive power dragging its heels on this? How much worse can it get before I finally get the break I need? Or am I losing my touch and my magic is fizzling out?*

"Undercover is a bitch, isn't it?" Blythe said, reaching over to rub Daryl's knee.

And that's the other problem. Being undercover with you isn't the hardship I wish it would be.

❖

"Do you think we sounded desperate enough?"

Daryl filled her mouth with a spoonful of strawberry ice cream and released such an appreciative moan at the taste that Blythe felt her insides clench at the sexy rumble. It took her a long moment before she could answer, too caught up in the look of pleasure on Daryl's face as she ate.

"I think we very succinctly put over our desire for a child, in between talking about our backgrounds, relatives, interpersonal relationships, job prospects, and hobbies." Blythe took a small bite of her own rocky road concoction. "Thank God the first thing that shot out of my mouth for hobbies wasn't gun range target practice."

"I think as long as you mentioned how expensive your gun was I don't think Grace would have batted an eye."

"He did seem rather money-grubbing, didn't he?"

"Maybe that's why he could be the money man. He has ample opportunity to work out who among his clientele are the ones wealthy enough to pay to get the baby they want." Daryl looked up over her dessert. "Thank you for coming here. I needed to just step away for a while."

"Are you finding the actual role-playing difficult?"

"I'm used to asking the questions, not being expected to have memorized answers that I need to keep front and foremost in my mind. I feel like I should be breaking down doors and dragging information out of suspects. Instead, I'm sitting in offices pretending I have the life this Daryl leads. I'm not used to this softly softly approach."

"You're playing the role well though. Our neighbors love you." Blythe playfully growled at her. "Some more vocally than others. I was stopped by Jenn yesterday who was extolling the virtues of you running round the block in your underwear."

Daryl frowned. "I do not! I wear a very decent pair of shorts and a T-shirt when I run. How on earth can that getup cause comments to fly?"

"It's how you fill out those shorts and T-shirt, sweetheart." She deliberately tagged on the endearment and enjoyed seeing the start of a blush color Daryl's pale cheeks. "You're causing quite the stir amid the femmes of Cranston Heights and giving a fair few butches something to think about."

"Think about what exactly?"

"How they can get a body like yours so their wives will stop their eyes from wandering in your direction."

Daryl returned to her ice cream. "Don't they know I'm already spoken for?" She held up her ring finger and flashed her wedding band at Blythe.

"I told her that. I think I played the possessive wife quite perfectly too." Blythe knew she wasn't exaggerating. She'd made it very clear that women could look, but the only one who'd be touching Daryl was her alone. Blythe acknowledged just how true those words had been. She'd seen Daryl leave the house ready for her daily run and come back suitably sweaty and breathing hard. Some mornings, Blythe had to keep her grip on the kitchen counter to stop herself from reaching out to pull Daryl close and test out her stamina. There was something about Daryl that Blythe found irresistible.

She told herself it was unprofessional to harbor such thoughts for a work colleague while in the midst of an investigation. She told herself a lot of things, but that didn't stop her heart from racing when Daryl wore running shorts that showed off the long length of her muscled legs. Or how her T-shirt clinging to her chest made Blythe want to run her fingers across the abs that could be clearly seen through the sweat soaked material. Now, watching Daryl as she finished up the last of her ice cream, Blythe was struck by how much she wanted to kiss the cool strawberry ice cream from Daryl's lips. She knew her desire must have shown in her eyes because when Daryl looked up she blinked at her in surprise. Slowly, she laid her spoon aside as if any sudden movement might break the charged atmosphere.

"What?" she asked Blythe quietly, capturing her lower lip between her teeth and driving Blythe's want a little higher at the unconscious gesture.

"I wish I'd known you before this assignment. That way I wouldn't feel so damn insubordinate every time I look at you and think how handsome you are."

Daryl reached across the table to take Blythe's hand. Blythe caught sight of a small droplet of ice cream on her knuckle. Without giving thought to their surroundings or who they were professionally, she lifted Daryl's hand to her mouth and licked the ice cream away with a warm tongue. Daryl's grip tightened and Blythe kept her lips brushing across those strong knuckles. She looked up to see intense blue eyes boring into her. When Daryl spoke, her voice was roughened.

"How much of this is make-believe?" she asked.

"I don't know anymore," Blythe answered honestly. She pressed a lingering kiss on the back of Daryl's hand. "I do know that it feels right when I'm touching you. It feels as natural as breathing to me."

"And the fact we're trolling round adoption agencies trying to procure a baby?"

"That's something we can discuss later when we've been more intimate." Blythe knew her own face burned as much as Daryl's did at her words.

"You see us being intimate?"

Blythe leaned across the tiny table to brush a kiss across Daryl's mouth. "I do; repeatedly."

Daryl's hand snagged behind Blythe's neck to draw her forward again for another kiss.

"Hi, girls!"

Blythe jumped, startled by the intrusion. "Mia!" She hoped Mia realized just how lucky she was that Blythe wasn't carrying her gun. Reluctantly, she slid back down into her seat.

"I thought I spotted you two canoodling here in the corner booth." Mia Connelly gave them both a warm smile, totally oblivious to what she'd unwittingly interrupted. "What brings you here sampling sweet treats?"

"We've just started the ball rolling at our first adoption agency," Blythe explained and had to smile when Mia clapped her hands together like a delighted child.

"How wonderful. Tell you what, how about you two come over to our place for a meal tomorrow night and I'll invite Liz and Claire too so you can swap adoption stories."

Blythe nodded eagerly. "That's very kind, thank you." *Perfect, those women are exactly who we need to interrogate in a friendly atmosphere.*

"No problem," Mia said. "Besides, it gives me the excuse to get to know you better. Daryl, it appears you like your desserts." She looked deliberately at the empty ice cream glass. "Do you like fruit pies?"

Daryl nodded. "I'll admit to having a bit of a sweet tooth."

Mia spared Blythe a knowing look. "So sweet things are the way to your girl's heart then?"

"It explains why I'm with Blythe." Daryl smiled across the table and Blythe felt her heart skip and stutter in her breast.

"Oh, you two are too cute for words," Mia sighed. "My Niki needs to take lessons from you, Daryl. Especially on how you get to keep so fit when you eat such sinful desserts."

"The answer is lots and lots of hot and sweaty...*exercise.*"

At Daryl's blatantly sensual tone, Blythe was assailed with visions that hinted more of exercise under the sheets than the pounding of the pavement in a pair of Nikes.

"Oh my God, you are so bad!" Mia chuckled, fanning herself comically. "No wonder Blythe wants to keep you all to herself."

"I like it that way," Daryl said. "I've been hers from the moment our eyes first met." Daryl reached across the table and Blythe linked their fingers together.

"Geez, the honeymoon never ended for you two, did it?" Mia shook her head at them. "I'll leave you to whatever you were doing, and I'll call later with details for dinner tomorrow night."

Blythe waited until Mia left the shop. "I swear we have magnets attached to our asses where that woman is concerned."

"She does have the unfortunate habit of interrupting us just as we're getting to the good stuff."

"But she has just opened up a channel for us to talk to Justin's mommies. I thought we'd have to bide our time for another week or so before we could approach them without it looking highly suspicious. I didn't want us being seen as too blatant in our desire to talk about adoption. Having just moved in and you saving their child's life seemed a little too much to then arrive on their doorstep asking if they'd tell us how they got him. At least this way you know Mia will do all the talking and we can slip in our questions around her."

"It's going to be a busy day tomorrow, apparently. We're meeting with the next adoption agency on our list and then dinner with the neighbors."

"It should make for an interesting evening. Especially now that Mia thinks your tight body comes from us having an exuberant sex life."

Daryl grinned. "Hey, I'm just helping to perpetuate our cover as a devoted couple who love each other with a passion."

"Do you think our attraction is due to these roles we're playing?"

"All I know is, when I walked into that office and saw you sitting there, my life hasn't been the same since."

"So what do we do about it?"

"We just take it one day at a time and not let whatever we're feeling jeopardize the investigation. The children have to come first."

Blythe had to laugh. "I swear you just channeled my friend Rafe for a moment." She recognized the warning though; the case had to come first. Then, and only then, could they explore what was happening between them.

CHAPTER ELEVEN

The office in Blythe and Daryl's home hummed with the sound of computers busy doing their job. Daryl sat before the screen recounting their latest interview to Agent Lake and the team.

"I swear, Nathan, the woman fell just short of coming right out and saying 'you're unfit to raise a child because of your deviant lifestyle.'" Daryl was still fuming at the derisive manner in which the adoption agency manager had treated her and Blythe.

"Do you believe that excludes her agency from the list?" he asked.

Daryl shrugged. "I don't honestly know. We got so many sympathetic looks as we came out of the office, no doubt looking shell-shocked, that maybe someone in there disagrees with her and goes behind her back to facilitate an adoption."

Lake nodded. "That would make sense. We'll probe deeper into Connie Hunt's staff. Let's see if we can find anyone with homosexual sympathies."

"We could have benefited from some of those sympathies in her presence." Blythe slipped into the chair beside Daryl, armed with the paperwork she'd just printed off. "She looked through our medical files and made the comment God must have had good reason to make us both barren."

"Fuck me," Trace growled. "How did you rein yourself back from punching her, Blythe?"

"I was too busy wondering if I needed to hold Daryl back first."

Daryl looked sheepishly at the screen. "If I could have arrested her there and then for a hate crime or discrimination I would have. The woman made my skin crawl."

Agent Lake looked over his shoulder at Caldow. "We'll run a check into her associates. A woman that devout in her beliefs has to run with a pack of like-minded people. And I'd say she makes enemies fairly easily."

"She told me I'd have a better chance of getting a child if I looked less like a man," Daryl added, silently amused by the shocked and furious faces that looked back at her from the screen.

"And how did you answer?" Lake asked.

"She politely told the bitch she could still be a good mother to a child whether she wore pants or not," Blythe said. "I'm telling you, the woman was a poisonous snake! Tell me what you can find out on her because I'd bet she's a spinster who's never spread her legs once!"

Daryl choked on the coffee she was sipping and hastily put the mug back down. Trace and the men on the other side of the screen all laughed, though Lake recovered his professionalism hastily.

"She made me mad." Blythe was justifiably indignant.

"We really didn't like her," Daryl said with a smile on her face.

"So Criton and Welch Adoptions didn't ring any bells except for the blatant homophobia they display?"

They shook their heads.

"I'm hoping for a more informative evening tonight in the company of Liz and Claire, the women who somehow acquired Matthew Malone. We'll have an informal setting, hosted by a very chatty neighbor who informed me that my wife has the neighborhood buzzing."

"How so?" Lake asked.

"Seems everyone wants to take up running so they can try to keep up with her."

Daryl sighed. "I don't see what all the fuss is about."

"Well, Angel Hair, you're six foot of gorgeous butchness. I'm surprised Blythe hasn't had to keep you under house arrest away from all the admiring eyes."

Daryl laughed then realized Trace wasn't joking. "Get out of here." She willed her face not to display her embarrassment but knew it was a lost cause.

"Maybe you should have handsome here ask your ladies the questions tonight, Blythe. She might get more out of them than you." Trace flashed Blythe a sly grin.

"I've considered that, especially as she's the one who saved Justin/Matthew from nearly taking a header into the fish pool. They might be more willing to open up to the savior of their child."

"It wasn't that big a deal," Daryl said.

"It was a very big deal," Blythe said.

Daryl heard the sound of someone mimicking a whip being cracked. She glared through the screen at Trace who just grinned like the Cheshire Cat.

"I'll expect your report in the morning," Lake said. "At the very least they should give you the name of the adoption agency they went through."

"I'm guessing it wasn't today's," Blythe said.

"Not with Ms. C. Hunt at the wheel," Trace said under her breath, making the c soft and sending Caldow into a fit of laughter that he hastily hushed when Lake glared at him.

Daryl cast an eye over the paperwork Blythe had rested on her lap. "Any new information from the hospitals?"

Browning shook his head. "We're checking out all the employees that have worked on the baby support area, but some of it is done on a voluntary basis and they don't keep detailed records for those who might just be filling in for an hour."

"Damn it," Blythe grumbled.

"The woman we're trying to trace gave all the women she helped different names, and so far, not one of those names appears in the hospital records," Caldow added.

"She's like a damned chameleon. She apparently can blend in with the hospital staff and no one notices she's out of place. She's obviously no threat to look at. You welcome her into your home to look after your child because she's proved she's reliable and safe. And then she strikes." Daryl rubbed at her face, annoyed that the woman seemed to have left no trace anywhere that they could follow up on.

"I'm running a program using the description of the kidnapper against anyone going in or out of the hospitals at any given moment." Trace gave them all a resigned look. "As you can imagine, it's spitting out every woman that has blond hair and the occasional dude with man boobs. I'm gathering the identities of them through the hospital IDs and the rest from the DMV files. Who knew there were so many blondes out there? I'm going to need a miracle to narrow it down if we're going to get anywhere on this line of inquiry."

"Do the hospitals know you have access to their security cameras?" Daryl asked.

"Not at the moment. I did get to watch a very fascinating operation yesterday courtesy of one cam. Oh, and a doctor providing a little 'hands on' experience with a young nurse. I'd like to think he was checking out his plastic surgery skills considering the amount of time he spent 'testing' her breasts." She demonstrated graphically.

Blythe burst into laughter and Daryl swiftly hid her smile behind a hand while Lake cut Trace a reprimanding look.

"Eyes only on what we need, Trace," he said.

Trace lifted her hands in surrender. "Don't blame me if Dr. Feelgood wanted to play 'hide the thermometer' right under a security camera's lens while I was scanning for blondes."

Browning muttered, "Call me next time, Trace."

"On that note," Lake said, speaking loudly over the agents behind him, "I hope you have a successful evening, ladies."

The computer screen went blank as their connection was severed and Daryl stared at it for a long while before speaking. "Why can't we find her? She's tied to the hospitals, has to be linked to an agency because of her knowledge of the desperate couples, and still she's invisible to us."

"She's good at what she does. She's done it five times now."

"Five times too many." Daryl pushed out of her seat and stalked from the room. *Five children, five babies taken from their mothers, and where is my Intuition? Showing me, directing me, but not once letting me stop her. I'm finding where the children are, slowly, oh so slowly, but just once couldn't I be shown who's behind it so I can stop them from terrorizing another mother?* Daryl stared out the living room window, not seeing the traffic going by, lost in her disillusionment. She was tearing herself up inside because she couldn't solve the case quicker.

She jumped as arms slipped around her waist and Blythe pressed herself against Daryl's back.

"Stop beating yourself up over this, Daryl. You're not omnipotent. You can't solve everything with the snap of your fingers even if you do have the stats that apparently prove otherwise."

Daryl could feel the length of Blythe's body pressed against her. Strong arms encircled her and Blythe's head rested on Daryl's shoulder. She felt oddly safe and secure in that hold. "I feel so useless," Daryl admitted.

"Undercover work isn't a quick fix. You can't expect everything to suddenly appear before us. We've got to investigate, interrogate, and at the same time never give ourselves away. As we gather more evidence things will become clearer."

Daryl sighed deeply. "I'm used to things happening a lot quicker."

Blythe nodded against her. "I know. I've read your personnel file. You're renowned for finding lost children. And you have here; you've located some of the missing children already."

"But not all of them," Daryl muttered. She'd only been able to physically account for Matthew Malone so far. But she *knew,* without a doubt, the others were near too.

"Yet," Blythe said. "But that doesn't mean you won't. You have some kind of uncanny sixth sense when it comes to finding children."

"I'm just doing my job," Daryl said, thankful that still, after all these years, her true ability still didn't make the reports. She was fighting the need to wrap her own arms over Blythe's to keep them around her. The comforting hold was a balm to her anger and she could feel herself relaxing and calming down. For a moment, she allowed herself the luxury of not thinking about the missing and instead just concentrated on the feeling of being safe in Blythe's arms.

"What's got you so wound up?" Blythe asked softly in her ear.

"I just want these people so bad, and I don't even know if it's more than the two we've already deduced. I hate guessing. I'm working on instinct, and I'm terrified I'm wasting the resources the DDU has entrusted to me."

"You're not wasting anything. We're gathering evidence like you'd do in any investigation. We're just going through it undercover and sneaky-like because no one will come right out and tell us why children are being taken from their mothers." Before she stepped back, Blythe pressed a quick kiss on Daryl's cheek. "You sure you're up to tonight's outing?"

Daryl nodded, now distracted by the gentle kiss and wishing they had more time to discuss what was sparking between them. It was both exciting and confusing. She missed the warmth and comfort found in Blythe's arms. Daryl didn't dare turn around because the longing she felt would be visible all over her face. She was trying so hard to remain professional, to keep her mind firmly on the case, but every innocent touch from Blythe was wearing down her resistance. Daryl was starting to look forward to when they were among others, playing the role of lovers. It was then she could look and touch without fearing she was crossing a line.

In company, it was expected of them to be demonstrative, and it was becoming as necessary to Daryl as breathing was. She loved the feel of Blythe's hand wrapped inside her own and how Blythe leaned in close and would rest her cheek against Daryl's shoulder. Daryl wondered how she'd feel once the need for this intimacy was gone. Blythe had said she saw them being intimate, but Daryl knew the case loomed between them before they could even take a step that close. And would she even get that chance? Once the case was solved, she would be heading back home to her own department, back to her own life. She needed to concentrate on the reason they were undercover and less on how much she was relishing the fact they were partnered together.

"You've gone very quiet, Daryl," Blythe said from behind her.

"Just thinking about the case," Daryl said, knowing that was only half the truth.

"Always the cop," Blythe teased softly.

I used to think so, until you appeared and made me notice so many other things instead. The Chandler-Kents have a life I never expected to experience. I'm finding myself envious of the love they share and yearn for even half of their life together. Daryl turned to find Blythe removing her earrings. She held one out for Daryl to hold onto while she fiddled with the stubborn clasp of the other. Such a simple task but it struck Daryl as oddly intimate.

"These are my serious earrings. For tonight, I want something a little more showy," Blythe explained, gently retrieving the small gold stud from Daryl's palm and heading for the stairs. "Do you want me to pick you out a shirt for tonight?" she called from the landing.

We're so domesticated. Daryl smiled reluctantly. *Yeah, I could get used to this way too easily.* She bounded up the stairs in Blythe's wake to prepare for the night ahead. To investigate, interrogate, and play the part of the devoted partner. Daryl brightened considerably; it really was the best of both worlds for her.

❖

Mia and Niki Connelly's household didn't allow for anyone to be shy and retiring. Mia ushered Blythe and Daryl in and Niki handed them a drink. Then they were reintroduced to Liz Mayer and Claire Benson. Blythe made a play of looking around the room for Justin. Liz laughed at her.

"Tonight is a rare evening for us. We get to have a child-free, adults-only night. We snagged Claire's younger sister to baby-sit and all but ran out of the house."

"You need time away for your own sakes, I bet." Blythe settled herself beside Liz and unobtrusively began to study her and her partner. Liz appeared to be in her early thirties, with long brunette hair. She was curvy but not overweight. Claire looked to be around a similar age, maybe a little younger, shorter, stocky built with short black hair styled into a floppy boyish cut. Blythe didn't have to employ too much of her profiling ability to deduce that since both women wore a large amount of designer label clothing that money was clearly no object for them. "I hope Daryl and I are as lucky as you two. We'd love a child of our own."

Liz's face lit up. "Mia said you were doing the rounds at the Cranston Heights adoption agencies."

"Have you walked through the valley of fire at the 'you're going to burn in hell' agency yet?" Claire asked.

"Criton and Welch?" Blythe laughed at Claire's all too apt description. "Oh yes, we had our baptism of fire and brimstone at that particular corner of heaven today."

"Do you think you'll get a call anytime soon?" Claire sported a knowing smirk.

"I don't intend to sit all day by the phone waiting for Ms. Hunt to get in touch anytime this century." Blythe let her humor fade deliberately. "How hard is it to want to give a child in need a loving home?"

"We were on lists for years before we were finally blessed with Justin," Liz said. "It took moving to Cranston Heights and settling here before we finally adopted."

"How old was Justin when you got him?" Daryl asked. "Because we've got our heart set on having a newborn and not an older child."

"He was just a few days old." Liz reached into her purse and took out her cell phone, scrolling on its screen and passing the phone to Blythe.

Blythe made sure she memorized the time stamp on the picture, reconciling it to the date she knew Justin had been abducted. It was literally dated for the day after he was taken. *Not much of a waiting period.* Liz began scrolling through more photos to show her child off. Blythe made all the appropriate noises that mothers like to hear.

Claire sighed. "You'll be there all evening because there hasn't been a minute of Justin's life that hasn't gone undocumented."

Liz huffed at her. "I've got all the photos, but who has the little video clips on *her* phone?"

Claire held up her hands in surrender. "Busted. I admit it. He's so cute. Everything he does has to be recorded."

"We'll be exactly the same. Especially Daryl." Blythe reached over to rest her hand on Daryl's knee and squeezed it affectionately.

"I'd kill to have a little one to love as much as I do their mother." Daryl covered Blythe's hand and kept it in place.

Mia nudged Niki as they sat side by side on an adjacent settee. "Oh God, Niki, we're surrounded by romantics. You might want to grab a pen and paper to take notes."

"I can do romantic. Wasn't I romantic last night?" Niki said with a playful leer.

"Sure, honey. You took your socks off for once." Mia's dry comment made everyone laugh.

Niki took their humor in good part and rose to top up everyone's wine glasses.

"Did you two go to Grace's Adoption Agency?" Blythe asked.

"The creepy guy with his female-only staffing policy?" Liz shuddered. "He gave us both chills just looking at him. He gave off serious serial killer vibes."

"He didn't exactly make us feel comfortable either," Blythe said.

"His costs were the highest we found for what he could offer. Some agencies charge double, sometimes triple if they sense you're desperate enough."

Blythe caught the swift look of censure Claire shot in Liz's direction. *Okay, so what are you hiding, Ms. Benson? What are you afraid Liz is going to reveal?* Blythe noticed Liz hadn't caught the look because she continued without hesitation.

"And if you want a specific kind of child you have to expect to pay top dollar."

"Did you want a specific child?" Blythe asked, wondering how much this couple would admit. Liz appeared to be the one who wouldn't hold back.

"I just wanted a baby boy who was healthy. I'd heard stories about gay couples getting children with questionable health problems."

"How questionable?" Daryl asked.

"Some agencies intentionally only offered us foreign children infected with AIDS or other diseases," Claire said. "Don't get me wrong; we know those children need all the love and attention they deserve, but we wanted a child that we could raise into adulthood. We didn't want to adopt a child who would wrap a hand around our hearts only to leave us too soon. I know that nothing in life is ever certain, but we wanted to at least have some chance of stacking the odds in our favor."

"Wanting a healthy child doesn't make you bad," Blythe said, wondering if health was a deciding factor in these kidnappings. She made a mental note to have the team double-check the health records of all the mothers.

"I'd really like a child that resembles either Blythe or myself," Daryl said, drawing every eye in the room to her.

"You want a little blond baby?" Mia asked. "Oh, can you just imagine how cute you'd look together?"

"I've imagined plenty," Blythe said with a dreamy smile. "Nothing would make me happier than to have a little blond kid to love as much as I love her mommy."

"Or a little black haired baby to carry on Blythe's coloring." Daryl settled back in her seat with a contented smile. "I live for that."

"What agency did you two get Justin through?" Blythe deliberately asked Liz the question while surreptitiously watching Claire's reaction.

"We went through Building Blocks Adoptions originally, but it went through some managerial restructuring and the name changed to Miller's Adoptions."

Blythe's heart picked up a pace. "That's who we go to see tomorrow. We have an appointment with a Serena Miller."

Liz nodded. "That's the lady who took over the agency. She's very nice."

"And she's the one who got you Justin to adopt?" Daryl asked.

Claire answered that. "Indirectly. She had links to children that were abandoned at hospitals, ones left outside churches. She said all those children needed to be counted too so she was in touch with other agencies. Many fingers in many adoption pies, was how she described it."

Liz shrugged. "I didn't really ask the details. I just wanted a baby, and when she called to say she'd found one for us, it was the answer to all our prayers."

Blythe nodded. *Why ask questions when you're being given what you most desire?*

"Were you ever told anything about his birth mother?" Daryl asked.

"Only that the poor girl died in childbirth and had no relatives to take the child on. He was heaven sent to us. I just wish his biological mother could see how much he's loved by us."

"No one can accuse you two of not loving that boy," Blythe said.

"He's our son," Liz said proudly, looking over at Claire and obviously not seeing the strained look on her face.

Blythe could see it. She was trained to notice gestures and facial cues. *Fuck. Now we have to investigate this couple as suspicious whether we like it or not.* She eagerly accepted the cell phone again as Liz found a more recent photo to show off. Proud parents with a terrible secret. Whether they both realized it or not.

There was a part of Daryl that wanted to leave the dinner party and run back next door to get the DDU team online. She wanted them to check into the backgrounds of both the Building Block agency and the one that had taken its place. She wanted to find out more about the supposed adoptions taking place of abandoned children. Was this how it worked? Were false papers drawn up to say these kidnapped babies had been left unwanted so that their adoption could be more easily facilitated? She also wanted to get Claire in a room on her own and question her until she broke. Daryl had caught how nervous she got when talking about Justin's adoption. She'd looked even more uncomfortable whenever Liz spoke up, but Daryl had seen none of the same subterfuge in Liz's demeanor. She wanted to lean on Claire a little harder to see what she was hiding. Apparently, from her partner as well.

There was a loud chime at the dining table and everyone looked up. Liz waved her phone sheepishly.

"Sorry. I asked the babysitter to let me know how Justin was doing at eight o'clock. He has a habit of waking up wanting something to drink, and then the little monkey thinks he can stay up and play for another hour. He's being a terrible two-year-old, testing his limitations." She checked her phone and held it up for everyone to see. A photo of a sleeping little boy in pajamas covered in fish was on display.

"May I see?" Daryl asked and was handed the phone. Daryl's gaze went to the screen, and she felt the familiar weight descend on her shoulders. Her vision sharpened and narrowed in on the photograph. *So there you are.* Daryl was grateful to reconnect with her Intuitive state. *Now tell me something I don't know, powers of mine. I know this is Matthew Malone, I know where he is, and that he's safe and loved. But where are the others and what is going on here?* The pressure eased from her leaving Daryl smiling at the sleeping child. "He looks so peaceful," she said then looked closer. "And his pj's are seriously cool."

"He loves fish, which is why we think he was drawn to the pond that time." Claire leaned toward Daryl. "We need to thank you again for what you did that day. He's sleeping safe in his bed tonight because of you."

"I was just the first to get to him. I'm really glad he's obviously no worse for what nearly happened."

"He now thinks he can fly," Claire muttered, shaking her head. "Thankfully, he's still too small to climb up the furniture to launch himself off it."

"So far," Liz interjected.

"True," Claire said. "I swear he's fearless. But he must have a guardian angel watching over him because we had only looked away for a second and he was at the pool ready to fall in."

"And you saved him." Liz's voice wavered and Daryl was horrified to see tears start to well in both Liz's and Claire's eyes. "How can we ever repay you?"

Daryl's detective brain began compiling questions, but she held them back. She wanted desperately to ask who had helped them get their hands on a stolen baby.

"You don't owe me a thing. I was just doing..." Daryl felt Blythe's hand tighten on her leg. "What oddly came naturally," she finished, slipping her own hand under the table to pat Blythe's. *I wasn't going to give myself away.* She smiled at Blythe and then over at Liz. "Guess someone up there felt I needed to get some parenting practice in. Starting with a crash course in 'never taking your eyes off them.'"

Mia took a long drink from her wine glass. "Once again, I'm glad Niki and I didn't have children. I swear she'd end up barbequing them."

Niki rapped on the table to catch their attention. "Are you sure this is really what you want in your life? Sleepless nights, endless crying, screaming, and I'm not talking about just the baby here."

Daryl and Blythe looked at each other then around the table. "Hell yes!" they said in unison. Startled, they laughed at each other. Daryl loved how that felt. She'd never had such a connection with another woman before.

"Then I think this calls for wetting the baby's head." Niki got up from the table and returned with a new bottle of wine.

"But we haven't gotten a baby yet," Blythe pointed out.

Niki paused in mid pour over Daryl's glass. "You're both young, good-looking, wealthy and live in Cranston Heights. What's to stop you from fulfilling all your dreams here?"

Daryl was beginning to wonder the very same thing.

Chapter Twelve

S eated in the fancy new office of the Chicago Deviant Data Unit, Detective Rafe Douglas was reviewing a file when her partner, Detective Dean Jackson, shot up from his seat, startling her.

"What the fuck?" She looked up and saw the reason for his speedy departure from his desk. Ashley Scott stood in the doorway, bearing gifts that Dean was already making himself welcome to.

"Hey, Detective, leave some for your boss," Ashley said, shooing him away from the large tray of doughnuts she was carrying. She handed him a coffee then shifted around him to bring the rest over to where Rafe sat. Rafe accepted her coffee with a grateful smile at Ashley and took a large mouthful. The hot liquid burned her throat, but she drank again thirstily. "God, that's exactly what I needed."

Ashley passed her a doughnut too. "You need to eat as well. You're still too thin." She ran her eyes critically over Rafe's body.

You haven't had any complaints when I'm lying on you, Rafe thought with a wicked glint. Ashley spotted it and favored her with a "don't you dare start" look back. Rafe made sure to stick her tongue out deliberately to slowly lick at the frosting on the doughnut. She was satisfied to see Ashley swallow hard at the sight. "With the amount of food you make me eat, I'm surprised I'm not a little butter ball." She took a big bite from her treat for show. "Should I be suspicious of why you're here bearing gifts?"

"Can't a woman come see her girlfriend at work and bring her and her partner frosted goodness?" Ashley eased a hip up on Rafe's desk and leaned forward to steal a kiss.

Rafe's whole body warmed at the quick tease of a tongue that brushed along her lips to lick away any remnants of frosting.

"I'm more than happy to see you, but you're not supposed to be so distracting when I'm trying to work."

"I'm hoping to do more than distract, Detective. I'm looking to take you away from all this." Ashley gestured to all the screens in the office with their displays of cases new and old. She then patted the files in Rafe's in tray.

"Take me somewhere?"

Dean snorted into his coffee cup. "Douglas is going on a dirty weekend…" he singsonged under his breath.

"Am I?"

Ashley patted Rafe's cheek. "Hold that thought, Detective. I'm here to hold you to your promise to take me to Connecticut."

"Seriously?"

"Yes, sweetheart. You and I are going to visit an old friend."

"Connecticut?" Dean mumbled around yet another doughnut. "That's hardly the most romantic of places to go."

"No, but I understand the nightlife is starting to get interesting," Ashley said with an all too knowing look at Rafe.

Rafe closed the file she had been looking through and placed it in front of Dean. "I'm going to see the boss for a few days leave. Keep the DDU running smoothly for me while I'm away."

Dean stared at the pile of paperwork before him. "Hey! You can't just up and leave us like this!"

Rafe was already getting her jacket on. "I'll keep my cell phone on. You can call me if there's a problem. Just think of me as working out of the office for a bit."

"I'll bring her back in one piece," Ashley said as she quickly hastened her steps to keep up with Rafe who was already at the door and ready to leave.

Once outside and away from other ears, Rafe asked the question that had been brewing since Ashley had arrived. "What have you heard?"

"There's demon activity in the same area that a DDU undercover operation is happening."

"Does Blythe know you're coming?"

"No. I'm just unofficially checking out the area for my own investigation. I have no links to the DDU or their investigation at all."

"Yet," Rafe said, knowing that their paths would have to cross sooner or later with Blythe and the kidnappings she was working on.

"Yet. And her unit can't be told there's another investigation occurring in tandem. So we've got to hope she doesn't mind working with us for a while and keeping it quiet. Hopefully, we can keep this strictly business and not have to mention a demon connection if we're lucky."

"And the actual chances of that?"

"Slim to nonexistent, but I hold out for that wafer thin hope. After all, not everyone would take the mention of demons quite as well as you did after your invitation was extended."

"Yeah, the kind of invitation handed to me personally by a killer demon in human skin." Rafe jabbed the elevator call button. "I didn't even get a chance to RSVP with a 'no thank you, leave me in ignorance, please.'"

"Sorry, but some invitations are non-negotiable once you open it...or chase it down an alley in your case."

They stepped onto the elevator and Rafe selected the floor she needed to speak to the head of her department. "She'd better let me have this time off."

"Tell her the truth. You're following a lead brought to you by a previous good source. That way, your back is covered should this all go to hell." Ashley laughed at her own joke while Rafe just glared at her.

"You're not funny, Sparky," Rafe whispered her own special nickname for Ashley. "What do we tell Blythe?"

"That you were just passing through?"

"Sure, I can see her going for that. I work in Chicago. I always take the scenic route through Connecticut on my way home." Rafe needed a plan of action before blindly heading off out of state.

"She can't report to her team that a senior member of another DDU is also looking into this case. They'd wonder why they hadn't been told. We'll just call her when we get there, arrange a meeting, and go from there. I know she's your best friend, Rafe, but I need to know I can trust her with the information we know. Demons don't come under a National Security heading."

Though they were alone in the elevator, Rafe still lowered her voice. "Are you really going to tell her about the possibility of demonic involvement in her operation?"

"Let's see what I find when I can have a look around for myself."

"Guess I'll be packing my Spear of Light," Rafe sighed.

"If we can just banish this demon we won't even have to disturb Blythe's reality."

"Can we still go see her though?" Rafe thought about how long it had been since she'd seen Blythe and was aware she'd really like to catch up. She was excited to introduce her to Ashley too. She made a mental note to take a new picture of Trinity with her phone so she could show Blythe that the damn cat she'd gotten her was still the best gift she'd ever received.

As if reading her thoughts, Ashley asked, "Have you got someone to look after Trinity while we're away?"

"God damn it!" was answer enough.

"That's okay; I've asked a friend to do it."

"You've roped in Eli, haven't you?" Rafe shook her head at Ashley's unrepentant nod. "You can't make an angel feed a cat while we're away!"

"Why not? He knows how to use a can opener."

"He's an angel!"

"And Trinity is one of God's creatures." Ashley stepped out of the elevator as it reached the necessary floor. "Besides, Trinity loves Eli."

"That's because she thinks he's a fucking huge bird with those massive wings he sports. She's just waiting to pounce on him like prey when he's not looking." Rafe had seen the cat eyeing Eli when he came to visit with Ashley. She knew Trinity didn't just rub on him for cat treats.

"They'll bond. It will be sweet."

"You make it sound like we're trying to integrate our kids so they'll get along and we can have peace."

Ashley laughed and sat in a seat outside Detective Stephanie Powell's office. She settled in to wait. "Go get your boss to sign you over to my team for a few days. We have things to do, places to be, demons to banish."

"This is so not the dirty weekend Dean wished for me."

"I'll see what I can do to fulfill your quota of down and dirty, Detective."

Rafe was thankful for the appearance of DS Powell's secretary who came out of one office and ushered her into another to be seen. Rafe hastily gathered her thoughts to find the most suitable way to ask for a few days off that didn't involve too much of the truth.

CHAPTER THIRTEEN

Serena Miller of Miller's Adoptions took copious notes. Daryl watched her as everything they said was written down. She liked how Serena listened, that she wasn't condescending, and was friendly but still entirely professional. Daryl felt herself relax as the tight band in her chest she had endured in every agency before loosened a little in Serena's presence. They'd gone over many of the same details that the previous agencies had requested. Here their bank balance had been given a cursory glance, noted, then moved past. Daryl took in the details of Serena Miler. She was small, slender, and had blond hair several shades darker than Daryl's. She was pretty, well dressed but not too showy for a woman well into her forties. Daryl liked that for all her professionalism she could still smile and make the intense interrogation not so much of the trial it had been at the previous agencies.

"Well, there's no doubt in my mind that you two are in love," Serena said, laughing softly at Daryl's flush of embarrassment at being caught staring at Blythe while she answered a question.

"Oh, it's been obvious right from the start for us," Blythe said, clasping Daryl's hand in her own.

Serena picked up their medical files, and her eyes were filled with sympathy. "Oh, you poor dears. How much pain you had to go through, both of you, to know neither of you could have children."

Daryl knew what was written in the files. Blythe had been diagnosed with endometriosis. The report spoke of the mass of scarring that affected Blythe's eggs from going to her fallopian tubes.

For herself, she'd been given polycystic ovarian syndrome, with its irregular menstrual cycles and an increase in male hormones. Daryl thought that was a nice touch with her being so much more masculine looking than Blythe. She heard Blythe's voice hitch as she told Serena about how much they'd both wished for a baby but had realized that physically, for both of them, it was never meant to be. The pain in Blythe's voice tore at Daryl's heart, and she couldn't look away from her. Just hearing the distress in Blythe's tone and watching her fight back tears upset Daryl immensely. She was startled as tears welled up in her own eyes and she had to swallow hard against a sob that threatened to break free from her chest. She brushed at her face quickly, but her actions were spotted.

"I'm sorry this is so rough on you both." Serena leaned over her desk toward them.

Blythe snagged a tissue from her purse and handed it to Daryl. "You'd think we'd be used to it, but knowing how much we want a child together and having neither of us able to carry one is the cruelest thing of all." She brushed at her own face and lifted Daryl's hand to her cheek. "It's okay, baby, I promise. We'll be okay."

Blythe's soft voice was nearly Daryl's undoing. She blinked back a fresh wave of tears and scrambled to her feet abruptly. "Is there a bathroom I can use, please?" she asked gruffly, not trusting her voice any further.

"Down the hallway to the right, Daryl," Serena said. "Take your time."

Daryl squeezed Blythe's hand, gave her a watery smile, and escaped the room. She was mortified by her reaction in the interview. *The medical files aren't even real.* Blythe getting upset on their behalf had obviously touched a nerve in Daryl she wasn't aware she had exposed. She found the women's bathroom easily and rushed inside. She forced the tap on and splashed her face with cold water, wondering where the emotion had come from. She wasn't known for getting upset easily. Was she taking the undercover role too far? Daryl soaked her face again and reached for a handful of paper towels.

The door behind her swung open, startling Daryl.

"Oh, sorry!" A small, mousey blond woman halted in the middle of the bathroom. "Are you okay?"

Daryl finished wiping her face dry. "Yes, thank you. I'm just a little…overwhelmed by this whole adoption process."

The woman stepped closer and patted Daryl's arm. "I understand. I've worked here a while. It's not an easy process to get to what you want most."

"I just needed to clear my head a little." Daryl threw away the towels and tried to get herself back together. She felt curiously calm again, as if nothing had happened.

"I know that feeling." The woman tapped at the dark glasses she wore. "I've been skirting a migraine all day. This is the only room in the whole building where the lights aren't incessantly bright." She shuffled closer to Daryl to impart a secret. "But there are only so many times I can leave my desk to escape into here without someone drawing attention to it and asking about my bladder weakness."

Daryl smiled. "I hope your headache eases soon."

"And I hope you get the child you deserve."

As Daryl left the bathroom, she paused at the woman's parting words. She turned to thank her, but she had ducked into a bathroom stall so Daryl left her in her privacy.

"You were brilliant!" Blythe crowed, hugging her tightly as they reached their car after leaving the agency. "Absolutely brilliant!" Her face shone with her happiness and Daryl was dazzled by her beauty once again. She melted into the hug and accepted it, for whatever reason she was receiving it.

"Why? What did I do?"

Blythe leaned back in Daryl's arms and beamed. "Getting emotional was a stroke of genius. Serena thought you were so sweet. She loved that you were as emotionally involved as I am."

"She didn't say anything when I came back."

"She'd told me that people who can show their emotions are the better parents." Blythe squeezed Daryl close once more then took the alarm off their car. She guided Daryl inside solicitously, leaving her a little confused and unsure what had transpired.

"If they have parking lot cameras, I'm making sure they see how sweet we are together," Blythe explained once seated in the driver's seat. "What kind of lover would I be if I didn't give my girl a reassuring hug?" She patted Daryl's knee with glee. "You totally blew me away. I never thought to use *your* tears as leverage."

"Glad to have helped," Daryl muttered. "I don't honestly know what came over me." She was still confused by her reaction. She couldn't remember the last time she had cried. It had to have been at the loss of her mother. She wasn't known to show much emotion, especially one that ended with her in tears.

"Well, you made quite the impression on Serena. She told me I was lucky to have such a tender sweetheart." Blythe guided the car out of the lot and onto the main road.

"She was the nicest of all the agencies we've investigated. I noticed she didn't make as big a deal of our finances like the other two did. She was more interested in us as a couple."

"Yes, she asked a lot of personal questions, which I think we aced, by the way."

Daryl had to laugh at how smug Blythe was acting. "You do realize that we're not really trying to adopt a child here?"

"If we were, we would be a shoo-in at that agency. I can tell." Momentarily, Blythe took her eye off the road ahead. "What upset you so much, Daryl?"

"I honestly have no idea. I never react like I did in that office. It was…a touch bizarre."

"You're not a big crier?"

"Nope, I didn't even shed a tear at the movie *Titanic*."

Blythe acted scandalized. "You are heartless!"

"It was hard to be shocked by the film when you kind of knew the ship was going to sink no matter how attractive Kate Winslet was."

"So today was what? PMS?"

"Not that I'm aware of. I just must have bought into the story and emotion of our apparent inability to have children."

"It breaks my heart to think that there really are women out there that suffer with the symptoms you had mocked up for us." Blythe stopped at a traffic light. "Do you know I have no idea if I can actually *have* children myself? I've never considered being a mother so it never even crossed my mind that I might not be able to."

"My dad would love grandkids," Daryl mused. "But he figured very early on that he'd never get them from me."

"This case is making me want too many things that I never thought I'd want," Blythe said then seemed to realize she'd spoken aloud. Daryl laid a hand on Blythe's thigh to reassure her.

"It's okay. I'm all twisted up and bent out of shape with this assignment too. At least you're not the one having an unexpected crying episode while trying to be professional undercover."

"I'll protect your butch image and tell the team you faked it to leave the room so I could talk alone with Ms. Miller."

Daryl squeezed Blythe's thigh in thanks. "Maybe my blood sugar is low. Could you eat pizza?"

"I've never known anyone to eat so much and stay so buff. You want pizza now?"

"We could eat early then report to Lake afterward. I think we deserve a treat after being placed under the microscope by three agencies in as many days."

"Pizza it is."

"With ice cream to follow?"

"I guess I can pander to your sweet tooth too," Blythe said with a smile.

"You're the best wife ever. "

"You bet I am, sweetie. Your momma would be proud of your choice."

My mother would have loved you as much as I'm starting to. Daryl stared out the windshield blindly as her words sunk into her brain. *God, my hormones must be wreaking havoc today. I feel like I'm acting so out of character that I don't know who I am anymore.* She closed her eyes against the sunlight as it streamed into the car. *Or, it would seem, who I want to really be when I'm around Blythe.*

CHAPTER FOURTEEN

Daryl clicked open another e-mail from her inbox. There were still no results back from the DNA testing of Heather's pacifier as yet. Lake had also forwarded all the findings on the background checks on the adoption agencies. She rested her chin on her fist and scoured every word for a clue.

"I can hear you sighing from the kitchen." Blythe entered the office carrying cups of freshly brewed coffee. She set one down before Daryl and leaned over her shoulder to read what was on the screen. "Well, I can't say I'm surprised to see that Mr. Grace has had employees reporting him for sexual harassment."

"The guy was a sleazeball, but it says here he was never charged."

"He's in a position of power and has quite a standing in the community. He's not going to let that kind of mud stick to his reputation. I bet Trace had to dig deep to unearth it."

"A man who covers up this many reports could be hiding other stuff too." Daryl took a sip of her drink. "Thank you for this. I was beginning to run on empty." She felt the warmth of Blythe's hand on her shoulder. She swore the touch seared right through to her skin. "Hunt seems squeaky clean. I'm kind of disappointed. I'd expected a little vigilante work on the side from her. You know, crashing Gay Pride rallies, that kind of thing."

"She's probably afraid that if she got close to that many gays and lesbians it would be contagious."

Daryl searched more of the report, but it didn't tell them anything more they could use. "There's very little on Miller here either. I think I'm going to have to do a little follow-up of my own."

"Who are you going to investigate, fair detective?" Blythe ran her fingers gently through Daryl's hair.

"Claire." Daryl was distracted by the hypnotizing brush of Blythe's fingers across her scalp. She wanted to close her eyes in bliss and turn into a boneless mass under every touch. She tried to keep her focus on the job, but it was proving less important with every pass of Blythe's gentle hand.

"She did seem to be trying not to have Liz say anything too damning, didn't she?"

"But I didn't get the impression Liz knew anything. So what does Claire know about the adoption that Liz was kept in the dark about?" Daryl knew if she were a cat she'd be purring up a storm as Blythe never stopped her soft caress.

"How would you play it? You can't exactly tell her that you could pick out every tell she had that gave her away."

Daryl chuckled. "*Every tell.* You're such a profiler, noting every tic and twitch that gives away that a person is lying."

"You noticed it too. You're wasted in Vermont, Detective. You'd be a valuable asset to my team."

"Has Lake given you instructions to soften me up toward that possibility?" She couldn't help herself; she leaned her head further into Blythe's touch.

"No, my softening you up is all for my own benefit." Blythe removed her hand, but before Daryl could protest, Blythe's soft lips captured her own. Daryl moaned into the gentle kiss.

"No one's watching us here, Agent," Daryl whispered as they finally drew apart.

"Then that kiss must have been just between you and me." With a smile that caused Daryl's body to tighten in desire, Blythe moved away to her own seat. "You said you were going to talk with Claire? When do you intend to do that?"

Daryl stared at her, feeling the lingering touch of Blythe's lips imprinted on her own. "I suddenly find I have other ideas running through my head."

Blythe smiled at her. "What happened to putting the case first?"

"I was all set to do that, but then you kissed me out of character. Now all I want is to carry you upstairs to that big bed of yours and make you mine for real." Daryl watched Blythe's face warm, and her eyes grew smoky with desire. Daryl thought she looked more beautiful than ever. Seduced by her scent and mesmerized by the half smile that curved her lips, Daryl wanted her. She was half out of her seat when the phone rang beside her. The glare she leveled at it should have blown the offending object into smithereens. It was Blythe who reached over to answer it.

"Caldow, what do you have?"

Daryl sank back onto her chair. She surprised herself by how much she needed Blythe and needed her right this second. She concentrated on bringing her breathing back to a normal rate and tried to listen objectively to Blythe's side of the conversation. She and Caldow were discussing Claire and Liz.

"Thanks for that. I think Daryl is going to see if she can get Claire to open up a little more. She was obviously hiding something and that withdrawal would support it." Blythe replaced the receiver. "Eighty thousand dollars was withdrawn from Claire's private account the day before they got Justin. There is no record of what that money was used for. They didn't have any work done to their home, there was no new cars purchased, and Caldow says there is no proof whatsoever of Claire leading a double life with another woman. There's nothing to show for where it went."

"You think it was payment for a stolen baby? That's some serious money to lay down."

"You'd pay the highest asking price to get what you desire the most. What was it Liz said? *Some agencies charge double, sometimes triple if they sense you're desperate enough.* So was she aware of the money being used to buy their child? Liz wanted a baby desperately; Claire got one for her. She wiped out her savings for that child of theirs."

"It's the price of building a family. I don't have that kind of money, and I doubt the credit cards furnished by the DDU would stretch to that kind of purchase."

"If we need the money, then we'll find it. Looks like it's the price you pay to get the child of your dreams."

"While unknowingly taking it away from its real mother." Daryl looked up at Blythe's silence and found her studying her. "What?"

"I'm not sorry for kissing you. It seemed natural and necessary. I can't help myself around you."

"I'm finding it hard too. We're blurring the lines between what we're portraying and what I'd like us to be doing together in reality."

Blythe reached across the desk and rested her hand on top of Daryl's. "Would you think less of me if I admitted I'm actually dreading this case coming to a close?"

"Why?"

"Because I've become so used to being with you, touching you, just sharing every day with you that I find I can't imagine life without you beside me."

Daryl swallowed hard. "We're in trouble, aren't we?"

"At the very least facing a severe dressing down should we get any more unprofessional," Blythe admitted.

Daryl slipped her hand out from under Blythe's and switched their hold. "I don't care about being professional. I can't imagine not being able to see you either, and that goes beyond this job we're doing. I felt it the moment I set eyes on you in the DDU conference room."

"Me too. What the hell are we going to do, Daryl?"

In answer, Daryl got up and purposely walked away.

"You're going to see Claire *now*?"

"No, because I wouldn't have a damn clue what to say to her because all that is filling my head and heart are thoughts of you. I'm going to go for a walk first and then see her."

"Oh, Daryl." Blythe rose to follow her.

"I'll be back soon, I promise." Daryl tugged Blythe to her and kissed her. Daryl traced the soft contours of Blythe's mouth, memorizing the shape of her lips, the taste of her. She thrilled to the soft moans that whispered from Blythe's lips and were breathed across her own.

"You come back to me," Blythe whispered, her hands clenched tightly in Daryl's shirt.

Always, Daryl promised silently and slipped out the front door before she put herself first and took what she desired most.

Blythe.

❖

The Mayer/Benson home was like all the others in Cranston Heights—elegant in build and screaming wealth. Daryl tried to shake off her cop instincts that instructed her to burst in the door, gun drawn, and demand to be told where Claire got Matthew from. *Who knew a normal life without the badge could be so hard to work around?* She walked up the driveway and rang the doorbell. She heard footsteps and then Claire opened the door.

"Hey, Daryl. What can I do for you?"

Trying to look embarrassed, Daryl fidgeted on the spot. "I really need someone to talk to, and I don't think I can talk about this with Blythe."

Claire opened the door wider to allow Daryl inside. "What's wrong?" She led Daryl into a spacious living room decorated tastefully but littered with a child's toys. Claire caught Daryl looking. "You'll have to excuse the mess. Cleaning up after Justin is a full-time occupation, and it falls to me today. Liz has taken him to visit his grandparents so I'm making the most of the quiet." She gestured for Daryl to take a seat.

Daryl made a show of taking a deep breath then spoke. "We haven't heard from any of the agencies yet, and I'm a bundle of nerves waiting. I have a feeling we won't hear from the religious right, but I'd hoped that we'd be called for a second interview pretty much immediately."

"These things take time. How long did it take for you to get your initial interviews?"

"Three weeks." Daryl had been chomping at the bit having to wait to start their rounds of visiting the agencies. It lengthened the time of their operation, but there was little she could have done to change it. Knowing she was having to waste time waiting for appointments to be made when the missing children were all around her had driven her crazy. "I guess I just need to hear it from someone who's been there, done that. I need assurance that we can do this and in the end get a child."

"You and Blythe are a perfect match for adopting a baby. I'm no expert, but even I can see you'd make fantastic parents. You've seen Miller, right?"

"A few days ago. She was lovely and very professional. She's the only one who made me feel comfortable in her office. I'm hoping she's the one we deal with."

"That's who we went through. It was Mia who suggested her actually. Said there was a sympathetic agency looking to place children with gays and we should check her out. She said Miller went out of her way to find the perfect child for her clients, and she was right."

Mia suggested? Daryl filed this away for later. "Perfect child?"

Claire hesitated for a moment. "In her second interview, she sometimes asks if there is something specific you are looking for, such as age, sex, coloring."

"Did *you* ask for something specific?"

"We wanted a boy. He had to be a newborn or just a few weeks old, and we wanted my coloring. Liz said she wanted the child to look like I was the daddy."

"So we could get the choice to specifically ask for a child that would favor either Blythe or myself?"

"Which I'm sure you'd want, yes?"

"Yes. I don't want a child that wasn't going to look like us. I want people to think this baby is naturally ours. Even though physically there's no chance in hell of that happening for either of us."

"*You* would have had the baby?" Claire sounded surprised.

"Both Blythe and I have faulty baby making equipment. But I'd have carried the child if I could have. Anything to give us the family we desperately want."

"Geez, that sucks, Daryl. I never wanted to be pregnant. We found out the hard way that Liz would never be able to carry a child to full term. We spent thousands on sperm donors, but after her fourth miscarriage, I begged her to look into adoption. It was soul destroying and taking a toll on her health losing a child every time. Then Ms. Miller took us on her list and listened to what we wanted."

"Was it that simple?"

Claire let the question hang in the air for a long time. She stared at Daryl then seemed to come to a decision. "What I tell you stays between us, okay? I trust you. You saved my son's life and I owe you for that."

Daryl wondered just what Claire was going to confess.

"I offered some serious money along with my list of what I wanted the kid to look like. I begged and pleaded for them to find me a match to make Liz feel whole."

"Money no object?"

"He was worth every last penny, and Liz doesn't know how much I sacrificed for him, so I need you to never talk about this in front of her or anyone."

Daryl nodded. "My lips are sealed. I've got some shares I can cash in if I need to, and my dad has some offshore investments I'm sure he'd trade in for a chance at a grandchild. Money is no object for me either. I want a child."

"Then when you get that second appointment make sure you impress on her that you'll do anything to have a family. Liz was ill the day of our appointment so I got to plead my case alone. Liz wasn't interested in the paperwork; she just wanted a child to love. Miller told me it would cost extra to get a specifically chosen baby, and I agreed to her price. I moved heaven and earth to get Liz her child and now he's our life. We couldn't love him any more if he was our own flesh and blood. He's my son. I'd die for him."

"Do you know where Miller got him?"

"To be honest, I never asked. When we got the call she had a child for us, Liz and I hightailed it down to the offices, signed the paperwork, and drove home in a daze with Justin between us."

"Was there ever anyone else with Miller?"

"Another person? No, not that I can recall. Miller had Justin in her office, all his health records, and the adoption papers to sign. She did say she'd gone through one of her outside sources to get him so he wasn't listed as being born in a local hospital." Claire smiled ruefully. "To be honest, I wasn't going to check the details. I didn't see anything past the little boy in the basket. There could have been a whole squad of naked cheerleaders in there and I wouldn't have seen them."

"Did you give her the money there and then?"

"No, I had to take it the next day because there'd been a holdup at my bank. I handed it over to some woman who was waiting for me. That was the last time I was in there." Claire paused for a second.

"She was a strange woman. She wore sunglasses even though it was dark and dreary that day."

Daryl's memory fired. "I think I must have met her briefly when we were there. She suffers migraines so she wears dark lenses."

"I remember her because she looked so ordinary except for these big ass shades she was rocking. She reminded me of Elvis with his white aviator specs!"

Daryl laughed. "Yes, I seem to remember they did cover most of her face. She was very nice though." A chill ran through her blood, but she tried to appear unconcerned in Claire's presence. *Is this our Good Samaritan? The woman in shades for migraines, when in fact, they could be the tinted lenses of the mystery woman's description?* "Everyone seems to be nice at that agency."

"You need to press the point home that no cost is too high for you to be a mommy. They are like any business; they respond well to the dollar sign, but you'll get what you pay for—a child that *could* actually be yours."

"I want Blythe to hold our baby in her arms, and I want us to be a family at any cost. I'll be sure to make certain Ms. Miller knows that."

Chapter Fifteen

The floral bouquet of lurid pinks, neon yellows, and bright whites accompanied in their wrapping by a small furry teddy bear wasn't Rafe's first choice for an undercover disguise to have her blend in. She cut a baleful look at Ashley beside her.

"Are you sure you don't want to carry the flowers? They'd look more natural with you." She wanted to be rid of the awful blooms and their sickly, cloying fragrance.

"No, thanks. You look awfully cute with them, and the teddy is a nice touch." Ashley just tightened her hold on Rafe's arm and led her down the length of a hospital corridor.

"Have you seen anything yet?" Rafe scanned the area for any kind of demon trace. For Rafe, demons glowed before her eyes. It was the lasting legacy from a demon who had been hell-bent on killing her. In human form or their natural vile skin, demons gave off a telltale glow that Rafe could see. It made her new demon hunting career easier and her normal life all that more difficult. "How many times do we need to walk the length and breadth of the maternity wing, Ash?"

"Just a little longer so I can get it memorized. Besides, Eli told me he'd join us in a moment or two."

Rafe was thankful she no longer suffered the intense pain and blindness she had first encountered when meeting Eli. The angel, who was for all intents and purposes Ashley's guardian angel, had glowed with such an intense bright white light that it had driven Rafe to her knees. Mercifully, he had helped her to be able to function in his presence. Rafe was still uncertain what exactly Eli had done when he'd put his hands on her head and miraculously altered something in her brain's synapses. It left her in awe of him and carrying a healthy fear also.

Ashley tugged on her arm to gain her attention. "This is the room that houses the Baby Aid charity thing I told you about, where you get coupons and freebies. Something tells me she's been here but not for a while."

"Could it be she only trawls the hospitals when they need a certain kind of baby to fulfill an adoption?"

"Ooh," Ashley breathed, mulling that over. "You mean like a specific kind of coloring or sex?"

Rafe nodded. "Personally, if I was going through the whole adoption route, I'd want a child that looked like us so there'd be a resemblance even if it wasn't truly biological."

"You'd want a kid that looked like us?"

Rafe leaned in close to Ashley's ear. "We'd negotiate the demon blood bit, seeing as both of us have that magical, mystical thing going on."

"I can just picture a little toddler looking like you with your brown hair." She reached up to pat lovingly at Rafe's slowly returning hair. "And with your beautiful dark eyes."

Rafe chuckled. "Flatterer. We could go for a little blond kid with your blue eyes and the ability to get their own way no matter how much I say no."

"You'll never say no to me, Rafe. You have too much fun saying yes."

The way Ashley breathed out that last word made Rafe's insides quiver in response. "Fuck, the things you do to me, and could be doing to me if we were back in our hotel room and not walking up and down every damn hospital wing in the Heights."

"I'll make it up to you," Ashley said, pushing Rafe down yet another corridor.

Eli silently made his appearance beside them. He wore his impeccable white suit and looked impossibly handsome with his blond hair fashioned just so. He was every inch the angel. Huge white wings were closed behind him and rested on his back. Thankfully, he was visible only to Rafe and Ashley and both made sure not to draw attention to the fact they were talking to someone no one else could see.

"She's not here," he said. "Or in the other hospitals."

"Damn it." Rafe gritted her teeth against saying something about wasting precious time and barely resisted the urge to throw the flowers aside. "I am not coming here every fucking day and staking out the maternity wing in the hopes someone pops a kid out so this demon can swoop in and grab it."

"I don't think it's exactly working quite like that, Rafe," Ashley said. "I think we need to talk with Blythe. I need to know where they are in this investigation."

"What if they are no further than we appear to be?"

"Then I'm in for a long stay in Connecticut and you're going back to feeding your own cat," Ashley replied.

Eli made a show of plucking a hair from his sleeve. "Black cat hair on a white suit is not the accessory I was looking for."

"Is she okay?" Rafe asked, knowing that her cat couldn't have been in better hands than a bona fide angel, but still anxious enough to ask.

"Yes, she's fine. She's been fed, watered, her litter box is fresh, and she's been petted. Oh, and we also played with the squeaky mouse she likes best." Eli released a long-suffering sigh, but the curving of his lips gave him away. "Felines are very soothing. I like the purring especially. It's restful."

Rafe had to smile at the look on his face. "Thanks for doing this, Eli. I know it goes above and beyond your calling."

He just nodded then turned to Ashley. "Are you certain you need to bring this matter to the attention of another human?"

"It's Blythe." Ashley emphasized her name. "I've worked with her before, and she's Rafe's best friend. I think we can trust her on this. I have to believe we can."

"Be mindful of where the truth is revealed, Ashley." Eli folded his arms.

"If this demon is stealing children then I don't care who finds out what the world harbors from hell."

Eli just regarded her. "Everyone is moving into place. You have more eyes and ears covering this territory now, and they are all at your disposal."

Rafe pulled out her phone and found Blythe's number. "Does this mean I can text her now and we can stop pacing the hospital floors like lost souls?"

"Speaking of which," Eli said as there was a flurry of activity around one of the areas they were walking through. Rafe watched as a doctor and nurses crowded around the seat of an obviously dying man who hadn't been given a bed in time. For a moment, the old man looked out at them blindly. His tired eyes widened then his features relaxed into the most beautiful smile ever to grace a haggard face.

"Go in peace," Eli whispered.

Rafe watched as the flurry around the man halted and the doctor pronounced him dead. A nurse ran to get a gurney so they could remove him from the waiting room. Rafe regarded Eli intently. "Tell me you don't moonlight as the Angel of Death?"

"No. For one thing, he wears much sharper suits," Eli answered, completely straight-faced. "For that man, I merely eased his mind so he could let go. He'd had a hard life; his afterlife will be much easier." On that note, Eli disappeared, his job obviously done for now.

Rafe didn't know how to comment so decided not to. She let Ashley lead them out of the hospital. She passed a young man searching through his wallet and counting his change outside the gift shop. "Here, save your money." She pushed the flowers and teddy bear into his arms and hastened out the building with much relief. It hadn't been so long since she'd had her own stay in the hospital. Just stepping inside one had made her feel sick to her stomach. She could only remember parts of her stay after being attacked, but she knew she was never more relieved than when they released her. She drew in a big lungful of air as they stepped back into the sun.

"Why didn't you tell me you didn't want to go into the hospital I've been dragging you around?" Ashley asked her softly, looking at Rafe with concern.

"We were investigating a lead. Those places just don't have happy memories for me."

Ashley crowded in close and slipped an arm around Rafe's waist. "I wish I'd known you then. I'd have visited every day and then stayed all night disguised as a nurse."

Rafe chuckled at the thought and pictured Ashley in a not so stereotypical nurse uniform and was thankful she couldn't read her mind. Though judging by the cheeky grin Ashley was giving her, she began to wonder. "That might have made my stay in the hospital so much more enjoyable. But we weren't destined to meet just then obviously." She leaned into Ashley's body. *No, you had to come save me from another brush with death thanks to that demon.*

"Call Blythe. Set up a meeting with her at our hotel room where we can have privacy to talk. We need to know what her DDU has found out about my case."

Rafe laughed softly at Ashley's proprietary tone. "Listen to you. *My* case. You two can fight over territory all you like. Count me out of that. I wouldn't know who to bet on for being the most stubborn." Rafe began texting Blythe on her private number. "I'm telling her to come alone too. No point pulling her undercover buddy in on this." She sent the message off, suddenly excited about seeing her.

"Look at you, all smiley at getting to see your BFF." Ashley bumped her with a hip. "Are you looking forward to seeing Blythe, sweetheart?"

"Yes, it's not the same over a conference call or talking on the phone."

"Do you think she'll like me?" Ashley's voice was quietly subdued, all traces of her teasing gone.

Rafe wrapped an arm around Ashley's shoulder and pulled her in close. "She's going to see how much I love you and how perfect you are for me. She'll witness how wicked smart you are and just how beautiful you are too. She already knows you're a brilliant investigator. What's not to like?" She kissed Ashley on the top of her head. "But we'll not mention the massive tattoo you sport on your back. She's a profiler; she'll lay all your secrets bare and leave you whimpering."

"Guess I'll save my best party trick until you think she's truly ready?"

Rafe nodded. "You always save the best for last, Sparky. And believe me, that trick is going to bring the house down."

❖

The unexpected sound of a text being received sounded loudly. Blythe was surprised to get it on her private phone and not on the Chandler-Kent cells they had been furnished with. She opened it and smiled.

"Everything okay?" Daryl asked from her side of the table. Since she'd returned from Claire's she'd contacted the team to get the courier to swing by in his fake FedEx truck to pick up the hair samples Daryl had snagged from Justin's hair brush. Blythe had been impressed that an excuse to use the bathroom had yielded them more new evidence thanks to Daryl's swift snag and bag tactics. Now they were both searching the Miller agency records for all female employees. No one was there that matched the description of their abductor. She'd been appalled that she'd come into contact with the woman and never realized it. Blythe had assured her that in the context of their meeting, she wouldn't have questioned the woman's identity either. Now they both sat in their office checking through the mundane details Trace had been finding on the Miller adoption agency. The hospital video feed had not provided them with anything they could use so far so it was back to research and digging through the employee records now that there might be a lead. Blythe and Daryl had been reading up on personal and professional lives of the staff, managers, and the secret investors of the Cranston Heights adoption agencies. They'd also been discussing whether Mia Connelly's involvement was deliberate or just plain helpful, which seemed to be her biggest personality trait.

"It's from Rafe. I don't believe it; she's *here*." Blythe read the message again to make sure.

"Here in Connecticut? I thought she operated out of Chicago?"

"She does, but this says she's here and wants me to meet her tonight."

"That's cool. We were just kicking back tonight anyway so take the car and go see her. Just be sure to come back with some kind of grocery bag or takeout box when you return. You know, just in case neighborhood watch is at the window cataloguing your movements."

Blythe knew Daryl wasn't joking. Mia didn't miss a trick in the street. She messaged Rafe asking what time she was free and where they should meet. "I wonder what she's doing here? It's usually hard to get her away from her desk in the Windy City."

"She's with the DDU too, isn't she?" Daryl leaned away from her computer screen and stretched her arms above her head.

Blythe watched the play of muscles underneath Daryl's thin T-shirt, and for a moment, she wasn't able to remember what she'd asked. The movement made Daryl's breasts lift, and Blythe couldn't tear her eyes away. She forced herself to concentrate and not be caught staring at such an obvious place. She came to her senses when Daryl relaxed and lowered her arms, shaking her shoulders a little to work out some kinks.

"Yes, the DDU in Chicago is Rafe's baby. It's a small team, but they're all fantastic investigators."

"Didn't they have that serial killer case recently? Where the guy was cutting open women's backs, revealing their spines?"

Blythe nodded. "That was Rafe's case. She had me do a profile for her. From what she told me after, I was pretty spot on." She recalled the call she'd gotten when Rafe had informed her that the killer had been caught. "The suspect killed himself quite dramatically too. Some psychopaths have such a flair for theatrics."

"So you worked on that case?"

"Not officially, but when Rafe asked me for help I couldn't say no. She knows I'd do anything for her, and I know she'd move heaven and earth if I asked her to for me."

"She sounds like a good friend."

Blythe smiled. "She's the best. Even if she is very by the book in her investigative style, which still drives me crazy sometimes."

"And you're such a maverick?"

"According to Rafe, I was in the academy. I'd like to think my subsequent years at the FBI have matured me so that I'm less exasperating to her."

"You're an agent who marches to the beat of your own drum; even I can see that." The look Daryl gave her made Blythe's insides spark and ignite.

"Whereas Rafe would want to check the sheet music first, examine the instruments, and then, and only then, let the music play to her specific rhythm."

"And you brought her a cat," Daryl said with a grin.

"She needed the spontaneity. Four paws and a purring engine provided that for her."

"Think she's here for a reason?"

Blythe shrugged, staring at her cell phone once more as if expecting to find the answer there. "I don't honestly know. Rafe never does anything without a reason."

"Do you think she's heard about our case?"

"I told her the basics when we first got the assignment, but I doubt there's a link between here and Chicago." She leaned back in her chair and considered this for a moment. "That would be too horrible to contemplate. I'd hate to find these kidnappings were more widespread than we have found so far."

"Even if the feds are chasing that angle. However, I was only shown here," Daryl said then added somewhat hastily, "What I mean is my investigation directed me here alone. I didn't find any links to suggest more kidnappings outside this area." She moved back behind her screen out of Blythe's eyesight.

"No one is questioning the research you did beforehand, Daryl." She wondered at Daryl's flustered words and sudden nervous demeanor. She tapped a fingernail on her cell phone screen, curious as to what had necessitated Rafe's message. "I guess I'll find out tonight what Rafe wants." She pushed the phone away. "Any preference on the food I bring back as a distraction?"

"Thai?" Daryl said. "And while you're gone I'll try and tidy up the front yard."

Blythe couldn't help herself; she laughed. "I'm sure you could wrangle any one of the neighbors with a green thumb to come over and tidy the yard to save you bothering."

"I'm enough of my father's daughter to know which way to hold a broom. The next-door neighbor's tree has shed all over the driveway. It's been bugging me."

"You're going to make someone a marvelous wife," Blythe said, enjoying the flush her comment brought to Daryl's cheeks. Blythe tried to ignore the pang in her chest at the thought of Daryl with someone else.

"Well, for now, I'm yours so they'll have to wait in line for my sweeping skills."

Blythe's cell phone buzzed as another message came through.

"I've got to meet Rafe at seven p.m." She brought up a map on her computer to check the address she'd been sent. "She's staying almost right on our doorstep." She printed off the map of directions to Rafe's hotel and sent back a text of confirmation. She couldn't stifle the feeling of disquiet that rumbled through her bones at Rafe's appearance. Especially since Blythe was deep undercover on a very sensitive case. She knew Rafe requesting a meeting had more than a friendly reason behind it. Now she was worried what that reason was. Rafe's health had been sorely affected by an assault she'd sustained at the hands of a killer. Blythe feared it was something connected to that which had prompted Rafe's out of the blue call to meet. For a moment, her blood ran cold as she feared the worst. She quickly tempered down her frightened thoughts and forced herself to continue reading into the case at hand. But the niggling worry that something was wrong plagued her and wouldn't calm down no matter how much she buried her head in the paperwork.

CHAPTER SIXTEEN

The hotel was easy to find and Blythe parked her car without a problem. Inexplicably nervous, she headed inside and walked straight for the elevator. It came quickly and Blythe tried to regulate her breathing to calm herself down. She watched the floors tick by intently. She felt Daryl's absence keenly and was surprised by how much she had gotten used to being with her at all times. She knew if Daryl had been there she'd have some calming words to impart to make Blythe feel less fraught. She stepped off the elevator and searched for Rafe's room number on the endless sea of look-alike doors. She knocked on one before she could hesitate further. The door opened and Rafe stood there looking healthy and happy. Blythe bit back a sob that had risen to her throat and flung herself into Rafe's arms.

"Well, hello to you too!" Rafe said, hugging Blythe tightly to her and laughing at the strong grip Blythe had on her.

Blythe pulled back and smacked Rafe on her arm. "That's for making me think you were here to tell me you were dying."

Rafe's eyebrows shot up her forehead. "Dying? Fuck, Blythe. I pay you a visit and you've got me buried six feet under instead?"

"You never just visit," Blythe said, wiping at her eyes and huffing at Rafe. She let herself be pulled into the room while Rafe closed the door. "And I'm on an undercover assignment. I'm not supposed to have people just dropping by."

Rafe nodded at that. "I know, and I'm sorry for this. I'd be pissed too, but I have a good reason why I'm here. Can I introduce you to someone first before I get into all that?"

Blythe realized that there was someone else in the room with them. A small blond woman with startling blue eyes was seated on the settee watching them in amusement.

"You'll have to forgive Rafe, Blythe. It's my fault we're here."

Blythe shook hands with the woman she remembered from the case they'd worked on years previous. "Ashley Scott, right? You're the private investigator."

"And my girlfriend," Rafe added with a smug smile as she settled beside Ashley and took a hold of her hand.

"So you're the woman brave enough to take Rafe on?" Blythe settled herself in a seat opposite them both.

"She wasn't so hard to tame," Ashley replied. "I've found she's a bigger pussy cat than Trinity is."

Blythe's amusement doubled at the look of disgruntled disbelief Rafe threw at Ashley. She could see the love Rafe had for Ashley. It was very clearly emblazoned on her face. It did her heart good to see Rafe so relaxed and obviously happy.

"Sorry, Blythe," Ashley said. "But your friend here is incorrigible."

"*I* am?" Rafe said with a wicked glint in her eye.

"I've waited a long time to see Rafe look this good, so no apologies are necessary." She leaned forward in her seat and rested her elbows on her knees to give Rafe a thorough once-over. "You're looking better than the last time I saw you over the conference video link."

Rafe ran a hand over her head self-consciously. "The scars are fading and my hair is growing over them. I'm feeling fine."

Blythe looked to Ashley for confirmation of this.

"She's doing okay, and I'm making sure she looks after herself."

"She's moved in," Rafe added. "Trinity has two mommies now."

"And to think you were so dead set against having a cat."

Rafe just grumbled at her. "You didn't exactly leave me with much of a choice. You spun your tale of woe of how she was the last in the litter and needed a home. Then you started in on how perfect she'd be for me and that I'd enjoy coming home to such a happy cat." She pulled out her cell phone from her pocket. "Look at her." She handed the phone over to Blythe. "Tell me she doesn't rule the house."

Blythe flicked through the photos featuring the very familiar black cat in various poses. She came across one that had Rafe and Ashley cuddled together with the cat between them like a proud child. She held this one up. "Who took this? It's wonderful."

"Ashley's friend Eli took it for us. He's on cat-watch while we're here." Rafe accepted her phone back and settled back in on the settee. "So how are you doing, Blythe? Enjoying your undercover lover role?"

Blythe wondered just how much she should admit. Ashley shifted slightly in her seat.

"I could leave if you two need to talk more privately?" she said.

Blythe shook her head. "No, it's fine. I'm just really finding it hard to separate work from what I feel for my new partner."

"This Daryl Chandler, is she having the same trouble where you are concerned?" Rafe asked.

"We're both very aware there's an intense attraction between us and we're trying so hard to toe the professional line."

"Playing lovers has got to be hard," Ashley said.

"It's difficult to know when the kissing can stop," Blythe admitted quietly. "But you're not here to hear about how hard it is for me to keep my hands off the detective I'm playing house with, so spill."

Rafe squeezed Ashley's thigh. "I told you she wouldn't do small talk."

"I want to know why you're here instead of back home in Chicago running your own DDU and feeding your own darn cat. And don't give me that lame excuse you were just passing though." Blythe looked to Ashley. "Unless your family is out here and you've just introduced them to Rafe, and if that's so then I apologize for being suspicious."

"I've no family to introduce Rafe to," Ashley stated baldly. Blythe was taken aback by the finality in her tone. "We're here for you, actually."

"Me?"

"You and your investigation into these child kidnappings to be more precise," Rafe said.

"The case is strictly need to know. We're operating undercover, Rafe. That means no trace of what we're doing is on record at the moment because of the feds' involvement and our blatantly going against them. I only told you because you're my friend and a *trusted* fellow officer." Blythe couldn't stop the bitter tone escaping.

"We don't want to involve your DDU just yet and I have no interest in the feds," Ashley said. "They're pursuing a line of investigation that is totally incorrect, but it will leave them out of your hair and ours while we investigate the truth here."

"Can you tell me why a private investigator is interested in a case that the DDU is already involved in?"

"I've been asked to look into this situation as just another pair of eyes," Ashley said simply.

"By who? Daryl came to *us* with her suspicions and we're not the only ones looking into these cases. The feds and the Connecticut FBI are doing their own investigation, right or wrong. So who has you on their payroll to do the same?"

"I'm not at liberty to divulge that."

"But you've had your girlfriend tell you what I told her?" Blythe took a deep breath to try to dampen her anger that was threatening to boil over. "Rafe, what the hell is really going on here? You don't operate like this. The DDU doesn't operate like this either, at least not in my unit. The feds stupidly kicked Daryl out of their investigation so I know they wouldn't take on another outside source. And to my knowledge, none of the mothers or their extended family hired a P.I. to investigate further into their child's disappearance."

"I never said it was a family member," Ashley said.

"Then who?" Blythe asked again, this time more firmly.

"Someone who wishes to remain anonymous for now. They're sending me in to investigate the places you can't while you're undercover as prospective adoptive parents."

"So am I to believe there's a third investigation running under the knowledge of the Chicago branch of the DDU that is flying under the radar of my own branch and the feds themselves?"

"I'm sticking to the hospitals and the Baby Aid stations," Ashley answered instead.

"We've had those under surveillance." Blythe couldn't help but wonder why Rafe was looking so calm in the face of her growing annoyance.

"Have you found anything?" Ashley asked.

"We're only working with a vague description of the woman involved in the actual snatching. We don't have a great deal to go on in the footage we've acquired so far. But we think we've narrowed it down to the agency she apparently works for."

"I need to know which agency," Ashley said, more to Rafe than anyone else.

"You can't just walk in on my case and take it over. I'm part of an undercover operation already set in place here."

"I won't infringe on your cover story, Blythe," Ashley said. "Do you remember the last case we were both involved with?"

Blythe nodded. "The pedophile ring. I know you were involved, but you were never a part of the team I was assigned to."

"Exactly. Your team went after the men and the children they had hidden. I was called in after the lowlife that was on the outer edge of the ring."

"You went after the distributor of the porn footage the guys were making from the house."

"Yes, and my investigation didn't tread on anyone's toes while you did your job and got those children free. The same will apply here."

"I heard the guy killed himself as your team went in."

The corner of Ashley's mouth twitched into a small smile. "A special place in hell was waiting for him no matter what path he took to get to it."

"What tipped Chandler to look specifically here, Blythe? I couldn't find anything definitive that pointed to this exact location. Yet, according to the feds' report, she came here and has already located a child in his new adoptive home and claims the others are somewhere there too." Rafe frowned at her. "That's some major league good luck."

Blythe bristled. "Daryl is renowned for her ability to find lost children. She has an almost uncanny knack for it." She caught Rafe and Ashley trade glances. "What? What was _that_ look for?"

"Blythe, how much do you know about this Daryl?"

"I'd trust her with my life, like I would _you_, Rafe."

"That's good because there might be something more going on here than meets the eye and I need to know you're safe. You're going to need to be clear-headed when we tell you our side of this investigation."

Ashley rested her head against the back of the settee to look at Rafe. "Are you sure?"

"Yes, I think she needs to be told."

Blythe stared at them both, confused and angry and more than a little uncertain what exactly she was being led into. "Rafe, please tell me what you're doing here. I don't understand any of this."

"Have you gotten any kind of feeling in this investigation that there's something not quite right about it all? Like the fact your main suspect can disappear without a trace until she reappears to take another child?"

Blythe considered Rafe's question for a moment. "It is very odd, but we're working on the premise she's connected to an adoption agency where someone works alongside her to help place the children she takes. The kidnapper, who hides in the shadows so much, needs someone who can stand alone in the light."

"I love that analogy. You have no idea how right you are." Ashley seemed to come to a decision. "Do you ever think that there's something more than man's depravity in the cases that pass by your desk?"

"Like what exactly?"

"Another influence, one not of this world."

Blythe's eyes widened as she let Ashley's words sink in. "Oh Christ, are you two hazing me as some kind of bizarre 'meet my new girlfriend' thing?"

Rafe laughed. "Okay, enough of the pussyfooting around. Blythe, I need you to promise me what we reveal to you now you'll never speak of outside this room."

Blythe stared at her cautiously. "What exactly are you going to divulge?"

"That when I was attacked in the alley it wasn't a man who tried to kill me."

"Then who?"

"More of a *what*. It was a demon," Rafe said.

Blythe didn't move a muscle. "A demon," she repeated.

"A demon who had taken human form and was living here among us."

"A demon," Blythe said again with some impatience. "And is this now when you tell me just how much brain damage you incurred in that alley because the Rafe I know—"

"The Rafe you know nearly died in that alley. The Rafe that lived through it came out seeing the world through different eyes." Rafe paused. *"Literally.* I can see demons, Blythe. Real live demons that walk the earth and we don't know they are here."

The white noise in Blythe's head did nothing to help her process what Rafe was telling her. She really thought Rafe was losing it. "You can't honestly expect me to believe you."

Rafe waved a hand at Ashley to take over. "Time for your party trick, sweetheart," she muttered. "Blythe, I've found out that there are more things happening on this planet than I could ever have envisioned. You always said I only ever saw life in black or white. You're my dearest friend, Blythe. I need you to know what we're up against."

Blythe didn't get a chance to question what the hell they were talking about. Ashley stood up and Blythe instinctively turned to her. In that instance, Ashley disappeared before Blythe's eyes and in her place was Angelina Jolie, dressed in her Tomb Raider shorts and a tight top, sultry eyes sparkling and her full lips curved into a laughing smile.

Blythe bolted up from her seat. "Holy fuck!" Her hand scrambled for the gun she usually had on her hip. Her hand found thin air instead of her holster. For an instant, she flirted with just passing out.

"Welcome to my shades of gray," Rafe announced dryly.

"Who do you see before you, Blythe?" Rafe couldn't see the transformation herself. When Ashley shifted to take another form, all Rafe saw was a golden glimmer that made up Ashley's "glamour." Everyone else saw the person Ashley changed into, heard their distinct voice, saw no reason to doubt who it was they were seeing. But Rafe saw right through to the woman beneath. She'd never seen anything but Ashley thanks to the injuries she'd received at the hands of a demon and the subsequent poisoning she'd suffered that had altered her life forever. Her blood's makeup now made it impossible for her to be blind to demonic or angelic forces.

"I see Angelina Jolie," Blythe blurted.

Rafe's mouth dropped open. "Dressed how?"

"Shorts and a sleeveless tee." Blythe shot her a look that asked why that mattered in the scheme of things.

Rafe leveled a disgruntled look at Ashley. "I don't believe it. You can conjure up Lara Croft and I can't see it at all? How fucking unfair is that?"

"It's for the best, Rafe; otherwise you and I would never be alone in the bedroom." Ashley rested a hand on her hip.

Blythe had let out a startled gasp. Rafe guessed Ashley's voice sounded exactly as it should for the body she was manifesting. *This is so not fair! I want to see Angelina too!*

"Please change back," Blythe said, staggering back into her seat with a thump.

The golden glimmer faded so Rafe knew Blythe could see Ashley again.

"What are you?" Blythe asked shakily.

Rafe was pleased to see no fear coloring Blythe's eyes, just an understandable uncertainty, and a growing curiosity. She knew Blythe would be too much of an investigator to let this opportunity slip by in terror.

"She's pretty unique." Rafe spoke before Ashley could answer and received a loving smile from her.

"I'm human, but with a twist."

"And this twist gives you some sort of magical powers?"

"Kind of," Ashley admitted.

"Should I be afraid of you?"

"No." Ashley moved to kneel before Blythe and took her shaking hands in her own. "I'm one of the good guys, I promise. You needed to see for yourself that not everything is as it seems, and I'm afraid that's the situation in this investigation of yours."

"Demons are connected to stealing these babies?" Blythe let out an abrupt laugh. "I can't believe I'm even hearing this, let alone considering it."

"Blythe, I now see demons on a daily basis. My orderly black-and-white vision of the world got smashed to smithereens along with some of my skull in that alley. This is why we're here. You need Ashley to find the demon that's here. You'll never see it, you won't be able to detect it, but Ashley will, and she can put a stop to whatever its role is in these snatchings."

"Why would a demon want to steal children and pass them off to someone else?"

Ashley shrugged. "That's what we hope to find out."

"And what am I supposed to do with this information? What do I tell Daryl?"

Rafe just shook her head. "For now, this has to be between us. With you aware of why Ashley is here, we can at least keep you informed of what we find and trade information without drawing the DDU into it." Rafe smiled wryly at her. "After all, the D stands for Deviant and not Demon in the DDU."

"I don't think your partner needs to know anything about this," Ashley said.

"I don't like keeping something like this from her. It's her case, after all."

"For now, let's keep her out of it. Let's see what turns up first before we start spreading the news of a demon infestation running amok in Connecticut." Rafe stood and drew Ashley up with her. She directed her attention back to Blythe. "Okay, Agent Kent, you've had the show, now it's time for the tell. Allow us to present to you a crash course in Demonology 101."

❖

Blythe was torn between utter disbelief and the inescapable acceptance of all that Rafe and Ashley had shared with her that night. Part of her had wanted to say *enough* and just walk away from the entire conversation. The other half found it fantastical, mystical, and downright terrifying. Blythe had never placed much faith in religion and spiritual beliefs. To find out in one evening that both heaven and hell existed and that hell was spewing out demons that were out to steal babies was more than she could cope with. Distracted, Blythe's attention was only half on the road. Something shadowy shot across the lane in front of her. She startled at the loud bang as something slammed down on the hood of her car. Blythe wrestled with the steering wheel, swerving to avoid hitting whatever it was in her path. She barely managed to keep the vehicle under control enough to stop from side swiping a line of parked cars. She heard a thud as her side mirror collided with another and was thankful not to hear the sound of breaking glass. She slammed on her brakes and sat hunched over the steering wheel trying to catch her breath.

"What in the hell was that?" She shivered as the weight of her words settled on her. Rafe and her demons. "Damn her!" She scoured the sidewalk and the road ahead for any sign of what had run into her path. The road was empty as before. She got out of the car to investigate. There was nothing on the front of her vehicle, no clue left behind to show that she had almost hit something. The street was curiously silent. All she could hear was her own ragged breath. With one last nervous look around, Blythe got back in her car and this time drove with more care and attention.

The lights shining from the windows of the home she shared with Daryl almost brought tears to Blythe's eyes. She pulled the car to a halt on the driveway, and for a moment, she just stayed behind the wheel. Blythe could feel a headache building behind her eyes. The night's revelations still thundered through her brain. She'd learned more than she ever could have imagined about a world she still couldn't comprehend *really* existed. She'd listened to Rafe and Ashley talk about the existence of demons, explaining their theories about why there was one attached to Blythe's case. *Like this case wasn't hard enough without this added complication. No wonder I lost concentration on the road.* The smell of the food sitting in a bag on the front seat stirred her into motion. She got out of the car and headed indoors, barely sparing a look at the dent gracing the side mirror. She figured she'd gotten off lightly. She shook off her disquiet at the door.

"Hi, honey, I'm home!" she called out more cheerfully than she felt. Her chest constricted with a pathetic relief as Daryl appeared out of the kitchen at the sound of her voice. Blythe hurried forward, not caring how it would appear, and pushed her way into Daryl's arms.

She felt Daryl's surprise, but her strong arms wrapped around Blythe and held her close.

"Hey, what's wrong?" Daryl rubbed a hand over Blythe's back soothingly.

"I…it was just upsetting seeing Rafe and her injuries up close." Blythe hated lying to her, but she knew she couldn't tell Daryl the truth. How could she explain that things she'd thought were confined to matters of faith and superstition were in fact real and running rampant in every state? She'd driven home looking at everything in a new and infinitely more frightening light. And that didn't begin to factor in the ramifications of it being a part of their investigation.

"Was she okay?" Daryl steered Blythe into the living room and eased her down on the settee. She took the bag of food from Blythe's unresisting hand and put it aside. Blythe loved how well she fit into Daryl's body. Even though they were nearly the same height, she felt small in Daryl's arms and protected. For a moment, Blythe tried to go back to the world she'd known. Before Rafe had tilted it off its axis and sent her spinning into free fall.

"She's okay, but I just realized how close she came to dying, and it was a sobering experience." Rafe had told Blythe all she had gone through at the hands of the demon and the murderous poison that she'd had coursing through her veins as another consequence. The fact that Rafe could talk so calmly about it only served to amaze Blythe more.

"Did you meet her girlfriend?"

Boy, did I. "Yes, she's quite a character."

"But Rafe's happy?"

Blythe thought about how Rafe had been. She'd faced death and stared a demon in the eyes. She'd had her brain scrambled in the attack and then touched by an angelic hand. She'd met a woman with shape-shifting abilities, whose father had been a fallen angel. Yet Rafe, surrounded by demonic influences and angelic assistance, had been the happiest Blythe had ever seen her all thanks to Ashley Scott.

"She's so in love. It was a pleasure to witness." Blythe pulled back in Daryl's arms at the sudden sound of a stomach growling noisily. "That sounds like someone needs to eat."

Daryl grinned sheepishly. "Sorry. I didn't have time for a snack by the time I was done outside and then I found some things inside that I thought I could work on."

Blythe reluctantly slipped free of Daryl's arms and pulled the bag close. She started laying out the trays of food. "Well, aren't you all domesticated? Let me grab some cutlery and we can eat. I'm hungry too." She went to gather the forks they needed and snagged a bottle of wine off the counter for them to open. When she returned, Daryl opened the lids and took a proffered fork gratefully. Blythe sat beside her, unconsciously wanting to keep her close. She hated the feeling of being afraid of the world. Being beside Daryl made her feel safe.

"Did they say why they were here?" Daryl asked between mouthfuls of rice.

Blythe hesitated for just a fraction of a second but remembered what Rafe had instructed her. *Keep it as close to the truth as possible, then you can never be caught out in a lie you can't remember.* "Ashley's here for an investigation, and Rafe had traveled down with her just for the hell of it." She managed not to cringe at saying *hell* so calmly.

Life really is never going to be the same again.

"Where's Ashley's investigation?"

"In the local hospitals, believe it or not. Seems someone is stealing from them, and she's been brought in to see if she can work out who it is and where they are selling the items." Blythe stuffed her mouth full of food. She figured if she wasn't able to speak it might stop her from feeling so bad telling a half-truth to someone she cared about.

"The same hospitals we're looking into?" At Blythe's nod, Daryl marveled, "Small world."

"Isn't it?" Blythe said and reached for the wine, pouring herself a very large glass.

CHAPTER SEVENTEEN

The streets were quiet as Daryl jogged. Ever vigilant, she kept a watchful eye on everything around her as she ran. The morning was warm, and she was enjoying the early morning sunlight on her face. There was a faint sheen of sweat covering her skin as she completed her regular course. For some reason, this morning she had decided to add another route to her circuit. Something was tugging her in another direction, and she had long learned not to ignore it so she continued running. Cranston Heights was block after block of impressive homes and affluence. Daryl never begrudged anyone their good fortune, but so many of the homes were so blatantly ostentatious it set Daryl's teeth on edge. She usually dealt with those who were much less fortunate and much less moneyed.

She jogged steadily, letting her feet pound the pavement and enjoying the ache in her muscles as she tested her endurance. Coming toward her on the other side of the road, she spied a woman pushing a stroller off a driveway. They were both heading toward a busy street, and Daryl slowed so she could cross it safely. She felt her steps falter, and her vision narrowed and focused without warning. The familiar weight pressed down on her shoulders, and she almost bowed under the pressure. Her sight zeroed in on the face of the baby seated in the stroller, happily swinging a wooly monkey back and forth in tiny hands. *Camille Weeks,* Daryl realized, as certain as only she could be. The pressure lifted and Daryl whipped out her phone. She held it up in such a way that it looked like she was reading a text and not focusing on the woman and child on the opposite side of the road. She made sure to take close-ups as they crossed over in a lull of traffic. As they got nearer, Daryl looked up at the mother. She waved her phone at them. "I swear I get more text messages when I'm out running than I ever do in my office."

The woman laughed at her. "You can't get a minute to yourself." She tapped on the stroller. "I know that feeling."

Daryl smiled down at the baby." She's a beauty. What's her name?" "Stasia."

Daryl's mind whirled. *Stasia, the name means shall be reborn. How appropriate.*

"Well, Stasia, you have a marvelous day while I try and outrun all these folk who couldn't find their own elbows unless I told them to roll their sleeves up." She bid good-bye to the laughing mother and picked up her pace to get across the road before the morning traffic halted her progress. She typed a text swiftly on the move, with Stasia's name, the street she was on and what house they had just come from. She then attached all the photos she had taken. She sent it off to Trace. Within seconds, she had a reply.

You're up early. Nice kid. Anyone we know?

Daryl texted back. *I believe its Camille Weeks.* She continued running, her mind whirling with the fact she had found another of the missing babies. She knew her running a different route that day had not been her choice after all.

How do you know? Trace asked in the text that arrived next.

Daryl read the words but didn't honestly know how to answer. *I always know my kids. I don't know how or why, but I recognize each and every one.* She thought back over some of her more upsetting cases. *Dead or alive.* She ignored Trace's query and typed back a question instead.

Have you identified the mother yet? She crossed over another road and began heading back in the direction of home.

Some of us have only just wheeled into work, Angel Hair. I'll get back to you once everything has been inputted. What are you doing out at this hour?

Daryl answered that with no problem. She smiled sadly when Trace wrote back *Do a mile for me.* Daryl assured her she would, and with renewed energy, ran. Buoyed by her discovery, Daryl switched routes again and added an extra side road to her routine. She noted the quiet street. It was almost *too* quiet. The hairs on the back of Daryl's neck and arms rose as she was assailed by a sudden bone-penetrating chill. She stumbled in her steady pace. The sense of unease continued as she looked around, desperate to find what was wrong. Out of nowhere, a figure dressed head to toe in black appeared right in front of her. Daryl didn't have a chance to pull up and braced for impact. Instead, she felt a fist drive into her chest. The blow didn't so much connect as impact as an *energy blast*. The force of it blew Daryl completely off her feet, tossing her backward into a wrought iron gate. She bounced off the metal, falling forward onto her knees. She felt the harshness of the sidewalk cut into them and watched as blood began to seep across the concrete. When she looked up there was no sign of what had just materialized before her.

Like my world couldn't get any weirder.

Gingerly, Daryl got to her feet, checking herself over for cuts and scrapes and wincing at the damage to her knees. She had no idea how she was going to explain what had happened to Blythe. She opened her water bottle she kept in her pack and washed away the grit and dirt from her cuts. Whatever had happened, Daryl had never felt or witnessed anything like it before. She didn't think she could explain it to Blythe without sounding completely crazy. She didn't want Blythe to see her that way. She needed Blythe to see her for herself without the added distractions she always had going on.

But this had been a first, even for Daryl.

❖

It took her a while to get back on her street. She dutifully waved to the neighbors who were getting ready to leave for work and smiled at the ones who were dragging their reluctant children to school. Daryl entered the front door and was assailed by the delightful aroma of something toasting. Her stomach tightened in reaction. *All I do on this assignment is eat.*

"You're just in time for bagels," Blythe called from the kitchen. Daryl padded through to join her.

"Do I have time to wash up first? I'm kind of sweaty."

Blythe blanched at the dried blood that covered Daryl's arms and legs. "What happened?"

"I took a tumble. It looks worse than it is. I just need to get cleaned up and break out the Band-Aids." She waved off Blythe's concern. "I'm okay. The sidewalk, however, took quite a beating from my knees."

"I can eat the first batch I've got toasting if you want to go shower." Blythe finished liberally spreading some cream cheese on a hot bagel. A worried frown creased her forehead. "Put some ointment on those cuts to stop any infection."

Daryl turned to head upstairs but remembered to hand Blythe her phone first. "Look who I met today." She brought up the photo of the baby and then hurried up the stairs two at a time, pulling off her T-shirt as she went.

"Is this one of the other missing children?" Blythe's incredulous voice followed after her.

"Yes, it's Camille Weeks, now known as Stasia."

"How on earth do you do that?" Blythe called after her, but Daryl pretended not to have heard her.

Daryl gathered up the clothes she'd left on her bed and hastened to her shower. Once in the room, with the water running, she asked herself the same question. She stared at herself in the mirror, but there was no answer there to be seen. There was, however, a large red mark in the center of her chest. She traced it gently. "Blessing or a curse, I can't really tell," Daryl muttered as she finished undressing and stepped under the warm water with a wince. "But as long as it means I can bring children home, or find some kind of closure for their family, then I'll bear the burden gladly." She grimaced as the water hit her battered skin. "No matter how much it hurts."

Over breakfast, Blythe questioned Daryl about the latest development in their case. Daryl was going through the photos she'd taken on her cell phone.

"What are the odds of you taking a longer route today in your regular run and finding what you believe to be another kidnapped child?" Blythe was more than curious as to how Daryl recognized these children without any hesitation. She wondered what lay behind Daryl's unwavering belief this was one of the children whose disappearance she'd been investigating.

"Tell me, Daryl, how can you single this baby out of all the babies you've no doubt jogged past every morning since we've lived here?" Blythe reached over to pluck the phone out of Daryl's hand and studied the photo on the screen. "I mean, all babies look the same to me. They're all small, wrinkly, and prone to be noisy."

Daryl picked up her coffee cup and took a drink. To Blythe's professional eye, she knew Daryl was applying a delaying tactic. It only served to raise warning flags in Blythe's mind.

"I've studied the pictures of all the missing children until they are all but imprinted on my brain. These cases have been with me every waking hour since the files landed on my desk."

"But children change, Daryl. Their faces alter as they grow and lose their baby looks and start becoming little people."

Daryl smiled at Blythe's description. For a moment, Blythe was distracted by how attractive that small lift to her lips made Daryl look. Daryl nodded toward her phone.

"Camille Weeks had a Latino father. Her coloring set her apart from all the other babies who were predominantly white. Her new mother looks Latino to my eye. If I'm right and this child is Camille Weeks, then tell me that baby wasn't stolen to order."

Blythe noticed Daryl hadn't exactly answered her question. For a moment, the investigator in her wanted to delve even more until she knew what lay behind Daryl's conviction that she could confidently pick one child out of many. The other side of Blythe wondered if she was pushing too hard for an explanation because suddenly her world wasn't as clear-cut as before. *Rafe's got me looking for demons around every corner.*

"Hey, are you all right?"

Daryl's voice cut through Blythe's racing thoughts and she looked up to find Daryl's concerned eyes on her.

"Sorry, I'm just…" *Just what? Trying to reconcile the world I thought I lived in with the world I'm now aware exists around me?* "I didn't get much sleep last night." She couldn't look at Daryl after that lie, and her eyes fell again to the laughing baby's face on the phone. Maybe Daryl had some kind of photographic memory. "Lake told me you had an unorthodox way of investigating." She saw an unguarded look of alarm momentarily flash on Daryl's face before she hid it.

"Did he now? Well, he's known me for many years. He's watched my investigative style evolve. I still do all the same boring investigatory stuff you do. I fill in the same seemingly endless reams of paperwork."

"But what makes you so attuned to these kids, Daryl? I mean, come on, you go out for a jog and just happen to stumble on one of the children we're looking for. Look at it from my point of view. Either you're the most amazing detective ever to wear a badge—"

Daryl interrupted her. "Or I'm imbued with superpowers, and when I'm not pretending to be your mild mannered spouse I'm leaping over tall buildings in one bound and saving the planet from evildoers. Sorry to disappoint you, *Lois*, but my superpowers weren't in action today." She pointed to her leg covered in Band-Aids.

At Daryl's lazy grin, Blythe felt herself relax for the first time since she'd come back from seeing Rafe and Ashley. She let herself be warmed by the humor she saw in Daryl's eyes.

"What do you think you possess, Detective?" Her chest tightened as Daryl began to laugh. The sound delighted her so much it was almost too painful to bear.

"I should have known that breakfast with a profiler would entail more than 'please pass the sugar.'" She put down her mug and stared at Blythe. "I'm not psychic and I don't converse with the dead. I just am drawn to certain places and people and instinctively know that's where I need to be."

She bit at her lip and Blythe had to resist the urge to lean over the table to kiss her. That small sign of insecurity weakened Blythe's resolve to be strictly professional. Having to put the job first was killing her. "You know when you're knee-deep in a case and you find that final clue that just makes everything fall into place?" Blythe nodded at her. "That's what I get around these kids. That certainty that this is where they are, this is *who* they are. I just know it deep down inside."

"You're amazing, do you know that?" She thrilled at the blush that colored Daryl's face.

"I'm just doing my job, and if that brings these missing kids back to their mothers' arms then it's a job well done."

Blythe squeezed Daryl's hand gently. "You know I'm going to add my voice to Lake's to get you to come work on our team. Because however you do it, your success rate shows it works."

"We haven't even solved this case yet. For all my convictions, I could still be totally off base."

Blythe scoffed at her. "You? Not when it comes to your kids; that's what you've said. And your record speaks for itself. You'd be invaluable on our team."

"And what about us?"

"I want this case solved and out of the way so we can concentrate on what we really feel as opposed to what we have to pretend to be for the sake of our cover." Blythe ran her fingers lightly over the top of Daryl's hand. She loved the strength she could feel, the long length of her fingers, the blunt fingernails. "You know you have a certainty in your investigation?" Daryl nodded, but she was watching Blythe's fingers tracing the top of her hand. "Well, I feel the same where you're concerned. I know what I feel isn't just emotions projected from our cover stories."

"Good, because I feel it too." Daryl lifted Blythe's hand to her lips and brushed a kiss across her knuckles.

Blythe's body warmed to the sweet touch, and she tried to lose herself in the peace Daryl wrapped around her. *Here I was thinking that the hardest thing I'd ever have to tell her is that I think I'm falling in love with her. But there's this little matter of demons and maybe even demon baby snatchers. Suddenly, the whole love dilemma seems so simple compared to the waking nightmare I find myself in.* She shivered.

"You okay?" Daryl asked.

"With you by my side, how could I ever not be?" Blythe caught a look on Daryl's face. "What are you thinking, Detective?"

"That I want to phone Miller and press her for another meeting. I want her to know that money is no object and we'll do anything to cut through the red tape and get us a child."

"You want to all but tell her we know she has a secret baby selling gig as a side line?"

"I'd try to not let her know that we're aware she is extorting money off those desperate to have a child by any means possible. Including, it appears, paying for stolen babies."

"You know we can't show our hand. We have to wait to get called back, *if* we get called back." Blythe shook her head gently at her. "Patience, Detective, this investigation has to go by the book so that we can catch the ones behind the baby snatching. If we charge in, guns a-blazing, we might scare away our only chance of solving this."

Daryl blew out an exasperated puff of breath. "I can't stand the waiting. I know those kids are here all around me. It's driving me crazy having to cool my heels and not knock on every door to find them and get them back."

Blythe squeezed Daryl's hand. "You'll get that chance, Daryl, I promise you that. But we have to wait on Miller to call us to take that next giant step into parenthood."

"Waiting sucks."

Blythe laughed at her, charmed by how cute Daryl looked with that particular moody pout on her lips. "Well, let's hope we're not going to have to wait the usual nine months for a baby of our own."

The horrified widening of Daryl's eyes only made Blythe laugh more.

CHAPTER EIGHTEEN

Rafe scoured the area through her night vision binoculars and let out an exasperated sigh.

"I've never known a demon hunter so impatient," Ashley said, taking a bite from her sub sandwich.

"I don't like lengthy stakeouts. I'm an all action kind of gal."

Ashley chucked softly. "Yes, you are, and in the right settings I love that about you."

Rafe lowered the binoculars. "Do not start with the sexual innuendos when we're camped out on a parking garage roof with nothing but two camping chairs and a cooler."

"I had Eli turn the security cameras off so we wouldn't get caught. We could use that to our advantage..." Ashley waggled her eyebrows suggestively.

Rafe stared at her for a long moment then put the binoculars back to her eyes. "Sorry, sweetheart, but sex in a deserted parking garage is not my idea of fun."

"Did you see that?" Ashley pointed toward the ground level.

"See what?" Rafe trained her sight on the building below. "What did you see?"

"I thought I saw movement in one of the windows on the bottom floor." Ashley pointed at the exact spot, and Rafe focused in. She waited for something to move.

"There's nothing there now. Was it something glittering or just cleaners do you think?"

"You know full well the cleaning staff left hours ago."

"Actually, I didn't. Was that before or after you'd sent me on a food gathering mission?"

"I watched them leave around eleven p.m. so yes; I guess that was after you'd very kindly gone to get me something more to eat. That office is supposed to be empty now."

"What do you think you saw?"

"A very brief glow, like something passed the window and glimmered. But it was too damn fast."

"Well, Blythe said this was the agency that seemed to be doing the questionable dealing in the baby trade. If the baby broker and the demon you're after are linked, then it stands to reason the demon would have access to the offices." Rafe lowered the high-powered binoculars and nudged Ashley gently. "I told you we did right telling Blythe about everything."

"Her text was a surprise. I didn't think she'd get a lead first. I had expected us to find the demon, banish the thing, and get out of Blythe's hair before anyone noticed us."

"It helps they got so friendly with one of the mothers that has a stolen kid. Mothers like to talk. I think it comes from having to listen to a kid babble all day. They'll run off at the mouth to any adult the second they get the chance."

Ashley chuckled. "You are so bad. Don't think I haven't heard you cooing in baby talk to Trinity."

Rafe stiffened. "It's not baby talk. It's coaxing for when the little bugger has coughed up a hair ball somewhere and I'm trying to get out of her where it is before I step on it."

"You interrogate your cat?" Ashley was laughing at her now.

"I'm a detective. It's ingrained on my soul. You dare tell anyone I coo at my cat and I'll have you sleeping on the sofa."

"Your secret is safe with me, Detective. All of them are." Ashley tugged Rafe's head down and kissed her gently.

Rafe smiled at the touch of Ashley's lips against her own. "Why were stakeouts never this much fun before you came into my life?"

"Because you were partnered with Dean, and you'd better not have been kissing him when on the job."

"You have nothing to worry about, sweetheart. Kissing on the job is something I've only discovered since being partnered with you."

"See that it remains so," Ashley said.

"I intend to." Rafe tugged Ashley to her and hugged her tight. "Back to the job at hand, P.I. Scott. Do you really think there's a demon hiding in the bowels of that adoption agency?"

"Nothing surprises me anymore. I'm just intrigued as to what a demon would be doing working in such an environment. They're not known for wanting to be around kids."

"Your father did, kind of." Rafe was still angry at Ashley's father who had looked after her only until his wandering eye had caught another woman in his sights. Then he had pretty much left Ashley to raise herself alone. Rafe's family hadn't been exactly picture perfect either, but she had still had their support until she was old enough to make her own way in the world.

"My dad was one of a kind," Ashley said wryly.

"True, but he created you, and I shall always be grateful for that."

Ashley burrowed more into Rafe and wrapped her arms about her waist. Rafe held on to her just as strongly.

"I'm the daughter of a demon."

"You're the daughter of a fallen angel. You can't argue that you came from perfection. I only have to look at you to see that. Your dad turned demonic later as his fate set in. But you, my love, are a child of light."

Ashley rubbed her cheek on Rafe's chest. "You've been talking to Eli."

"Maybe I have and maybe you need reminding that although you spend most of your life in the darkness hunting down demons, you are *not* one of them."

"My brother was."

"Your *half* brother wasn't born of the love your dad had for your mother. He gave up heaven for her. He was a fallen *angel* when he met her. You are a product of that love." Rafe squeezed Ashley to her.

"What would I do without you?"

"You'd eat less because I'm the only one you can send to get your midnight snacks." Rafe yelped as Ashley pinched her side. "Yow!" The sharp ache was quickly dispelled by Ashley's hand slipping between Rafe's shirt buttons and rubbing her stomach. Rafe gave herself up to the loving touch.

Ashley spoke softly into Rafe's ear. "You are so much like your damned cat it's a wonder you aren't purring." She spread a line of tender kisses down Rafe's jawline and then nipped her chin gently. "Before that hand of yours finishes what it's starting," she removed Rafe's hand from off her belt, "we'd better at least pretend we're staking out that place."

Rafe pulled away reluctantly and watched as Ashley straightened her belt and then set to re-buttoning Rafe's shirt. "We really shouldn't be let out together. It's too fucking tempting to just give in to what I always want to do when I'm with you."

"Which is what, Detective?"

"Get naked with you and fuck you senseless just so I can hear you say my name."

"*Raphael*," Ashley breathed seductively into Rafe's ear.

Rafe pulled back sharply and frowned at her. "Not that one, you bitch!" she grumbled at the detested full usage of her name and smothered Ashley's laughter with a bruising kiss. "Stop laughing or I'll damn well leave you up here." Rafe pushed Ashley from her and made a show of standing an arm's length away from her. She picked up the binoculars and tried to be professional when all she really wanted to do was finish what they had started. "I hate to break it to you, sweetheart, but I think that glitter you saw might have been one of the agency's nightlights on the fritz."

"So much for us finding the demon baby snatcher swiftly so we can go home."

"What do you think the deal is with this Chandler woman?"

"She's a cop following her leads."

Rafe considered that. "You don't think that maybe there's something more to it? I mean, she's pinpointing the exact location of stolen children where no other physical evidence has turned up. I've read the same case files as she has, and I read the presentation she gave to the DDU, thanks to Blythe sneaking it our way. She had knowledge of a kid here, but she still had to come here to prove it. What I want to know is how did she know to come here in the first place?"

"Are you saying you think she's involved somehow?" Ashley frowned up at her.

"No, I'm not saying that. From what I could find out about her, she's as squeaky clean as a soap bubble. But she has a fascinating affinity for solving anything to do with children, and it borders on the spooky."

"You think she's got something else going on?"

"I think I'd like to see her in action. Maybe see if this detective playing house with Blythe has a little glitter going on."

Ashley's jaw dropped. "You think Daryl is a demon? For fuck's sake, Rafe! That's one hell of an excuse to dig up for her not to be good enough to be with your best friend!"

"No, it's not that. Okay. So maybe I investigated her once Blythe told me her name because I needed to make sure my friend wasn't sharing a love nest with a psycho with a badge and gun. She isn't, but let's be honest here; the woman is obviously an investigative genius. I'd like to at least know what her trick is."

"Maybe she puts time and effort into her work and follows the leads."

"And if there are no leads pointing the way? Her paperwork is a detailed working of her investigation. They are too detailed, Ashley. It's like she needs to fill in the blanks to stop questions from being asked. No one really reads those reports once the case is solved."

"But you noticed something."

"If being with you has taught me anything it's that nothing ever looks like it seems."

"Blythe is going to kill you if you investigate Daryl, you know that don't you?"

Rafe shrugged. "I need to know she's safe and I need to know why this detective's cases have brought us here to where a demon is involved." She lifted the binoculars to her eyes again and waited a moment until she could confirm what she had thought she'd seen. "Got you, you shiny bastard. I have confirmation that there is indeed something in that building, glowing before my eyes like a disco glitter ball." Rafe let out a small sigh as proof of their demon was finally sighted. It just galled her to know there was nothing she could do about it right that second.

"I'll let Eli know." Ashley got out her cell phone.

"What are the chances of us going back to our room now and having your guys pick up the surveillance? Seeing as we can't bust in there and banish the demon ASAP because Blythe's team needs to conclude their side of the investigation first?" Rafe looked around and above her into the starlit night. "Surely by now you have the angelic eyes in the sky on alert?"

"I suppose we could ask nicely and leave them to it. They know they can call me if they need me."

Rafe shook her head. "Who would believe that angels use cell phones?"

"They don't exactly run a *1-800-Call the Divine* hotline, Rafe. Eli is the only one who uses one to contact me, seeing as he can be earth-bound. I'm not exactly hooked up to the angelic mind meld."

"Something I'm eternally grateful for because it's annoying enough having the phone ring when we're getting down and dirty without you getting telepathic messages as well. That would just be creepy."

Ashley reached for her phone as it chimed in her pocket. "Eli says for us to go."

Rafe looked into the night sky. "Do they listen to every fucking thing we say?"

"No, just the relevant bits."

"How do they differentiate?"

"Can't say I've ever really asked. Right this moment, do you really care?"

Rafe hefted her belongings together. "Let's go. I hear a bed calling me back to it and you calling my name in it."

"You know Eli probably heard that."

"Good, then he'll know to leave us in peace."

CHAPTER NINETEEN

It had taken a week before the Miller Agency had called Daryl and Blythe in for another meeting. The waiting had been almost impossible for Daryl to cope with, and now, seated in the Miller Agency's waiting room, her patience was wearing thin. Daryl couldn't help but twitch nervously at her tie. Blythe reached over to catch Daryl's wandering hand and held it securely in her own.

"I don't know why I'm so edgy," Daryl whispered.

"Because this might be the meeting that decides if we get our baby," Blythe whispered back and pressed a fleeting kiss on Daryl's cheek. "It's like waiting to see if the blue line says we're pregnant or not."

The door to Serena Miller's office opened and she waved them in. Serena smiled as Daryl hastily shot to her feet and tugged Blythe up with her.

"I'm so glad you could come here at such short notice." She ushered them into her office.

"That's one of the perks of being our own bosses," Blythe said as she settled herself into a chair and reached to take Daryl's hand in her own. "But we'd have dropped everything to get here."

Serena's smile widened. "You two are so sweet. It's a pleasure to see." She made a show of rustling through the papers on her desk. "You are going to make extraordinary mothers."

Daryl let out an audible gasp as the bait was finally taken. Thankfully, Serena mistook it for something else and chuckled at her.

"You, my dear, are going to be an amazing parent." She leaned back in her chair. "For legal reasons that are too many and too intrusive to go into, I had to run background checks on you to make sure you are suitable adoptive candidates. You two are perfect."

Daryl sent up a silent prayer of thanks to Trace and her computer wizardry that had obviously led Serena to the fake identity trail they had set in place.

"I can get you on our books straight away for an adoption and have you go through the legal ins and outs that the government adoption rules have in place. That can sometimes be a lengthy process."

"How lengthy, Ms. Miller?" Blythe asked softly.

Serena smiled at her. "A lot longer than I want you two to have to wait. So I'm going to offer you something I only offer to people of your standing in the community."

Daryl read "standing" as wealthy, but made sure her derisive thoughts didn't show on her face.

"I run a legitimate business here, and nearly all of my adoptions are through the government. But I am in a position to offer women like yourselves something a little more."

"More?" Blythe asked, leaning forward in her chair.

"I deal with ladies who, for reasons that are their own, choose to give their babies up to families who can provide a better life for them. These women don't want to go through the usual channels for getting their babies onto adoption lists. They prefer a private adoption where the adopters pay the mothers a fee."

Daryl felt her heart beat quicken at this news. *This is exactly what Claire told me about!* "And how private for *us* would this adoption be?"

"If the adoption went through these channels, you wouldn't have social services coming to check on you. The baby would be yours as much as if you had given birth to it yourself." She leaned forward conspiratorially. "And there's something else for you to consider."

Blythe edged almost off her seat. "What?"

"Because we have a wide range of mothers, there stands a very good chance that one would be blessed with either hair as dark as your own, Blythe, or as pale as Daryl's."

Daryl stared at her. "We could really have a child that would resemble us?" Finally, they were getting somewhere. This was what they needed. Serena Miller was opening the door to them to have a baby stolen to order.

"If that's the way you want to go. You can go through the state-run adoption should you wish. But a private one through me would give you exactly the kind of child I know you two wish for."

"A child that looks like one of us," Blythe said with a hitch in her voice. She looked eagerly at Daryl. "It's what we dreamed of."

"How much would the mother need from us for her fee?"

"Ninety thousand dollars," Serena quoted without hesitation.

Daryl's first thought was the price had gone up since Matthew had been kidnapped. Her silence had Serena rushing to explain.

"The money helps the mother start over after giving her baby away. They sign agreement forms that waive their rights to the child forever. They get sixty thousand as their termination of rights fee. I personally take control of what is kept on file here for that adoption. Because of the privacy I…" She hesitated briefly. "I alter the name of the birth mother so that no record of her ever exists. On paper, you will have a legal binding contract of adoption from me. It just won't be entirely truthful, and I'd require that particular piece of information to be kept between us." She seemed assured by Blythe's and Daryl's hastily nodding heads in agreement. "The rest of the money I keep because of the risk I am taking forging the paperwork so that no true record of the birth mother can ever be found."

Lining your own pocket by stealing babies, and with a hefty profit to be made considering how the price has gone up since Matthew's snatching. "So the mother remains anonymous, and we and the child would be unknown to her also?" Serena nodded at this. "That's a good system for anonymity. I wouldn't want anyone suddenly appearing trying to get more money from us or trying to take away the child."

"It's a one-off payment. The mother disappears without knowledge of who has her child or even where the child is. She can start her life over without the burden of the child she didn't want. And you, my dears, get to have a child that is all yours and no one can dispute that. The adoption is legal on paper, just like any other adoption is, but you have the added comfort of knowing that the mother will never ever touch your baby's life."

Blythe clutched Daryl's hand to her chest. "Sweetheart, I want that. I want the security of knowing no other mother is going to have claim on our child."

Daryl read the need in Blythe's eyes. For a moment, it looked so real that Daryl could easily forget they were only pretending. "I want that too." She turned her attention to Serena who was watching them with great interest. "Why us? Why do we get this opportunity?"

"Honestly? You can afford to do this. I only offer it to those who can. There are a lot of children out there that need homes. You can afford to get a more specific child, one that would fulfill your dreams to complete your family."

"And you know we wouldn't tell anyone about the forging of the mother's name because we want the child so much." Daryl couldn't help but smile at Serena. "We keep this secret together."

Serena smiled. "Exactly. You'd have a lot to lose too if the truth came to light. I choose my clients wisely. Not just anyone gets this deal. You're wealthy and respected in your field. You're committed to each other and wouldn't risk being apart should this ever come to light or, God forbid, go to trial."

Daryl heard the razor edge to Serena's soft tone and recognized a threat of jail when she heard one.

"I know you wouldn't want to jeopardize all that. After all, this way, you get exactly what you want."

"A child that would be ours alone," Daryl said.

"*Your* baby," Serena impressed upon them.

"Our baby," Blythe echoed. She gave Daryl a dazzling smile.

"Our baby," Daryl said, smiling back at the pleasure in Blythe's eyes. "What do we do to start this process, Ms. Miller?"

"Please call me Serena and just tell me which do you prefer? A boy or a girl?"

Daryl looked at Blythe, unsure what to answer.

Blythe smiled at Serena. "Either, both. We really don't care. Whatever comes first so we can bring them into our world."

Daryl smiled at Blythe's explanation and realized she'd just made it a little easier for them to find the birth mother who would have her child removed. Not having to look for a specific sex would save them some investigative energy.

Serena took more details and then told them she'd be in touch once she'd got a suitable candidate chosen.

Daryl rose and stuck her hand out to shake Serena's. "Can I say how wonderful you all are here at this agency? The last time we were here I met one of your colleagues. A small lady, blond hair, wears dark glasses?" She watched a flicker of something race across Serena's face before she hid it well. "She was so kind to me. I was still a little shaky from getting upset in here and she was very nice. Would you tell her I appreciated her kindness, please? I'm afraid I never caught her name."

"Oh, that would be Lailah; she's someone who works closely with me. She's a lovely woman, has been quite a godsend to me in many respects. I'll be sure to pass on your sweet words."

Lailah, Daryl thought as she and Blythe bid farewell to a beaming Serena. *Now we can delve into your background and see what secrets you are hiding.*

❖

The discordant sound of a flurry of texts hitting Rafe's cell phone brought her crashing back to consciousness with a groan.

"Geez, how come you're so popular?" Ashley muttered into Rafe's chest. Her head was resting against Rafe's breast while her arm was wrapped around her waist, effectively pinning Rafe to the bed.

Rafe snatched up her phone. "Let me just see who is trying to clog up my inbox. I hope to fuck it isn't the big boss wondering when I'm coming back."

"Do you think she bought that you were helping on an investigation that might have DDU undertones so you were checking if it was a case you might be brought into?"

"I think so, but she seemed a little suspicious I was so far away from my desk."

"Because you so rarely left the office until I appeared and showed you the wider world out there." Ashley pressed a kiss to Rafe's skin.

"True, you introduced me to love and joy with a smattering of demonic activity. My life is blessed." Rafe checked her phone. "It's Blythe." She read out loud the texts that Blythe had sent her.

"So this Miller woman has taken their baited money hook and is going to snatch them a child," Ashley said. "It was a smart move to not limit the search to a specific sex of the child. I'll have Eli warn the others to watch over the mothers at the hospitals. Then we can start watching them as they go home in case they have the Good Samaritan trying to help."

Rafe read out the next text. Ashley sat up.

"Say that name again."

Rafe repeated it. "Lailah. That's the one Blythe thinks abducts the kids, the one you believe to be a demon."

"Oh, she's a demon all right."

"Blythe says that she's got her team looking into this woman. They're checking to see if she has a record."

"They can look, but they won't find her name on any database. She won't appear anywhere, not with that name. That's her *true* name."

"What do you mean?"

"This demon, hidden in a woman's guise, has taken on an angel's name. Lailah is the angel in charge of conception, and she guards over babies' spirits at their birth."

"She's flaunting what she's doing by giving herself that name."

"And no one is the wiser because to them it's just a name. But for a demon to take an angel's name is blasphemy. It's the most disgusting thing possible, and banishment is too good for her. The true Lailah is a protector. This demon debases that."

"Can't we just walk into the offices, ask to meet her, and I'll Spear of Light her right then and there?" Rafe was hoping Ashley would say yes. Rafe liked Connecticut well enough, but she missed the bustle of Chicago where she had her own demons to banish.

"As much as I'd like that, we can't because of Blythe's involvement and her case that we have kind of hijacked. She needs to capture all that are involved. Until then we have to cool our heels and then go spear this bitch and send her to hell."

"It doesn't seem fair, when we know who she is now."

"We have humans and demons working together here. Something tells me that Ms. Miller doesn't realize that. Twisted, kindred souls have met on this plain. We need to capture them in their sordid act, the human and the demonic, and bring both to justice."

"So what do I reply to Blythe?"

"Tell her we'll do our own research into Lailah and that we know where she hides out."

"Are we going back out there tonight to make sure?" Rafe sent the text off and watched the screen darken.

"I'm going to want all eyes on that agency building. When she snatches Blythe's baby, I want us following her every step she takes. Lailah protects children. This imposter doesn't."

Chapter Twenty

After the debriefing with Lake and the rest of her team, Blythe had cajoled Daryl into joining her at the gym. They'd signed up for regular sessions at the nearest one and had found it frequented by half the neighborhood. Usually that was something Blythe used to her advantage, chatting with the neighbors, learning what she could about the area they were investigating.

Today, Blythe just wanted to be left alone to work out. She was hyped up after their meeting with the adoption agency. It had gone exactly how they had wished. The adoption was finally in place; now they waited for the horrendous act of a child being snatched. Blythe was trying hard not to think of that eventuality. She could only hope that Rafe and Ashley fulfilled their side of the investigation and found the mother and the snatcher before the damage was done.

Just thinking of Rafe made Blythe hit the punching bag harder. She had enough on her plate with the whole stolen babies to order thing without adding the side dish of demons that Rafe had placed before her. She'd managed to text Rafe earlier with the details from the adoption meeting and had been surprised to get a text back telling her that they thought Lailah was the demon and she'd been spotted briefly at the agency building. Blythe honestly didn't know what to do with such information. She desperately wanted to talk this over with Daryl but was mindful of Rafe's request to keep it silent. Knowing that a baby was going to be taken for her supposed happiness and that there was some ungodly creature hiding at the Miller agency that was central to the snatching was more pressure than Blythe could process. She put all her energy into punching the bag.

"You got some inner demons you working out there, Blythe?" Mia Connelly asked as she cautiously edged into Blythe's line of sight.

Blythe halted her furious pounding and hugged the bag. "Just imagining it's the face of one of our clients who is a major pain in the ass."

Mia laughed. "Well, I for one wouldn't want to get on your bad side with a punch like that. I managed just one mile on the treadmill and I'm ready for a stiff drink."

Blythe knew Mia was a new addition to the gym. She got a sneaking suspicion that most of their neighbors were there because of a certain blonde. She looked over to spy Daryl who was running on the treadmill as easily as if she was taking a gentle stroll.

"I couldn't even begin to keep up with your wife. She's got the stamina of a racehorse." Mia eyed Daryl appreciatively. "And the legs to match."

"Are you cruising my girl right in front of me, Mia?" Blythe asked.

"Hey, I'm not the only one it would seem." Mia jerked her head toward a trio of women who were all pretending to be stretching and warming up but were all surreptitiously watching Daryl.

Blythe felt her temper start to rise. It shocked her, but the possessiveness didn't. This was *her* Daryl they were ogling. "They can look all they like. She's mine."

Mia snorted. "Well, duh! You only have to see the way she looks at you to figure out that girl is taken and damned happy about it too."

Blythe digested her comment greedily. She'd done enough watching herself as Daryl had worked her way around the room using all the equipment. Blythe was well aware of the strength in Daryl's body, but viewed in her workout clothes she was a truly powerful sight. Blythe again wondered what it would be like to feel that body pressing into her own as Daryl lay upon her. She felt her heart race at the thought and hoped the blush she could feel building would be taken for the flush of exercise. She'd held Daryl close, but the need to be flesh on flesh was clawing at her insides like a hunger needing to be satisfied. Protocol dictated that she wait, that the case came first and foremost before her baser desires. But as Blythe watched Daryl move from the treadmill to pick up some free weights she couldn't help but wish for the millionth time that they had met outside of this case.

Mia was dramatically fanning herself with her hand. "I swear, the way you look at her…"

Blythe grinned sheepishly. "She's gorgeous, both inside and out."

Mia chuckled. "Looks like someone has been drawn by the outside packaging and wants to check out the quality for herself."

Blythe watched as a woman sauntered over to where Daryl sat lifting arm weights. She recognized her as Jenn from the welcoming party Mia had thrown for them. She stood by seething as Jenn sparked up a conversation with Daryl who continued in her routine. But it wasn't until Jenn reached out and touched Daryl's arm, wrapping a hand around her bicep, that broke Blythe's patience. She pulled off her boxing gloves. Without even a backward glance at Mia, she strode across the room.

As if sensing her, Daryl looked up from her repetition and smiled at her. Blythe noticed, even in her red haze of jealousy, that Daryl's eyes were trained solely on her. She vaguely registered Jenn looking up and hastily dropping her hand from Daryl's arm.

"Hi, sweetheart. You all done?" Daryl asked, lowering the weight to the floor.

Blythe nodded and before she could stop herself, she reached out to cup the back of Daryl's neck and tilted her head up. She kissed Daryl soundly, feeling Daryl's gasp of surprise against her lips before her mouth opened under Blythe's and she deepened the kiss. Blythe tugged the tie that kept Daryl's hair back. She combed her fingers through it until it was loose to her touch. Their kiss continued until they finally had to pull apart to breathe. The look of undisguised desire colored Daryl's eyes. They had darkened to an almost denim blue. The force of her stare hit Blythe like a fist to her chest.

Demons be damned.

"Take me home," Blythe said. Daryl was on her feet quickly, her eyes never leaving Blythe's face. Blythe slipped her hand into Daryl's larger one and led her out past the fascinated throng.

She was done wanting, yearning, and waiting. Life was too short. *Protocol be damned too.*

❖

Blythe drove them home in a heavily charged silence. Daryl had spoken only once since they'd left the gym. After their separate showers and changing back into street clothes, Daryl had asked Blythe if she was sure. Blythe's huskily delivered yes had sealed their fate.

Once Blythe had parked the car, they gathered up their gym bags and walked hand in hand to the front door. Blythe barely got through the door before their bags were tossed roughly aside and Daryl was reaching for her. She grasped Blythe around her waist and pulled her tight to her own body. Their eyes met, and Blythe knew there was no going back for either of them. Her hands were in Daryl's hair pulling her down to kiss her. She dimly heard the door kicked shut behind them, then all she heard were the soft sounds of moans as they kissed each other like they were starving.

"Please don't change your mind now," Daryl muttered against Blythe's lips as she slipped a teasing tongue over Blythe's own, teasing her, tasting her.

"I want you," Blythe said and began steering them down the hallway toward the stairs. Their lips were still locked together and they stole kisses from each other as they climbed the steps.

"Any second thoughts had better be voiced now," Daryl said, "because I don't think I could stop now if I tried. I want you so damn much."

Daryl's rough voice made Blythe tremble, and she captured Daryl's mouth in a fierce kiss to show that she had no intention of stopping. "I want you too," she said as her fingers dropped to start unfastening the buttons on her shirt. She saw Daryl's eyes fix on what she was doing, and when Blythe deliberately spread open her shirt to reveal the lacy black bra beneath, Daryl's groan of appreciation made Blythe's skin tingle.

"Oh my God, you're so beautiful." Daryl's voice cracked with emotion. She trailed one finger slowly along the lace covering Blythe's breast. They stood at the threshold of the master bedroom where Blythe slept, neither moving, as if both realizing that last step would change everything.

Blythe couldn't stand it any longer. "I need you, Daryl, please."

Daryl roughly pulled her T-shirt from her jeans. They shed their clothing in a trail into the bedroom. Their eyes never left each other's as they stripped. Naked first, Blythe hurried to help Daryl get rid of her underwear, and only when she stood nude before her did Blythe fully appreciate how truly beautiful Daryl was. Muscular and solid yet still essentially female, she captivated Blythe like no other woman she'd ever known.

"Do you like what you see?" Daryl asked hesitantly, watching Blythe with nervous eyes.

"I love what I see. I'm just trying to decide what part of you I want to touch first." Her palms itched to cup Daryl's small, firm breasts. She was about to lean forward to suck a tight pink nipple in her mouth when Daryl surprised her.

"How about all of me?" Daryl scooped Blythe up in her arms and carried her to the bed. Astounded by her show of strength, Blythe did what she'd seen Jenn do. She wrapped her hand about Daryl's bicep and squeezed.

"You've got some major muscles there." She smoothed her hand over Daryl's arms that so easily cradled her then let her palm squeeze Daryl's shoulder. "And here."

"All the better to hold the weight of the world," Daryl said with a wry twist to her lips.

Blythe wondered at her comment, but it was quickly forgotten when Daryl laid her down on the bed then swiftly covered her with her entire length. Blythe wrapped her arms about Daryl's neck to keep her in place. "Lover, you feel so good." Blythe caressed everywhere she could reach and accepted Daryl's penetrating kiss. The swirl of Daryl's warm tongue against her own made Blythe's arousal soar. She eased her legs open to let Daryl slide between them and rub against her mound. Daryl gasped into their kiss and began to rock slightly, adjusting her position until their clits brushed, sparking off a rage of shudders in them both.

"Oh God!" Blythe moaned, clutching Daryl's broad shoulders then moving down to grab Daryl's hips to keep her firmly in place.

She was rendered almost senseless as Daryl's kisses stole her very breath away. Daryl's lips moved down Blythe's neck, allowing her to gasp for air, and she licked and sucked at Blythe's pulse point making Blythe moan in pleasure. Then she kissed her way down until she reached the top of Blythe's breasts. The pressure eased off Blythe's clit and her eyes flew open in dismay. Daryl shifted so she could caress Blythe's breasts. Her hands cupped the ample roundness and squeezed gently. Daryl's fingers began tracing rough circles over the flesh, working her way around Blythe's aureoles until they puckered and forced her already tight nipples to thicken more. Daryl's tongue drew lazy patterns over and on one tight red bud while her fingers pulled and gently twisted Blythe's other nipple. Every suck and tug sent lightning bolts straight to Blythe's core. Daryl shifted her weight again and rubbed her thigh against Blythe's wetness. They both groaned.

"You are so amazing," Daryl said, sucking a nipple in deeper to her mouth and letting it pop back out. Her tongue licked over the distended flesh, and she laid a kiss on it before covering the other nipple with her mouth to mete out the same treatment.

Blythe was in constant motion beneath her. She arched her back to press more of her breast into Daryl's hungry mouth, her hips jerked to rub desperately against Daryl's firm thigh pinning her down.

Daryl taunted Blythe's nipples a little more before laying a trail of kisses and soft bites down to her stomach where she nipped at the soft curve of Blythe's belly. Blythe couldn't keep still. She felt as if each kiss was a hundred volts and that Daryl was sending her into sensory overload. The roughness of Daryl's hands only heightened Blythe's desperate desire and the intense pleasure/pain of those sure fingers tugging at her sensitized nipples made Blythe widen her legs more. Daryl moved down further and just stopped. Blythe lifted her hips in the hopes Daryl would get the hint.

"For God's sake, don't stop now," she pleaded, grasping desperately at Daryl's shoulders to push her lower.

"You are beautiful." Almost reverently, Daryl's finger brushed over Blythe's dripping folds, slowly, gently as she explored the swollen flesh. She lowered her head and ran her tongue the length of Blythe's sex. Blythe's body bowed, her eyes slammed shut at the eroticism of Daryl's seeking tongue. Blythe's hips bucked as she tried desperately to get Daryl's mouth where she needed it the most. But Daryl obviously wasn't going to be rushed.

"Suck me," Blythe said, pressing at the top of Daryl's head.

Daryl chuckled against her flesh. "All in good time. I want to taste you first." She pressed a tender kiss to Blythe's clit, causing her to gasp and shudder beneath her. Blythe felt Daryl's fingers run over and around her lower lips, tugging at them, gathering the sticky moisture that coated them, exploring her with lips and tongue. Then, before Blythe could scream from the anticipation, Daryl eased a finger inside her and began thrusting deep. Blythe thought she'd go crazy as Daryl stopped then would continue, giving her no proper rhythm to follow but making her hips jerk as she tried to keep that teasing finger inside her.

"Please, please," fell from Blythe's lips while Daryl's brushed against her thighs and soothed across her belly. Then her torturous mouth moved down once more to wrap around the hooded flesh that was hypersensitive to every touch. Daryl slipped in another finger and Blythe sighed at the added pressure, loving how it felt as Daryl filled her. She couldn't stop her voice from rising as Daryl rubbed against the rough patch of flesh hidden. "Oh God, yes, just there."

Daryl's name spilled from Blythe's lips in a litany. All she knew and felt was the strength of the body poised over her, the power of her fingers stretching and pumping against her soaked walls and the tug of firm lips sucking her clit. "Oh God, oh God, Daryl, please make me come." With tender care, Daryl brushed her teeth over Blythe's swollen clit, and Blythe exploded beneath her. Her body jerked and spasmed, racing through the orgasm and then shaking uncontrollably at the countless aftershocks that sucked Daryl's fingers in deeper inside her. She dimly was aware of soft kisses being pressed against her soft tangle of curls below her belly and Blythe managed to lift her head off the pillows to peer down at Daryl. The indecently self-satisfied look Daryl wore made Blythe smile. "Oh my, Detective, you can find what turns me on as expertly as any case you lay your hands on!"

Daryl grinned at the compliment. She eased her fingers gently out of Blythe and wiped their stickiness on the bed sheet. She then captured Blythe's face between her palms and kissed her thoroughly, leaving Blythe breathless and enraptured even more.

"That was amazing," Daryl said as she lay down at Blythe's side and cuddled in close. Her hand began wandering over Blythe's chest and cupped around a breast. "You taste divine." She ran her tongue over her lips and Blythe blushed at the sensuous act. She quickly regained her energy and shifted so she could lean over Daryl and kiss her. She wrinkled her nose a little at the very obvious evidence of her excitement still covering Daryl's face.

"Are you blushing, Ms. Kent?" Daryl asked, obviously enjoying Blythe's sudden attack of shyness.

"I'm surprised I have any blood left to heat my cheeks seeing as it all went south and was pounding through the same place where you had your fingers buried deep." She smoothed a hand over Daryl's handsome face and just stared at her for a moment. "You really do take my breath away, Daryl. I could seriously get in trouble over you for what you make me feel."

"Then we'll go down together," Daryl replied and then, obviously realizing what she had said, blushed to the roots of her pale hair.

Blythe laughed and ran her fingers through Daryl's soft hair, cradled her face, and kissed her warm cheek. "I love the sound of that," she said breathlessly across the swollen softness of Daryl's lips and slipped her tongue inside to deepen her kiss. Daryl groaned into her mouth, pressing closer, clutching at her back, and pulling Blythe to her.

Blythe didn't release Daryl's lips; she poured all her passion into her kiss, and only when they needed air did she pull back. She gazed into Daryl's eyes, loved the red flush that covered her upper chest and neck, and decided to lick her way down Daryl's neck to explore further. Blythe palmed Daryl's breast, loving that they were smaller than her own and obviously more sensitive. She watched as Daryl bit her lip to keep in a groan as Blythe brushed a fingertip over a straining pink nipple.

"No, don't stifle what you feel. I want to hear you," Blythe told her and she flicked her tongue out to roughly lave at the pale pink tip. She watched the flesh darken as it tightened, and she sucked it in greedily, making Daryl cry out. She sucked as much as she could into her mouth then did the same for the other nipple, leaving a wet trail of kisses along Daryl's breastbone. She flicked a nail across a taut nipple, wondering if Daryl preferred soft touches or could get off on being treated a little more roughly. The spark that flared in Daryl's eyes gave her the answer she needed. Blythe enjoyed letting her passionate side out to play; she had to be so buttoned up and controlled in her work. When it came to lovemaking, she wanted to play hard and wring the passion out of her encounters. She'd found few who would play, but looking into Daryl's face she thought she saw something that matched her own passion. She pushed Daryl down into the bed and delighted in the fact that Daryl resisted for a moment.

"Let me have you," Blythe whispered against Daryl's ear. Daryl turned her head to capture Blythe's lips. Blythe pulled away with a smile. "You've had your way with me, now it's my turn. Are you going to let me take you or do I have to fight you for it?"

Daryl's eyes darkened even further. Blythe's elation made her chest tighten as she thrilled to finding someone who would be an equal to her finally.

"And if I submit?" Daryl asked gruffly, her hand slipping between their bodies and cupping Blythe's sex. Her fingers moved to trap Blythe's clit between them, and she squeezed softly making Blythe see stars.

"Then I would see to make it worth your while." Blythe rocked her hips into Daryl's hand and coated her palm with her excitement. "I promise you, you can do what you like with me. Just let me have you now and show you how much I want you." She eased off Daryl's hand reluctantly and gasped when Daryl put her fingers in her mouth to suck at the sticky wetness. When she removed her hand, Blythe kissed her, pinning her to the bed and roughly fondling her breasts. She loved how Daryl shifted beneath her as her ministrations turned her on.

"Turn over," Blythe ordered and Daryl frowned a little. "Roll over on your stomach." She helped Daryl over to rest up on her elbows, leaving her back bare for Blythe's perusal. She lightly ran her fingernails down Daryl's back, loving how the muscles twitched underneath her. Blythe straddled Daryl's buttocks and spread herself open on top of her, rubbing herself gently against Daryl's tight ass. "I have been fascinated by your ass from the moment you walked into that office in your fitted suit." Blythe rocked a little more, moving easily on the wetness she was leaving behind. She knew she could get herself off on the firm muscle, but that wasn't her intention. She eased off reluctantly and Daryl looked over her shoulder, obviously disappointed too. Blythe squeezed each cheek of Daryl's ass and then settled between Daryl's spread legs. "I know that my first time with you should be gentle and sweet, but I really want to just fuck you and make you mine."

Daryl's face flamed and her eyes bore into Blythe's. "Gentle and sweet can wait," she said.

Blythe ran her palm over a cheek and squeezed. "Do you know how furious I felt today when I saw Jenn touch you?"

Daryl frowned. "Jenn? When was that?"

"In the gym today, she had her hand on your arm." She watched as Daryl tried to recall. "You don't remember?" She was rewarded with a blank look and a shake of Daryl's head.

"I remember watching you on the treadmill and thinking how long your legs were and how much I wanted them wrapped around me as I fucked you. I remember watching you take a drink from your water bottle and some trickled down your neck and I wanted so bad to lick my way down your throat and into your cleavage to get it. And I remember watching you boxing and feeling myself get wet as I watched you move and release your power." Daryl's eyes never shifted from Blythe's. "I don't remember any other woman because all I could see was you."

Blythe stretched up Daryl's body and kissed her hard. "I don't like other women coming on to you."

"I'm here with you. I only want you. Make me yours. Mark me as yours and they won't bother you again because you'll know I'm taken."

Blythe tugged on the soft flesh of Daryl's ear. "I can be possessive."

"Good, so can I where you are concerned. Don't think I didn't see those women in the gym checking you out too. It drove me crazy seeing them eye your body when I was no better and doing the exact same."

"You've had me. You've had your fingers inside me and made me come." She smiled against Daryl's back as she reacted to Blythe's words.

"Yes, I have and I want to do that again." She made to move, but Blythe stilled her.

"My turn, then you can fuck me." She loved how responsive Daryl was to her words and her touch. The lengthy groan Daryl expelled spurred Blythe on to do what she had been fantasizing about. She kissed a line down Daryl's back and then bit down on a tight butt cheek making Daryl suck in a breath. Blythe licked at the bite then marked the other buttock the same. "Mine," she said and then spread Daryl's legs. She slipped her hand between them and found Daryl's sex. Her fingers slipped in the abundance of arousal. "You're so wet," she said.

"That's because you're driving me insane." Daryl rose onto her knees at Blythe's insistence and lowered her head. "Please," she whispered, widening her legs further.

Blythe ran her hand through Daryl's soaked lips. She captured the distended clit and pulled gently on it, then rubbed over the head making Daryl jerk into her hand. With her other hand, she pushed a finger inside Daryl; it slipped easily inside so Blythe returned with more and filled Daryl up. She could tell Daryl wasn't used to being penetrated. She was tight, and she could see how Daryl's body tensed at the intrusion. "I have you." Blythe rubbed her cheek against Daryl's ass and began pushing inside her again, making Daryl follow the rhythm she was setting. Daryl's clit grew longer and firmer in her grasp, and she tugged it harder, feeling Daryl clench around her fingers. She let go and heard Daryl's moan of disapproval smothered into the pillow. She couldn't hold back a grin. Blythe took another bite at Daryl's butt and sped up her fingers. Daryl's groans were muffled, but she pushed back against Blythe's hand, seeking to push her fingers in further. With her hips rolling erratically, Daryl's moans left no doubt how desperate she was to come.

Blythe withdrew her fingers, and in a swift move, flipped over and positioned herself between Daryl's legs. She pulled Daryl down onto her mouth. Daryl shouted out Blythe's name and bucked against her lips. Blythe's tongue speared inside Daryl's opening; pushing in as far as she could go. Then she lazily dragged her tongue up to lick over Daryl's exposed clit. Blythe barely had a chance to marvel at how beautiful Daryl was before she felt Daryl's thighs tighten around her and she began to erratically pump against Blythe's mouth. Daryl's climax came quickly and Blythe greedily lapped up the wetness that escaped in Daryl's pleasure. She clamped on to Daryl's hips and refused to let her go as she rode out her orgasm.

Her face buried in Daryl's sex, Blythe could feel the spasms pulsing through her. She flattened her tongue on Daryl's clit and felt it move against her as it twitched with every last orgasmic beat. She pulled back just a little to let her eyes focus on Daryl's most intimate place and pressed a kiss to the hard clitoral head that was barely covered by the hood of flesh it rested in. No wonder she's so sensitive, Blythe marveled, as it jerked beneath her lips. She felt Daryl try to dismount from her face, and she reluctantly helped her, letting her ease onto her back before swinging a leg over her hips to keep her anchored in place.

"Oh my God," Daryl gasped. "No one has ever done that to me before."

Blythe's fingertips traced idle patterns along the bright red flush of orgasm that painted Daryl's sweat streaked flesh. "What? Had you hump their face?"

"Taken me from behind and then let me ride their face for my pleasure." She sucked in air greedily. "That was…" She shook her head in wonder. "Mind-blowing!"

Blythe laughed. "Glad I could help. How long has it been since you've made love, Daryl?"

Daryl hesitated. "Why? Was I really bad or something?"

Blythe's chest ached at the sound in Daryl's voice. She liked her lover confident and forceful. Her heart broke when Daryl sounded unsure of herself.

"No, you were fantastic, and I have a few toys at home I really want to have you wear and take me with." She could feel the heat from Daryl's blush warm her as she pressed a reassuring hand on Daryl's face. "I ask because you were tight and I was worried I might have hurt you."

"You didn't hurt me at all. I don't…" Daryl hesitated again, and Blythe raised herself up on an elbow to be able to see her face. "I don't usually have lovers inside me. They don't expect me to want it, and I kind of got used to not having it done."

"Did I make you uncomfortable doing it?"

Daryl shook her head. "No, you made me realize what I have been missing. God, Blythe, you made me come so damn hard I still have fireworks burned on my retinas!"

Blythe snuggled into her, satisfied she hadn't hurt her. "I love how hard your clit gets," she said, resting her hand over Daryl's sex and rubbing her fingertip just inside where she could feel the hooded bump. "I love how it feels between my lips."

Daryl groaned and trembled at Blythe's husky words. "I loved it when you sucked on me too, but unless you want me to come again, I suggest you take your finger off it." She removed Blythe's hand and placed it on her stomach, pinning it in place. At Blythe's moan of displeasure, she said, "I don't think I could come again just yet. You'd give me an aneurism."

"How do you feel about all this?" Blythe asked. "Because I have to say that I feel this was meant to be between us, and I'm thankful I've finally found someone who can match my passion."

"You're quite the dominant in bed, aren't you?" Daryl said, smiling.

"I submitted to you without any argument," Blythe said. "It was my idea to come home and get naked and you took my best laid plans for fucking you and took me first!"

"Equal partners in all things, Blythe. I'll give as good as I get and, if that was anything to go by, your lovemaking is so good I may never leave this bed again."

"I like the sound of that." Blythe snuggled into Daryl's arms. "I can do soft and gentle too, just so you know."

"And I can strap on a cock and drill you into the mattress springs whenever you wish."

Blythe thrilled to the devilish grin that Daryl wore. She shivered at the thought of Daryl doing exactly that to her. "This partnership just got so much better than I imagined."

Daryl's eyes grew serious. "I don't want you ever worrying about another woman, Blythe, do you hear me? I fell for you the minute I saw you. You're all I want." She remained silent for a moment then said softly, "I love you, Blythe."

Blythe's heart beat so loud that for a moment she feared she hadn't heard right. Daryl leaned up and kissed her gently. Smiling down at her, Blythe finally was able to admit what she felt. "I love you too, and that has nothing to do with being your wife here. It's the simple truth in my heart."

Daryl's smile was so beautiful it made Blythe want to cry. "Then I'm yours if you want me."

Blythe pressed her lips to Daryl's chest, right above where her heart beat. "Oh, believe me, I want."

Chapter Twenty-one

Daryl lay propped up on her side, brushing a hand over Blythe's curly hair. The soft, silken strands slipped through her fingers and captivated her. She couldn't touch enough. She was almost afraid that if she stopped feeling Blythe's skin that somehow she'd disappear and Daryl would be left achingly alone again. Blythe lay on her back gazing up at her, her own hand tracing patterns on Daryl's arm.

"Tell me something about you no one else knows," Blythe said.

Daryl blinked at the request. "Like what? You already wheedled out of me my favorite sexual position."

Blythe laughed. "It didn't take much wheedling when you were more than willing to share it with me and we found that it's now a favorite of mine too." Blythe brushed a fingertip over Daryl's smiling lips. "Tell me something you've never told anyone else."

Daryl thought for a long moment. She felt that she could trust Blythe with all that she was. Even if Blythe would never truly understand what Daryl could do when it came to her ability to find missing children. She'd never trusted anyone before, but she felt she could trust Blythe with her life. She nodded once, deciding to share herself fully with Blythe. "You know I said I have these gut feelings about finding the missing children?"

Blythe nodded, her hand stilling as she listened intently to what Daryl was opening up to tell her.

"I also said I'm not psychic or anything like that. I'm not, but I did have a dream once. It's never happened again, but the memory of it remains so vivid in my head that I can't dismiss it."

"What was it about?"

"I was among a squad of agents going into a house. I wasn't part of them. I wasn't an actual member of the team, but I was just there, following. I remember the woman in front of me had curly hair like yours, tied back and it hung long over the back of her Kevlar vest. The guy in charge silently signaled for everyone to take their positions, and we burst into the house, guns drawn. Inside, there were men in various stages of undress, and we swept the rooms, finding children in some with other men. The place wasn't well kept and it had many floors with what seemed like hundreds of rooms. I followed behind the woman the whole way.

"She went down some stairs to a basement, where the dark walls were lined with bunk beds. Children were everywhere, curled up on the mattresses and terrified by the noise of us coming in. There were shouts from the agents and the men as they were captured and it all echoed around the house. It was deafening. I'm guessing we'd just stormed in on a pedophile hideout. I remember the agents gathering the children and hurrying them out up the stairs. One little boy kept crying for his mother, and the woman had to scoop him up in her arms. He clung to her so tightly, like she was his savior. I guess she was. It was an awful dream."

Daryl's eyes weren't seeing the prettily decorated walls of the room she was in. Instead, she was back in the basement seeing the filthy conditions the children had been subjected to. She didn't even want to think about what they had been put through in the rooms above. "The weird thing was, my dream abruptly changed just as the woman in front of me was about to turn around. Then I was suddenly at the door of another house with a small blond by my side. She had the prettiest face, was surrounded by a sunshine glow of light, and had the brightest blue eyes I have ever witnessed. She went in alone and confronted a man at a computer. I remember worrying he would hurt her because she was so small. Then the weirdest thing happened."

Daryl shook her head. "It sounds so crazy, but it was just a dream after all. He began to change before her and these huge horns sprung from his head. Horns, just like a goat has. I swear I must have watched a horror film before I slept because he changed into a monster right before us, and this woman never even flinched. The last thing I remember is seeing him jerk as if something had stabbed him and he just disappeared." Daryl looked down into the widened eyes of Blythe who barely seemed to be breathing.

"I woke up with a start, my heart racing, but feeling oddly at peace. I went into work the next day and put out some calls to my buddies dotted around on the forces to see if a ring had been busted. Sure enough, there was one and they'd caught the guy behind the distributing of the films too. I've never had another experience like it, before or since, but I swear I was there and saw it all happen." She shrugged self-consciously at Blythe. "I've never told anyone about it because it's too damn bizarre and I'm considered weird enough with what I can do. I really didn't need to draw any more light in my direction telling people I'd had this dream." She watched as Blythe licked her lips and seemed to be struggling for words. "What's wrong, baby?"

"I was part of that bust, and the child who wouldn't let go of me left little finger sized bruises on my arms that took weeks to fade." She sat up slowly and Daryl did the same. "He was barely five years old, snatched from outside a grocery store and subjected to terrible abuse for the four months they had him in that house. He screamed when I had to leave him in the hospital, but I couldn't stay because I had to finish my job. But I wanted to stay and keep him safe until his parents could be informed he'd been found. I wanted to give him back to them, make sure they realized what a gift they had having him back alive. But I never got the chance; I had to be debriefed."

"You were there?" Daryl couldn't believe it. She ran her hand over Blythe's hair, trying to reconcile what she'd seen in the dream with the woman she had beside her now.

"My hair was longer back then."

Daryl frowned, trying desperately to process what Blythe was telling her. *The dream had been real and Blythe had been in it?* "This doesn't make sense."

"The blonde you saw was Ashley, Rafe's girlfriend. Her part of the job was to go after the porn distributor. And I really need you to meet her now because your dream obviously wasn't just a fluke."

"What do you mean?"

Blythe took a deep breath. "Rafe and Ashley are here working on our case as well."

A flame of anger ignited in Daryl's gut. "This is my case. I only involved your team. Since when are they investigating?"

"They're following up leads on Lailah. She's who Ashley is after."

"How does she know about her? It's only through what we've found out that Lailah's part in these snatchings has come to light." Blythe looked as if she was bracing herself to say something. Daryl frowned at her. "What else have you not told me?"

"They think Lailah is something not quite human."

"Something not quite human," she repeated carefully, not entirely sure she'd heard correctly.

"Like as in a demon," Blythe said.

Daryl searched her face. "You're joking, right?"

"No joke. I was as surprised as you are when they told me. Rafe was nearly killed by a demon and now she can see them."

Daryl couldn't believe she was hearing this.

"Daryl, you have some kind of special power with what you do. Surely you, of all people, can see beyond what looks normal and maybe see something else?"

"Like *demons*? Are you saying you think I'm possessed when I find these kids?" Daryl flung herself off the bed to stand beside it, trembling with anger. "Is this what you really talked about when you met your friend? That you all think I have some kind of supernatural power that I call upon to find the children?"

Blythe got to her knees on the bed quickly. "No, I never said that, but these demons…"

Daryl raised her hand to cut Blythe off. "*Don't*. I have spent all my life hearing whispers behind my back about my ability and how weird I must be to be around. I have hardly any friends, Blythe, because of it. I focus on the children and it takes over my life. Who can compete with that? I've hidden myself away in my office and dealt with the cases that have crossed my desk and done it alone because, that way, I can't be judged. But I brought this case to you all and hoped I'd be treated with respect. I know what I do scares people." She brushed a hand over her face horrified to find it wet with tears. "It scares *me*. But I thought I could trust you with me, *all* of me, but instead I find you're talking about my case behind my back and wondering if I'm conjuring up demons." She began snatching up her clothing and pulling them on roughly. "I thought you would know me better than that."

"Daryl, wait, please—"

Feeling betrayed and so heartsick she could barely see straight, Daryl fled the bedroom and ran down the stairs. She slammed out the front door and ran as fast as she could down the road. Leaving Blythe behind tore at her soul, but she felt exposed and blown wide open to the suspicions about her strange ability. Daryl couldn't explain it. She'd never known how she could do what she was able to. Only her mother had ever seen it as a blessing. Everyone else viewed her as plain strange. And now with Blythe talking of demons, Daryl didn't know where to turn. *I thought she'd understand me. I thought she'd be different. I thought I could trust myself with her. I've just put my job and reputation on the line with her.* Daryl's feet pounded the street as she tried to run as fast as she could, knowing she was leaving her heart behind.

❖

Rafe picked up her phone on its first ring and listened to the sobbing that echoed down the line. She held the phone away to check the caller ID. "*Blythe?*"

Ashley looked up from her laptop, concerned at the sound of Rafe's voice.

"Okay, we're on our way over. No, stay in the house in case she comes back. We'll sort this out. Try to take a deep breath and calm down. Give me your address. We're coming now." Rafe snapped her cell phone shut and reached for her coat. "Come on. There's trouble in paradise."

CHAPTER TWENTY-TWO

The drive to Blythe and Daryl's house didn't take Rafe and Ashley long once Rafe employed police tactics and surpassed the speed limit every chance she could.

"Wow, talk about lifestyles of the rich and the famous." Ashley pressed her face against the glass of the car's window and whistled. "And I thought your neighborhood was pretty spiffy, but, sweetheart, this makes your place look like a cardboard box from the Jiffy Mart."

"You got that right. Can you imagine having the money to live this kind of lifestyle? Where one yacht or two is the biggest worry you'll ever have."

"Maybe when you get promoted to head of the DDU we can move here," Ashley teased.

"That's what I love about you the most, my love. Your wild imagination." Rafe pulled up outside Blythe's home and got out of the car. She scanned the area quickly but couldn't see any sign of anyone or any*thing* in the street.

Ashley led their way up the path. She paused at the car parked on the drive. "There's demon residue on the hood. Faint but still there. What do you think that means?"

"Maybe one of them tagged a Class M demon while out. They're squishy enough to leave a mark. One less for us to worry about if they did." Rafe was about to knock on the door when Blythe threw it open and all but collapsed in her arms. Rafe steered her inside quickly. "Okay, now you can tell us exactly what happened today that made your partner take off like the hounds of hell were chasing her."

"I told her about the demons," Blythe said.

Rafe smacked a hand dramatically to her forehead. "Oh, for fuck's sake, Blythe! That's not exactly pillow talk!"

Blythe addressed Ashley. "She knew about the pedophile ring we worked on. She saw me. She even saw you in a dream she had."

"Daryl *dreams*?" Ashley exclaimed. "Well, that might go a long way to explaining her gift."

"No, she only dreamed that once, and she says she doesn't have a gift, just these gut feelings."

"I think she has more than that, Blythe, judging by her success rate and notoriety in her field." Rafe was pacing back and forth, furious that Blythe hadn't kept her word but intensely curious as to what made Daryl the woman she was.

"I need to see her, to make sure she's not—" Ashley almost inadvertently blurted out what was obviously on her mind.

"Make sure she's not what? A *demon*?" Blythe's voice rose. "Oh, my God, Rafe! What have you dragged me into that I can't even trust my lover anymore?"

"You've slept with her?" Rafe didn't think Blythe would have crossed the line like that. *This Daryl must be someone special.*

"She's all I've ever wanted, and I don't care what she is. I need her. I *love* her."

"Even if she's different?" Rafe said. Loving a woman who possessed special powers came with its own set of challenges. She spared Ashley a glance. However, it was worth it when it was the right woman to share your life with.

"I don't care about that. I just care about her. I have from the very second I laid eyes on her." Blythe sat on the settee and put her head in her hands.

"Any chance Daryl could be her One?" Rafe asked Ashley.

"She could be. You know how that whole thing works. It's never who you expect." She smiled at Rafe sweetly.

"My what?" Blythe said.

"Your One, your soul mate, your eternal flame, your main squeeze."

"There's really such a thing?"

"Oh, believe me, the things this one can tell you all about things like that." Rafe gestured to Ashley. "She could fill a book on this one true love stuff."

"You're my One," Ashley said to Rafe, "And you know it."

"Yes, I do and I'm forever grateful for it."

Blythe leaned her head against the settee cushion. "Soul mates… angels…demons. How does your head not explode with all this?"

"I think Armitage cracking open my skull allowed me to take all this in with little fuss. When you've stared down a demon, being told that a gorgeous little blonde is going to be the love of your life is much easier to take."

"I swear I thought this case was just going to be routine."

"Nothing will ever be routine from now on, Blythe. That particular genie is way out of the bottle."

"So Daryl's my One." Blythe sounded tired. "The one I can't live without and would give up my soul to be with. And yet she's not here."

Ashley patted Blythe's knee soothingly. "She will be. You're her One as well, it would appear." She cocked her head toward the sound of the front door opening and flashed Blythe a reassuring grin. "See?"

They all looked up as Daryl took a step into the room and stared at them warily.

"Don't worry. This isn't an intervention." Rafe took a step forward and held out her hand. She was relieved to note that Daryl had no glimmer of any sort around her. She shook Daryl's hand and introduced herself and Ashley. She caught the flash of hesitation in Daryl's eyes before she quickly covered it. She still eyed Rafe a little distrustfully and Rafe was hard-pressed not to bristle at her. She watched as Daryl acknowledged Ashley and froze.

"It really is you," Daryl gasped. She looked to Blythe then back at Ashley. "What the hell is going on here?"

Ashley smiled at her. "I understand you saw me in a dream?"

Daryl turned on Blythe accusingly. "That was a secret for only you to hear."

"I'm sorry, but I felt they needed to know." Blythe didn't look away from Daryl's obvious anger.

"Know what exactly? That I dreamed of you years before I met you? That I saw a case you were working on as if I was right there with you? Or that I saw Ashley make a monster disappear? What did they need to know, Blythe? That I'm obviously not normal because I can see these things and do things no one else seems capable of and even *I* can't explain how?"

Both Rafe and Ashley let out a gasp as another person appeared before them out of thin air.

Rafe recovered first. She let out an annoyed sound. "Well, well, doesn't that just figure? Here I was worrying that Daryl might be a demon, and instead she's got something entirely different going on." Rafe shook her head at the handsome man dressed impeccably in a luxurious white suit who had materialized behind Daryl. His huge wings unfurled and framed them both. He bowed his head in greeting at Rafe.

"Well, just fuck me now. I wish you'd told me she had an angel on her shoulder, Blythe."

CHAPTER TWENTY-THREE

Ashley felt deeply sorry for Daryl. To be accompanied by an angel and have no idea of his presence seemed to her an unimaginable nightmare. She could see the imagined betrayal on Daryl's face, obviously heartsick that Blythe had shared her secrets with them. Not knowing that, out of everyone she would ever meet, she and Rafe were the only ones who would truly understand her. Daryl looked around her, desperately searching for what Rafe had spoken of.

"You can't see him at all, Daryl?" Ashley rose from her seat to reach out a hand to Daryl to calm her and to take a closer look at the angel peering silently over Daryl's shoulder.

Daryl shook her head, the look on her face warring between fear and disbelief.

"What exactly are you seeing, Rafe?" Blythe asked.

"I'm seeing that the love of your life has a winged accessory bigger than a bread box standing behind her." Rafe shifted her gaze to Daryl. "Detective Chandler, this is your home. Please sit down and let us sort out this mess so that Blythe can hold you again without you thinking she betrayed you to the DDU's version of the X-Files."

Daryl sat in an armchair guided by Ashley. She cautiously eyed everyone, braced as if expecting an attack. Ashley's heart bled for her and at what she had to do now and how it would change Daryl's life forever. It wasn't every day you found out you had been followed by an angel for most of your life.

"Blythe told you we deal with demons, right?" Ashley asked, edging closer to kneel before Daryl and draw her attention directly on her.

Daryl nodded. "I saw you in my dream. I saw you go into a man's house. You made him disappear. He turned into a monster and you made him disappear." She cast Blythe a baleful look. "But it was just a dream."

"Did you see anyone else there with me?"

Daryl shook her head. "Just you and…whatever he was."

Rafe sighed. "So she can't see angels. That would explain why she's oblivious to the fact she's being tailed by this big white-winged guy. Who is curiously reticent for an angel." Rafe stared at him suspiciously.

Ashley noticed he took everything in they were saying but hadn't once opened his mouth to speak. Ashley looked over Daryl's shoulder to the angel who stood behind Daryl's chair. "Identify yourself." Out of the corner of her eye, she caught Daryl flinch as she realized Ashley wasn't directing that sharp bark of an order at her.

The angel inclined his head and smiled at Ashley but didn't utter a word. "He's an *Impressor*," Eli said, appearing at Ashley's side.

"And what exactly is an Impressor?" Ashley was sure that to both Daryl and Blythe it appeared she was talking to empty air. She tossed a wink at Daryl. "I have an angel too, only I can see mine in all his glory." She bit back a smile as Daryl's mouth dropped open before she quickly schooled her surprise. Ashley again wished that everyone could see what she saw, perhaps then she'd look less certifiable when she was caught conversing on her own.

"An Impressor is an angel who mentally impresses on their charge what they need them to see. Impressors are usually the ones who humans get answered by when they pray for a guide to show them the road to take in life. An Impressor will steer them to the right path."

"Great, he's a winged GPS," Rafe grumbled. "So he's doing what exactly with Daryl? She's not asking him to show her the right path. He's helping her in her investigations. How?"

Eli shrugged. "I have had very little contact with Impressors. I'm not familiar with their, how would you investigators put it? Modus operandi?"

Rafe snorted and even Ashley had to smile at Eli trying on cop speak. Ashley looked at the angel over Daryl's shoulder. "You can hear me, right?" The angel nodded eagerly. She looked at Eli. "So why can't I hear him? I can usually hear angels speak."

"Because he doesn't talk at all. To you, he is mute, but he talks to Daryl in his own way. He's been guiding her to find the children."

Daryl, obviously getting more and more agitated by all the talking directed above her head, rose from her seat angrily, nearly knocking Ashley over. "This is ridiculous. What game are you all playing? Am I supposed to believe what you say you see just because you talk to thin air? What the hell did you do to Blythe to convince her? Because after one evening with you two she believes that there are things running wild on our streets?"

Deliberately ignoring Daryl's outburst, Ashley questioned Eli. "What's his name and what is his connection to Daryl? I'm guessing you guys still have your telepathic link even if he is silent."

Eli nodded. "His name is Virgil and he is Daryl's guardian. And he says he's sorry Daryl can't see him because her mother could."

Now that's interesting. "Daryl, did your mother ever have powers like you?"

Daryl's whole body stiffened. "No, she never saw anything, but she was never frightened by what I could do. She said I was blessed."

Ashley smiled. "That's because, according to your guardian angel, your mother could see him." Eli whispered something in her ear. "Especially when she was so ill at the end. He stayed by her bedside with you to watch over her."

Tears welled in Daryl's eyes at the mention of her mother. "She was very sick. I sat with her every chance I got."

"You weren't alone."

Daryl looked about her. Ashley was desperately sorry Daryl couldn't see the two angels so prominent in the room.

"At the end when she was slipping away from us, my mom said something that Dad and I never understood. We thought it was her mind wandering, the mutterings of a dying woman, but it never made sense to us."

Ashley nodded, listening to Eli tell her what had transpired. "She said, 'Watch over her, Virgil.'"

Daryl clasped her hand over her mouth to stifle a sob. Blythe was instantly on her feet and at Daryl's side, wrapping her arms about Daryl's waist. Daryl all but collapsed into her hold.

"Virgil is the name of your angel, Daryl," Ashley told her.

"My mom could really see him?"

"She said all along you were blessed. She knew what you had by your side."

Daryl brushed away tears from her face. She tightened her grip on Blythe, and Ashley was heartened to see Blythe melt into Daryl's chest with relief.

"How long have I supposedly had an angel?" Daryl asked quietly.

"Since you first yearned to find a missing child and Virgil heard your call. He's been with you ever since. God sends angels to those who call for their assistance."

"And he just stayed?"

"You could hear him even though he never spoke a word to you. That's rare for a human. And together, you find the lost. It's your calling, Daryl, and Virgil's too."

"You're like any cop with a partner," Rafe spoke up. "Only you're lucky. He doesn't bore you rigid with his whining about his crappy home life, and you always get the last doughnut."

Daryl rested her forehead against Blythe's hair. "I'm sorry I didn't believe you. And I'm even sorrier for my anger and my storming out after…."

Ashley snuck a look at Rafe who was rolling her eyes and mouthing "love's young dream" at her. Ashley shook her head at her, knowing full well Rafe could be just as romantic when she pushed her cynicism aside.

Blythe was smoothing a hand over Daryl's cheek. "I wouldn't have believed me either. And you haven't even seen what Ashley can do yet."

Ashley grinned. "I promise I'll show and tell all you need to know. But I'm curious about something. How do you and Virgil communicate when you find those children and he never says a word?"

Daryl shrugged. "All I know is I get a crushing weight on my shoulders and then my eyesight narrows like I'm focusing in on something. My sight highlights a location or a person that I investigate. It's hard to explain. It's so second nature for me now."

Eli spoke. "Ashley, ask Blythe to step back please. Virgil wants to demonstrate."

Ashley did so. She'd never come across another human, fully *human* at that, teamed with an angel. Most angels just visited, assisted their human, and returned to their other duties elsewhere. But Virgil had stayed, set himself up as a partner to his human charge, and had even stayed by her side when Daryl's mother had been dying. She looked at the handsome face of the angel that moved to stand directly behind Daryl. They both had the same shock of pale hair.

"You have angel's hair," Ashley said without thought.

Daryl looked surprised and Blythe just laughed.

"That's what Trace calls her."

"Trace doesn't know the half of it," Ashley said.

Virgil's large wings opened to their fullest extent. He tipped them forward and effectively covered Daryl with the brilliant white feathers. The weight of his wings rested upon her shoulders, and Daryl reacted to the familiar pressing on her body. Ashley marveled that Daryl stayed upright with such a burden literally resting upon her. Then Virgil pressed his face into the back of Daryl's head. Ashley sucked in a breath as Daryl's eyes changed as her eyes became Virgil's. It was over in a split second, but Ashley was trained to notice such things. She couldn't miss the bright flash that signified Virgil commandeering Daryl's sight.

"Fuck," Rafe said. "That's fifty shades of downright disturbing."

"He's impressing himself onto her," Ashley said and explained to Blythe what she was witnessing.

"Daryl, does it hurt?" Blythe asked, her hand instinctively reaching out to her but pulling back at the last second as if fearing she'd disrupt what was taking place.

"It just feels like an enormous pressure on my shoulders trying to press me into the floor. My eyes are focusing like a zoom lens. Usually, this is where I focus in on a street name or on a location on a map. It doesn't exactly hurt as just feels really strange. I've gotten used to it." She shifted slightly and the feathers rippled on

Virgil's wing. "I'm just a little freaked that Ashley and Rafe can see something that I only feel."

"Okay Virgil, point made. Get your face out of her head. You're freaking me out," Rafe grumbled before addressing Eli. "Damn glad you don't pull that kind of stunt with Ashley."

Eli raised a pale eyebrow at her. "Indeed."

Daryl shrugged as the pressure eased off her shoulders as Virgil stepped back. Ashley noticed her eyes were back to normal and she didn't display any lingering effects of what had just taken place. Ashley had never seen an angel interact with a human in quite that way before, and she was doubly impressed by the fact Daryl took it all in her stride and had never really questioned it.

"So now we know. Daryl has an angel who is a child finder. Could this job get any fucking weirder?" Rafe said.

Daryl reached out to catch at Blythe's hand and pull her close. "Could you see anything?" she asked her.

Blythe shook her head sadly. "Just you getting a very intense look on your face. So now can you two let Daryl in on your part in her case?"

Ashley shot a look at Rafe who was looking resigned. "I think we have to, so there are no more misunderstandings."

Blythe had the grace to look sheepish. "I'm sorry, but it's been horrible hiding secrets from Daryl. I don't want us to have that." She lifted Daryl's hand to her lips and kissed her knuckles softly. "We're a team now."

"Tell me what's really happening here," Daryl said. "I think I have a right to know what is going on concerning my case."

"Your case is more than you'd ever realize." Ashley couldn't stop looking at Daryl's angel. He was as handsome as Eli but not as tall. His light didn't shine as brightly either, and he seemed younger, although she knew that angels never aged. He and Eli had some kind of silent conversation and then they disappeared. "Okay, the angels have just departed. It's just us here now, and I think Daryl needs to be brought up to speed."

Blythe leaned forward. "Are you going to show her what you can do? Because I think you might need to get all the fantastical stuff out of the way before you lay all the facts on her."

Daryl's eyes fixed on Ashley. "What can you do? Isn't it enough you say you have a guardian angel too?"

Rafe let out a sharp laugh. "Oh, believe me, Detective, you haven't seen anything yet." She nudged Ashley. "Go on, blow her mind." She leaned in to whisper in Ashley's ear, making her shiver at the warm breath that tickled her. "And no Tomb Raider this time. It's not fucking fair!"

Ashley laughed at the disgruntled look on Rafe's face. "What's your favorite film, Daryl?"

"*Aliens*."

Rafe groaned. "Oh come on! You can't pull a Weaver and not have me see it."

Her disgruntled pout made Ashley chuckle.

"Sorry, Rafe, it's another of your dream girls. One kick ass Ripley coming up," Ashley announced and got her glamour on.

Chapter Twenty-four

Her head pounding from the stress that the evening had piled upon her, Daryl scrambled for some pain-killers from the medicine cabinet. She shook two tablets from the bottle and tossed them into her mouth, swallowing them down with a large gulp of water.

"How are you feeling?" Blythe asked from behind her.

"She turned into Sigourney Weaver right before my eyes. I mean, *right* before my eyes. How the hell do you ever explain that away?" Daryl closed her eyes but couldn't exorcise what she had seen. From one second to the next, Ashley had changed into someone else. "I swear it feels like my head's going to explode from all this."

"It's a very cool trick she has, isn't it?"

Daryl appreciated Blythe trying to make it seem fun and exciting, but she didn't think she could cope with any more. I *have an angel. Oh my God, I have an angel.*

"It's terrifying. I mean, honestly, between that and the whole 'we're surrounded by angels and demons' discussion I was privy to tonight, I have no damn clue who I am any more. I don't know how Rafe copes. Her girlfriend shape shifts and is the product of an angel/human coupling." Daryl picked up the bottle of pills again to see if she could take another dosage. Blythe took them firmly from her grasp.

"Rafe loves her and they have a great thing going. They fight demons together."

"And what are we supposed to do now? Just continue on as if nothing has changed? I have an angel, for God's sake. What kind of freak does that make me?"

"We do our job as usual. Only now, both of us are aware there's an extra element to the case. And you are no freak. You never have been. You're still you. Nothing changed except you know now where you get your talent from."

"Lailah is a demon, according to Rafe." Daryl still wasn't sure if she could believe any of what she'd been told.

"Specifically a child-snatching demon working with a human partner who traffics the children on to new parents."

"God, what did I start here?" Daryl leaned her head against the cool wall tiles and closed her eyes tight.

"You didn't start anything; *they* did. You're the one who's going to put an end to it when we catch them in the act of giving us a child."

Daryl cracked one eye open to look at Blythe. "How can you be so calm about all this? They announced I have an angel who follows me around and you don't flinch."

"I've known for a while that there was something special about you, darling. Today only confirmed it. Angel or not on your shoulder, I still love you."

Daryl felt her heart soften. She needed to hear Blythe's reassurance when her world had just been altered irrevocably. "Even though I stormed out like a five-year-old?"

"Oh, honey, wait until I pitch a fit over something. My mother used to say I had a temper as dark as my hair when it flares. As long as you always come back to me, nothing will change my love for you. I don't care what superpowers you possess, what angel impresses on you, or any of that. I love *you*. I also need you to know that I didn't reveal your dream to my friends to embarrass you. I did it because I felt it would help them understand you and, hopefully, help you too. I'd never do anything to hurt you, sweetheart, because I love you too damn much." She laid a soft kiss on Daryl's lips to seal that promise.

"I have to admit I felt betrayed."

"I know, and I will never forgive myself for hurting you like that. It's killed me keeping these demon secrets from you. I want to share everything with you. When you mentioned your dream, I thought I had the perfect chance to tell you what I'd been told."

"Today started off so well," Daryl muttered, leaning her head against Blythe's shoulder seeking comfort. Blythe wrapped her arms around Daryl's shoulders and cuddled her.

"Yes, we got our name on the baby snatching list and we made love. That was the best part of the whole day for me. You're a fantastic lover. And your body is seriously hot, even in these unnecessary pajamas." She plucked at the soft material Daryl was wearing.

Daryl grinned despite herself, her pulse starting to race as she remembered what they had shared together. She tightened her grip on Blythe's hips, enjoying the feel of the soft silk that was Blythe's short nightshirt. "You turn me on like no one else. But then I spoiled it all."

"We'll both take the blame and move on from it. What I really want us to do now is what my plan was for us this afternoon."

"Which was?"

"To go to sleep with you in my arms." Blythe drew Daryl's head back so she could look into her eyes. "You need to rest. I can see the pain in your beautiful blue eyes."

"It's been a stressful day. Finding out my mom could see this Virgil as she was dying just blew me away."

"I'm glad she did. That was the thing that made you finally believe what they were telling you, wasn't it? That your mom knew your angel's name."

Daryl nodded. "The rest all just sounds like something from a horror film, but I was there when my mom died and I heard her last words. They make sense now." She smiled sadly at Blythe. "Everything makes sense now."

"Do you think you can cope knowing you have a silent partner?" Blythe led Daryl to the bedroom.

"I don't honestly know. I've been alone so long, or so I thought, in my investigations that to realize there's always been someone else helping me is a bit much to digest." She shook her head in disbelief. "That's without even going near the whole angel business that just boggles me beyond belief." She got into bed, letting Blythe direct her. She was too tired to fight anything any more. Lying in Blythe's arms, her head resting against Blythe's breast, Daryl just wanted to close her eyes and go back to when Blythe had first told her she loved her.

Just to freeze the moment and savor it. It had been perfect, and then all hell had broken loose.

Literally.

Blythe brushed her hand across Daryl's brow. "Stop thinking so much. Close your eyes and sleep now. We'll see what tomorrow brings soon enough."

Daryl tightened her hold on Blythe's waist and cuddled in closer. Everything she knew to be real was in her arms now. Everything else scared her and baffled her. She had a fleeting thought of her mother's last words. *Watch over her, Virgil.* Now they made perfect sense, even though the situation hadn't. *I hope you're watching over me too, Mom, because I don't know how to believe in angels. That was your thing, not mine. You were the one that believed, and you taught me to respect, but I never truly understood your conviction that if you prayed you would get heard. Someone heard me, Mom, and I don't know how to deal with that. I wish you were here to guide me.* For a moment, Daryl felt something as if it had been spoken aloud to her, a conviction that left her in no doubt.

You already have a guide.

Daryl squeezed Blythe a little tighter, hoping that if she held on tight enough Blythe could keep her anchored to her side. It was the only place she felt safe now. Her safe, orderly world had shifted. There were angels and demons in attendance, and Daryl had never given them any thought in her life. Now they were all she could think of.

"Shush," Blythe whispered, leaning over to turn out the light. "I can hear your thoughts from here clamoring inside your head. Get some sleep, and tomorrow we'll face the new world together."

Daryl laid her lips on Blythe's breast and listened to the steady sound of her heart beating beneath her ear. It soothed her until, finally exhausted, she fell mercifully to sleep.

❖

Even in slumber, Blythe's arms had held Daryl close. Daryl awoke after a night where she'd swung between bouts of fitful sleeping and jerking awake with anxiety gnawing at her chest. Restless, she shifted back a little so she could feel Blythe's body tighter behind her. She could feel the softness of Blythe's breasts pressed against her and feel her breath tickling the back of her neck as she slept. The weight of Blythe's arm across her hip was comforting. Reluctantly, she opened her eyes to the morning and began searching the room for the angel she was said to have attached to her. She saw nothing, felt nothing. She couldn't even sense another presence in the room. Sighing, she leaned back even more into Blythe's space and sought comfort from their position.

"You're thinking too much," Blythe said sleepily. "You haven't slept more than a few hours either." She shuffled closer to nuzzle Daryl's ear. "Try to go back to sleep now. There's nothing we have to do today. Just snuggle with me and sleep."

Blythe's voice was husky with fatigue. Daryl closed her eyes again, but her head was already wide-awake and processing all the information it had received the night before. Her eyes shot open as once again she surveyed the room.

"You know full well you can't see him." Blythe butted her head against Daryl's shoulder.

"How the hell did you know my eyes were open?"

"Because I can feel you tense like you do when you're working. You switch to investigative mode and your whole body becomes alert. It's too early in the morning to be that alert." She butted Daryl again. "Switch your brain off."

"How can I believe in something I can't see, Blythe?"

"You don't have to whisper, darling. Remember Ashley told you he was only around you for the investigations and in times of stress."

"Oh, I'd class this as a time of stress, wouldn't you?"

"She stated that the angels do not watch over us in intimate times like the bedroom or the bathroom. Your angel is a 'going to work' angel, so the rest of the time you're on your own." She squeezed Daryl around her ribs. "Unless you're with me, and then you're never alone."

"How can you believe so easily?"

"I've known Rafe for way too many years. What she told me sounds like something from a B-list horror movie plot, but she has never lied to me. I saw what Ashley can do. That's not normal. I can't explain it, I don't think I can entirely wrap my head around it, but I know it's real."

"How can you be with someone who has something like this hanging over her?"

"Oh, sweetheart." Blythe crowded in and rested her chin on Daryl's shoulder and held her so tightly Daryl could only take small breaths. "Nothing would ever stop me from loving you. I knew you had a talent in your job before all this. It didn't stop me from falling in love with you. It hasn't changed you. You were special in my eyes way before it was revealed you have angelic assistance."

"I'm frightened by what this means." Finally admitting it out loud, Daryl closed her eyes and hugged Blythe's arm to her.

"It just means there's more to this world than we ever knew. We've always probably known, deep down, that there's so much hidden from our human eyes. Now we're aware of it."

"But I can't see it. If I can't see it, how can I truly believe?"

"I think it's a little something called faith, Daryl. Faith to believe in yourself and what you know to be true."

"I don't think I know what is real anymore."

"Rafe had this information forced upon her because of nearly dying at the hands of a crazed demon. You, my sweet love, were gifted with it as a blessing. Your angel sought you out. He heard your prayer and came to assist you in finding the missing children. Maybe you don't need to see him because you already see the truth of what you two can do together. You've seen him all along with your heart."

Daryl digested this. She'd always felt safe when the weight had descended on her shoulders. She'd never felt frightened by the power she'd had gifted to her. "I really wish I could see him though. Ashley says he's a handsome man with hair my color. I've never seen anyone with hair as pale as mine."

"I think it's cool you share that. It shows that this is meant to be. You have an angel, Daryl. But even if you didn't, I'd still love you because, angelic BFF or not, you are all I could wish for."

Daryl had to laugh at the *best friend forever* dig. "You're picking up Rafe's sarcastic wit," she grumbled, turning in Blythe's hold to face her. "I've always been different. From the time I began to aid my dad finding these kids, I've always been seen as a little odd. But I got the results so the comments were kept hushed and the cases were directed my way. I've always known it wasn't just me. I tried to hide that fact by pouring all my energy into investigating the leads I got so that I wasn't just pointing to a map and saying 'let's go here now' and not having anything to back up my claim. But no matter what, even with this knowledge, I'm still the odd one who can find children."

"So you're considered odd." Blythe softened her words with a gentle kiss on Daryl's mouth. "But you do your job. Your purpose on this planet is to find missing children. You have an angel who guides you to them. You have a calling. Not everyone can claim something so great."

Daryl stared up at her. "Do *you* think I'm odd?"

"I think you're gorgeous." Blythe's kiss developed into something much more amorous as she lowered herself onto Daryl's chest and pinned her down. "I also think that if you're not going to let us go back to sleep this morning that I should use the time more productively."

"What do you have in mind?" Daryl was already tugging at the nightshirt that had ridden up Blythe's hips and was in the way of where Daryl wanted her hands. She'd had enough thinking about her "calling." Her libido was calling loud enough to drown her insecurities and fears out for now.

"I think I need to show you I can do soft and slow."

Blythe's lips took Daryl's in a very soft, increasingly slow, sensuous kiss that dragged a moan from deep in Daryl's chest. She gasped for breath when Blythe finally pulled back a fraction. "What if I don't want soft and slow? You turn me on so much and I've been waiting for you for so long, all I want is for you to take me fast and hard to make up for lost time." She loved the look that lit up Blythe's dark eyes and made them smolder. She wanted to get closer to that flame and burn in it.

"I can do that too." Blythe got up on her knees and whipped the nightshirt off. "Someone is determined that we aren't going to sleep in late today so I should have plenty of time to do everything I want to do to you."

Daryl shivered at the promise. She roughly tugged at her pajama shirt and was struggling with the shorts when Blythe's mouth descended on her breasts and began to mercilessly tease at Daryl's nipple. "Oh God," Daryl moaned as the sensation sent shockwaves straight between her legs. She redoubled her efforts to get her shorts off fast.

Blythe raised her head. "Hey, no invoking a deity. Look what happened the last time you called for help; you got yourself an angel." With a sly wink, Blythe flicked her tongue over the hardened nub of flesh that peaked Daryl's breast.

"You're the only angel I need at the moment," Daryl said and hissed when Blythe's teeth captured her nipple gently.

"Oh, honey, I'm no angel."

The wicked look on Blythe's face made Daryl grin. She pulled Blythe's head up to kiss her roughly.

"I thank God for that, sweetheart, because you're about the only thing I truly believe in now."

CHAPTER TWENTY-FIVE

Rafe looked up briefly as she heard the door open over the sound of Detective Dean Jackson talking in her ear. She waved the phone at Ashley when she walked further into the room seeking Rafe out. She put the phone back to her ear reluctantly.

"Yeah, yeah. No, I am listening to you. The line must have cut out." She rolled her eyes at Ashley's wagging finger as she silently told her off for not paying attention to her partner. "Look, just get me all you can find on this Lailah woman and her cohort Miller. Yes, I know this was supposed to be a vacation for me. Yes, I also am aware how long my desk has been left empty." She covered the phone with her hand so she could talk to Ashley. "I swear this guy is a bigger fucking nag than my mother." She turned back to the call. "Dean, I've already cleared this with Powell. She's on board. She knows I've got a DDU case here and that I need to stay for a little longer to sort it out. So you need to quit grumbling you don't get to see my face every day and how much you hate doing my share of the paperwork and just get Alona to work her magic." Rafe finished up the conversation quickly by not letting Dean get a word in edgeways. She ended the call with a terse good-bye and tossed the phone aside.

Ashley moved in to settle herself in Rafe's lap. Rafe latched onto Ashley's hips. She surrendered to a kiss that was everything she'd missed while Ashley had been out. When Ashley drew back, Rafe groaned, missing the warmth of Ashley's lips.

"We can do this later," Ashley said as she pressed another kiss to Rafe's smiling mouth. "I have news. Lailah finally stepped out of her hidey-hole today. I was able to follow her to a Baby Aid clinic and watch her sniffing out her next targets."

"That's fantastic news. It's about time she crawled out from the bowels of the agency. We've been waiting long enough. Were any visible donors for Blythe and Daryl's offspring?"

"Not at the first hospital I tailed her to, but she was on two calls today and the second Aid clinic has a young woman there who is uncertain about being a single mother. She has very dark hair, it could pass for black, and it's all natural from what I could tell." She paused for effect. "And she's carrying a healthy baby that is due any time now, which is right on the top of our requirement list."

"How did you get so close?" The minute the question was out of Rafe's mouth she mentally berated herself. "Oh my God, you went in as a pregnant woman didn't you?"

"I walked in as a heavily pregnant woman who already has two kids under foot and whose husband has just lost his job so we're looking for any aid we can get."

"You can glamour a pregnant bump?"

"I can glamour myself into anything human, so looking suitably blooming is no problem. I was two different women today, spinning out a different line while watching what this Lailah does to gain such trust. She's very good. She listens, sympathizes, and offers her personal support. For some of the women there, that's what they need the most—a shoulder to cry on and a person to lean upon."

"Does she look demonic?"

"She glitters to my sight, but she's got a very good human shell on. She passes for human with no problem whatsoever, but I'd like to see what's hidden behind her dark lenses."

"What do you think they hide?"

"It's said the human eyes are the windows to the soul. Demons are soulless creatures, so in creating their human forms they sometimes have trouble getting the eyes correct. Many wear contact lenses to hide their true eyes."

"So behind her dark shades she's sporting demon eyes. No disrespect, Ashley, but I sometimes miss the simple human garden variety of evil."

Ashley planted a kiss on Rafe's forehead. "I know you do, baby, but you can't banish those kinds of crazies."

"I'll admit that is a drawback." Rafe mentally went through their options. "You know Blythe's team is going to come back here for the handover, don't you? Blythe and Daryl can't go in alone. They'll need backup."

"We can't have them here. They could get in the way of our side of the investigation. We've already got two more than we needed having knowledge of things they shouldn't be exposed to."

"You can't really count Daryl though. After all, she's more on our side than she realizes. It's a pity we can't have Eli talk to Lake to get him to step back. It would take a ton of pressure off my shoulders."

"I'll be sure to ask him if he'd run interference for you with the DDU, but I wouldn't hold your breath. He'd probably say that was more in your realm of things to do."

"So if we can't use a little angelic nudging to have the New York DDU step back a bit then I guess we have no choice but to call in the bigger guns."

❖

SSA Lake's fury was barely restrained as he relayed over video link the news he'd received. Blythe understood his anger; she was still smarting herself at the turn of events in what was initially their case alone, but she at least knew the truth behind it all.

"So this Detective Stephanie Powell from Chicago has asked for you guys to report to her on this case?" Daryl asked. Blythe listened as Daryl feigned annoyance. She wondered just how much of it was real. "This is my case. I brought you guys in on it, not some team working in Chicago of all places."

"Chicago is a fledgling unit, Nathan. What's their deal here?" Blythe asked.

"Seems a detective and a private investigator have a vested interest in the kidnapper. They want in on the takedown and we've no choice but to step back and let them take her."

"Can they do that?" Blythe knew damn well no one would stop Rafe from taking anything she wanted.

Lake nodded. "Yes, apparently. Somehow they got wind of what we were doing here. The units work together, and it seems their priority over the kidnapper exceeds ours, so they want in on the case."

"But we stop the adoption ring no matter what, yes? Shut down Miller and Lailah will be dealt with anyway, right?" Daryl asked.

Lake nodded. "Yes. Powell just wants her people in on the takedown, not us, so while we will still be heading our investigation, at the last minute you'll be dealing with the Chicago branch." Lake looked up from his papers. "Looks like you've got an old friend coming to take your case, Blythe."

Blythe hoped she looked suitably surprised enough. "Are they sending Rafe Douglas in on this?"

"And some P.I. called Ashley Scott. I didn't know the DDU ran cases with outsiders now."

"It must be important if Rafe's on hand, sir. I know her very well. There must be a very good reason for her to want in. She isn't the kind of cop to take someone's case from them."

"You'll find out soon enough, as they are due to contact you tonight about this. I don't need to tell you to keep any meetings away from your cover house and away from prying eyes."

"I'll make sure they don't come here and expose us, sir." Blythe inwardly cringed over the fact she'd already had Rafe and Ashley in their home. Rafe's persona just screamed cop, but when Daryl had walked out, Blythe had never given a thought to what the neighborhood watch would think.

"Keep me posted with their intentions. I don't like getting calls from other teams telling me they not only want in on the case but also to take the lead." Lake's displeasure made Blythe squirm.

"We will, sir. At least with it being Rafe I know I won't get the runaround. She's brutally honest and very professional. She'll help us solve this case no matter what the reasons are behind their involvement."

"You make sure you emphasize this is Daryl's case," Lake said.

"Believe me, Agent Lake, I'll make damned sure that fact is recognized," Daryl said. "I'm not above fighting for my territory, and I'm not DDU so I don't go by the same rules you guys do. But I'll be civil and see what these folks have to say concerning a case that came to *my* desk."

Blythe heard the steely determination in Daryl's tone. She knew it was just an act, but it thrilled her anyway. "We'll contact you as soon as we've met up with our new team members." They said their good-byes and concluded the chat. Blythe disconnected the screen and blew out a noisy puff of air. "Geez! I hate hiding information from my boss."

"Well, we can't admit that we know exactly why Rafe and Ashley are here. Lake already has some ideas about me, obviously, and what I can do. To bring up angelic assistance might just have him withdrawing his offer for my personal parking space at the DDU."

"It's a good thing Rafe warned us she'd have to find a way to step in on the takedown. I wonder what she means by banishing and just what we'll see."

"We'll probably see a whole heap of nothing, as usual. I got the impression that they can contain the area, but if your team were here they'd be too involved to not realize something was wrong. And there's something just a little odd about watching Rafe and Ashley talk to something other than themselves."

"It must be hard on Rafe not seeing Ashley shape shift into other people."

Daryl nodded. "Now that was something I still can't get over seeing. I mean, one minute she's a tiny blonde, the next I'm looking at Ellen Ripley armed with a big ass-kicking alien gun."

"How do you honestly feel about Rafe coming in on this case? *Your* case?" Blythe asked.

Daryl shrugged. "I'm more than happy to defer to her and Ashley for many of the aspects that this case has revealed. After all, they alone can truly see the evil one of these women possesses." She leaned back in her chair and stretched. "I don't care how it's done. I just want these women brought to justice. If that means jail terms, I'll take my day in court. If it means banishing by some kind of mystical spear that Rafe carries around with her disguised as a writing implement, then I can live with that too. I may never fully understand it, and it all sounds fucking crazy, but as long as I can get those babies back to their real mothers I will rest knowing I did all I could do."

"With the help of Virgil," Blythe added wryly.

"Yes, with the help of my own angel." Daryl shook her head. "I still can't wrap my brain around it."

"But you're beginning to believe."

"I'm beginning to believe in a lot of things." Daryl clasped Blythe's hand in hers. "But I believe most in you and my love for you."

Those simple words stole Blythe's breath away. "You are too good to be true, Daryl Chandler." She brushed her lips over Daryl's cheek. "You have surprised me though. Most cops would be pitching an absolute fit over having their case hijacked."

"I figure after learning that all my child finding cases have been shadowed by another being assisting me, what's two more coming in to find these kids with me?"

Blythe scooted her chair closer so she could cuddle into Daryl's side. "You're amazing. I can see why Virgil stayed."

"Why?"

"Because you have a good heart. I'm guessing that's a rare thing."

"I may have an angel, but I'm not one, Blythe." Daryl shifted uncomfortably by her side. "I'm no poster girl for all that's good in the world. Far from it."

"Well, I have to say I loved your wicked side this morning. How about we explore both sides of you while we wait for Rafe and Ashley to officially introduce themselves to your case?"

Daryl got to her feet and led the way from the office. "You know that Lake would have a cow if he knew we were fraternizing on company time."

"Oh, honey," Blythe drawled, tugging Daryl up the stairs with her. "We're doing something that begins with an F, but it sure ain't fraternizing!"

Chapter Twenty-six

Two nights later, Daryl accompanied Ashley to the rooftop of the parking garage opposite Miller's Adoption Agency. It was supposedly under the guise of inter unit unity, but Daryl had a feeling Ashley wanted to talk to her alone. One angel bearer to another.

"So this is where you first caught sight of Lailah?" Daryl lifted the high-powered binoculars that Rafe had loaned her and trained them on the building opposite. She couldn't detect any movement in the building.

"She's not in there yet. There's no ghostly glitter trail going from room to room. She's a bit of a wanderer when the cleaners leave." Ashley placed her elbows on the wall in front of her and rested her chin on her hands. "As soon as I spot her I'll give you the heads up."

"Blythe told me what happened to Rafe that makes her see the glitter trails. It must have been terrifying for her."

Ashley smiled softly. "My girl is made of strong stuff," she said with an edge of pride. "She's tackled plenty of demons since then and isn't exactly shy about standing up to angels either."

Daryl shifted uncomfortably and let out a sigh that came out more heartfelt than she wished. "Ah yes, *angels*."

Ashley turned to regard her. "I'm guessing you're still a little shell-shocked. I can understand that. It's a lot to take in after a lifetime of having a power that you couldn't explain and then it's revealed as angelic interference."

"I wasn't expecting an angel," Daryl admitted, finally lowering the binoculars so she could look at Ashley. "I was actually more concerned I was possessed by something less...."

"God-given?"

Daryl roughly ran a hand through her hair. "I've never given much thought to stuff like this. My mother was the religious one. She had her beliefs but never forced them on to me as a child. She always said I was too much my father's daughter. I'd need evidence and a signed confession before I'd put my trust in any belief system." Her chest constricted as she remembered her mother. "I wish she were here now so I could share this with her. I think it would have shown I had a part of her in me too."

"Virgil revealed his presence to her when she was close to death. The very act of dying opens humans' eyes to the existence of angels around us, but he wanted her to know you had him beside you."

"Just like she always believed."

"Exactly. By the way, he apologizes for making you cry."

Daryl's eyebrows rose in surprise. "Excuse me?"

"In the agency, he told Eli he made you feel an emotion so powerful it made you cry. It was the only way he could think of to get you out of the room and into the bathroom where he was aware Lailah was heading."

Daryl was stunned. She remembered vividly the strength of her emotions that day. The uncharacteristic crying that had suddenly taken her over had been surprising to say the least. "Virgil made me get upset so I could cross paths with our suspect?" Ashley nodded at her. Daryl had to smile. "I really wish he could have just written something on the bathroom mirror so I could have gotten a clue as to what I was doing in there and why. And I hated the fact it made me look weak in front of Blythe."

"Oh, Daryl, I don't think Blythe sees you as weak at all. That girl thinks the sun rises and sets on that pale head of yours."

Daryl knew her cheeks were reddening under Ashley's frank appraisal. "How can I expect her to be with me when I have an angel at my shoulder and an obvious calling to find lost children? That's quite a bit of extra baggage to take on."

"How can you not expect her to jump at the chance? You're not meant to forge a path through life alone. Can you honestly admit to wanting to return to your 'normal' life after spending however many weeks it's been at Blythe's side?"

The terrible ache in Daryl's chest almost made her gasp out loud at just the thought of having to step away from Blythe's side. Ashley obviously saw the pain in her eyes.

"I thought not. So you come with an angelic attachment. It's no biggie. I do too and Rafe wouldn't have it any other way. It's who I am, what I do."

"But it's not safe for her anymore with me. I'm more connected to your world now, thanks to Virgil, than I could ever be to hers. She doesn't need to be sucked into a world where demons are the standard. With me, she stands no chance of a normal life."

"So you do what? Leave the love of your life behind because you need to face this demon-infested world alone?" Ashley shook her head. "Believe me, Daryl, finding that someone who accepts you for all you are is the sweetest blessing life can bestow on you."

Daryl nodded, but she knew she wasn't the same person Blythe had met back in New York. Daryl didn't even feel the same herself. And Blythe deserved to be with someone who didn't have a calling to find children that was obviously *heaven* sent.

"Can I tell you something?" Daryl asked, steeling her courage to do so.

"Sure."

"When I was out on a run a week or so ago I was….*attacked*."

"Attacked?" Ashley frowned at her. "I'm getting the sense you don't mean mugged for your running shoes."

"Something dressed all in black hit me with such a force I was blown off my feet and left bruised."

Ashley stepped closer. "Where did they hit you?"

Daryl pointed to her chest. Ashley held her hand up.

"May I?" At Daryl's hesitant nod Ashley rested her hand where Daryl had indicated. She closed her eyes and her fingers spread out warmly across Daryl's chest. Ashley opened her eyes and gave a sigh. "You got hit by a demon."

Daryl's huffed. "Why am I not surprised?"

"So who was driving the car when the other one got tagged?"

"Excuse me?" Daryl was confused.

"I spotted demon residue on the front of your car the night we came over. One of you had a close encounter with a demon. Its glitter trail was still visible on your hood."

"I'll ask Blythe. God, how much have we been keeping from each other for fear of sounding crazy?" She reached for her cell phone. "And today we both started receiving these." She held the phone out for Ashley to read the text.

There's no child for you here. Look elsewhere.

"So there's no child for you here? Someone obviously knows you're in line for one. As for the 'look elsewhere' part, there's a nice little warning if ever I read one. You get attacked, Blythe apparently has a run-in while out driving, and now texts." Ashley seemed to deliberate for a moment then said, "Get your tech girl to try and trace these. But you might want to leave out the details of the hit and run and you being attacked from your DDU guys just yet." Ashley got a look on her face Daryl couldn't decipher. "Curious. I wonder why you two are being targeted. This wouldn't fit the kidnapper's M.O. She needs to pull you in, not push you away."

"But would it fit the demon's?"

Ashley grinned. "Oh, you are smart. I like that in a fellow angel host."

"It's the only explanation. Someone also tried to break into our car last night but the alarm went off. When we checked the security footage, all we saw was a black figure. I think we're being targeted."

"So why is she trying to scare you off? That's an intriguing development."

"Damned if I know. But Blythe and I are both on edge. These are personal attacks, directed at us both. And they started once we were accepted for adopting a specific baby."

"Let me ponder that for a while." Ashley was silent for a time until Daryl couldn't take the quiet any longer.

"What's it like to be able to shape shift?" Daryl didn't mean to change the subject quite so obviously, but she didn't want to think about being attacked by a demon any more.

"It helps me get the job done. I've shifted since I was a baby. It's as natural as breathing is to me. What was weirder to me was having Rafe see right through my glamour. God, that was bizarre. But it was nice too. To know that finally there was someone who could see me and *only* me." She nudged Daryl gently in her side. "I bet Blythe makes you feel that way."

"She's not fazed by the whole angel thing at all. I'm still having a hard time believing, and she's so matter-of-fact about it. Like every detective from Vermont comes armed with an angel." Daryl tried not to sound aggravated about it, but finding out about Virgil had really thrown her life into disarray. Yet Blythe had taken the news a lot more calmly.

"She's a cop. They're like that."

"I'm a cop too," Daryl argued.

"Yeah, but you're a cop who's had angelic Impressor influences in your life. That kind of takes you off the usual 'just the facts, ma'am' list and places you higher on the weird and whacky column." Ashley just shrugged at Daryl's aggrieved look. "It makes you mysterious. Girls love a woman with a bit of mystery."

Daryl mused over Ashley's words. Her mind went back to the scene at the barbeque right at the start of their investigation. "Are Eli and Virgil here?"

"Just like American Express, can never leave home without them!"

"The day of the barbeque...." She stopped as she watched Ashley take on the familiar look of hearing a comment from someone else.

"You saved a kid? That's cool." Ashley listened some more. "Oh, you want to know how in the hell you managed to get to the baby in time before he took a header into the pool?"

"I was like everyone else. I wasn't aware of him until a split second when I focused in. Was that Virgil?"

Ashley nodded. "He did something new that day too. He loaned you his wings."

Daryl's jaw dropped. "No wonder I shot across the yard like a bullet." She couldn't get her head around the implications. "Well, fuck me."

Ashley chuckled. "You're going to have to tell me what that felt like. Eli has never blessed me with that trick."

"Virgil got me to the pool in time to stop Matthew from falling in. Wow. That's really something."

"I like you, Daryl Chandler," Ashley said. "You are so less confrontational about how your world has changed."

Daryl didn't know how to answer.

"Rafe was a major pain in the ass. Actually, she still is, bless her. But she fought and clawed her way around the whole heaven and hell thing until I finally wore her down." Ashley gave Daryl a saucy grin. "It was worth every minute too. But you're much calmer, even though I'm sure your brain is still firing off wild neuron firework displays in shock and disbelief."

Daryl liked that analogy; it was very close to how she felt. Mentally, there was a whole Fourth of July explosion going off in her head.

"And I like that I have finally met someone else with an angel. It's kind of lonely being the only one." Ashley's voice sounded so wistful that Daryl unconsciously moved closer. "And you haven't done what Rafe would have done had she found out she had an angel. She'd have been compelled to do the whole *my angel is bigger than your angel* thing. That's why I think you're the perfect person for an Impressor. You're calm. You have a very restful soul, Daryl."

"Thank you. I wish I felt it at the moment."

"It will return once you've gotten your head around all the angel malarkey, and then it will be back to business." Ashley peered over the side of the roof. "This demon has two women in her sights picked out for you and Blythe. From what I've witnessed, I guess she figured it was easier to look for Blythe's coloring than yours."

Daryl pulled at the edges of her lightweight coat and shivered a little. "Is it just me or is it oddly cold around here?" She caught the swift look Ashley gave her. "What?"

"Have you always been sensitive to areas?"

Daryl thought about it. "Not that I'm aware of. Why?"

"It's cooler here because there is a demon in residence. You're sensing it. Maybe you've never noticed it before because you've not been in contact with demons much."

"I wouldn't really know one way or another would I? I can't see my angel, so I certainly won't see a demon. And whoever hit me seemed very human but with a strength I've never seen before. Come to think of it, I did get cold right before they popped out in front of me."

"I think you're going to become more sensitive now because you've opened your mind to the possibilities of what is really occurring on good ol' planet Earth."

"I can see why ignorance can be seen as bliss."

"You've got an angelic guide and a rudimentary knowledge of demonology. You're way past the ignorance stage."

"And the bliss?"

"You get that with Blythe I'm sure. What more could you wish for?"

Daryl couldn't help the smile that escaped her lips and she laughed even while Ashley kept prudently quiet for once.

"By the way, Virgil wasn't with you when you got jumped, otherwise he'd have protected you. I'm reliably told he's going to stick a little closer to you now that he's aware you're being singled out."

"I'd rather he watch over Blythe. She's more precious to me."

Ashley grinned at something she was told. "He says his wings are big enough for the two of you."

"I'll bear that in mind," Daryl said.

"Here she is," Ashley announced suddenly, pointing down to the street below.

Daryl squinted in the darkness and tried to sort out Lailah from the few other bodies milling about on the street below. "Let me guess, you can see her sparkling."

"She's got a shimmer that is shinier than the Christmas tree on Rockefeller Plaza."

Daryl brought the binoculars up to get a closer look. She zoomed in on Lailah and followed her path as she walked right past the agency's main door and instead disappeared into a side door. "Strange she doesn't use the main entrance."

"I don't think they know she lives there. I'd wager she has a nest in the basement."

"A nest? Like a bird or something?"

"More like a snake. Some demons shed their skins like a reptile. Mostly the lesser demons that have to swap their forms. Some who can remain in character keep their flesh but don't want the sense of human normality like a home and stuff. Some have a different purpose coming up from hell." Ashley's eyes never left the building, and Daryl wondered what she could see that Daryl just couldn't. "Looks like this Lailah is specifically stealing children for some purpose we just can't see yet."

"You think there's something more to it than her fulfilling Miller's need to place children with ones she sees more deserving of a child?"

"Demons always have a purpose that is purely selfish. It's in their nature. I don't see what Lailah is gaining that is for her own satisfaction in this act. And believe me, demons are all about the satisfaction they receive."

"So demons are just as hard to figure out as human criminals. I'm not entirely comforted by that thought."

"Take comfort in the fact you probably won't have to deal with many demons in your line of work. After all, you don't appear to have been involved with them before now. Otherwise, I'm sure our paths would have crossed at some point."

"So Blythe and I get to go back to our own world knowing all this is out there? While you and Rafe do what?"

"We continue seeking out the demons and sending them back where they belong."

Daryl was uneasy with the knowledge that she was supposed to just go back to her life and pretend everything was normal. Nothing felt normal now. "The New York DDU is pissed at the Chicago involvement."

Ashley laughed. "And they don't know the half of it."

"I just want all the lost children found. I know they are here. I guess I just need Virgil to help me find them."

"Well, while he's looking into that, this is for you." Ashley rummaged in her pocket and handed over a USB stick. "You're going to need this for your staff meeting tomorrow."

Daryl held the small USB between her fingers. "What's on here?"

"Pictures of Lailah in action at the Baby Aid clinics. It's amazing how easy it is to get candid shots of her eyeing potential victims. I watched her today. Like I said, she's got two women she's hovering around like a demonic mother hen. I think one of them will be her target for you two."

"I hope we get the call soon. I want this brought to a close. She can't keep taking children."

"Just this one last time and then we can stop her. Then I can send her back to hell where she belongs."

"I like the sound of that. Even though I don't quite know what that will entail or even look like."

"It will look like a blessed relief to all expectant mothers out there who won't have Lailah preying on their children."

CHAPTER TWENTY-SEVEN

Blythe was sitting up in bed watching the TV when Daryl padded into the bedroom quietly. Her attention was diverted from the screen by Daryl disrobing before her. Daryl unbuttoned her shirt and tossed it to a chair. Blythe greedily took in Daryl's taut stomach and strong arms. Her eyes dropped as Daryl's hand lowered to unbuckle her belt.

"Did you have a productive night?" Blythe managed to ask while listening to the soft popping noise of Daryl unfastening her button fly jeans.

"We've established Lailah has a nest at the agency."

"A nest?" One part of Blythe's brain was able to follow Daryl's answer while the other was engrossed in watching her gather up her sleep clothes and wander into the bathroom they now shared. She had left the bathroom door open enough to continue talking so Blythe was afforded tantalizing flashes of Daryl as she prepared to join her in bed.

"Believe me, when Ashley talks nests, you don't want to know." The sound of running water could faintly be heard over the sound of the TV show Blythe was no longer interested in. "What are you watching? It's late."

"A *Fringe* rerun. I like the leading lady." She smiled as Daryl wandered back into the room dressed in a soft sleep shirt and shorts. Blythe knew those wouldn't stay on long.

Daryl looked up at the TV. "The blonde?"

Blythe grinned. "Yes, but she's not as blond as you, my love." She reached out to pull Daryl down beside her. Blythe pressed a kiss to Daryl's forehead. "I missed you tonight."

"I missed you too, but I learned some things and have come home armed with a USB full of faces for your team to investigate for us."

"Ashley has some potential candidates for our baby mama?"

Daryl grinned at Blythe's comment and Blythe was once again taken by how gorgeous she was. She kissed her again.

"She does indeed. According to Ashley, we're likely to get a baby with your coloring, as opposed to mine."

"You're one in a million, sweetheart. I can see why it would be difficult to match you."

Daryl laughed. "Yeah, right. Anyway, Ashley has been trailing Lailah all day, switching characters so Lailah would never see the same face twice." Daryl looked up at Blythe. "Can you imagine how amazing it would be for surveillance teams to have that gift? Anyway, she has two women down as the potential kidnap victims and she got us addresses and everything she could gather from the Baby Aid station and from her own investigation." Daryl burrowed into Blythe's side. "I'll say this for her, she's a marvelous investigator."

"Especially when you consider what she investigates."

"Do you think you can honestly go back to the DDU with what you know now and not say anything?"

"Well, firstly, I'd like to keep my job and not be pensioned out early after a psych evaluation. But I don't honestly think my world is going to ever be the same after what we have learned. Can I take that back to the DDU? I honestly have no idea."

"I don't think I can, in good conscience, not do something more now that I know I have..." Daryl faltered.

"Angelic interference?"

"Exactly."

"So...you'll do what? Team up with Rafe and Ashley and take on Gotham?"

Daryl's surprised laughter sounded good to Blythe's ears. "I don't see myself as a caped vigilante, Blythe. But you'd look amazing in a Catwoman suit."

Blythe groaned and captured Daryl's mouth in a ravenous kiss. The heat simmered between them as they explored each other's mouths with teasing flicks of their tongues and soft nibbles until they both finally had to pull back for air. "So what's your plan? Solve this case then see what other demons need to be sought?"

Daryl shook her head. "I don't know. But if Virgil can help me find children and there's a demon connection, I might want to be involved. I think I need to be." Daryl pressed her lips to Blythe's cleavage

"I agree now that we know what else is out there that we need to be aware of it." Blythe moved wantonly under the hot kisses Daryl was ghosting over her breast.

"I'm more aware of you at the moment." Daryl began tugging at the nightshirt that was stopping her from exploring Blythe's body further. Blythe lifted her arms so that Daryl could get it off and out of the way.

"No more talk of demons in the marital bed," she whispered as she pulled Daryl's shirt off and flung it to the floor.

"You're so bossy. I like that." Daryl let out a gasp as Blythe's fingers captured her nipples and squeezed. Her face flushed, Daryl surrendered to Blythe's touch. "God, I do love you."

"Good," Blythe said as she plucked at the tightening nubs. "Now come here and make it up to me that you spent most of the night in the company of another woman."

Daryl stripped off her shorts in haste and shoved aside the sheets to reveal Blythe's nakedness. "I thought of you the whole time," she whispered as she ran her hands over Blythe's curves.

Blythe tugged gently at the flesh she had still captured between her fingers. Daryl's hips jerked with each pull. "And what were you thinking?"

"How much I wanted to come home and make love to you." Daryl trailed her hand up Blythe's thigh and rested it on the soft curls that covered her sex.

Blythe opened her legs wider to invite Daryl's touch. "Then enough talk about the outside world. In here, it's just you and me." She released Daryl's flesh and took Daryl's hand, moving it to where she wanted it to be. She relished the sound that escaped Daryl's chest.

"You're so wet," Daryl groaned, slipping two fingers deep inside Blythe and pressing in hard.

Back bowing, Blythe surrendered to her love. "I've been thinking about you all night too."

❖

"Waiting for a woman to give birth to a dark-haired baby so a demon can snatch it apparently takes longer than I had envisioned," Blythe said as she cleared up her paperwork off her desk.

Daryl sat in a chair opposite, a frown marring her forehead.

"What's got your attention so bad?" Blythe filed her papers away and shifted to peer over Daryl's shoulder. She recognized the papers in Daryl's grasp. "Oh, honey, you can't keep going over the maps like this. You know as well as I do, when Virgil finds the other children, he'll impress it upon you."

"But I still need to look too. I've been out every day jogging around the Heights, even though I'm terrified of being knocked off my feet again. But if they're here I need to find them. I can't leave any loose ends. These children all have to be returned home."

"You will do that. I know you will, but please remember what Ashley told you Virgil said."

"That he couldn't see the last ones because they weren't being revealed to him either."

"Which he has his own theories on that he wouldn't share."

"Which is damn annoying," Daryl grumbled. "I hate and detest withholding information."

Blythe could appreciate how frustrated Daryl was. The last week had been a lesson in patience waiting for a woman to give birth so they could effectively take the child away from her to finish their case. Blythe didn't like the nasty taste in her mouth that revelation left. The threatening texts had continued to arrive daily, at all hours. They'd been traced back to numerous disposable cell phones. Blythe was exasperated that lead got them no further forward. "You'll find the missing children, Daryl; I have no doubt of that. I know this waiting is driving you crazy. I'm getting antsy too. We know from

Ashley's daily reports that the woman on top of Lailah's wish list is due to go into labor any time soon."

"It seems like forever since Ashley pointed them out as the ones Lailah was grooming."

"It's only been a week. At least your boss and mine understand the time this is taking. I hear Rafe has to perform some fancy footwork to get her boss to let her stay here and keep my team at bay until the last minute."

"Your guys should have been here for the takedown, shouldn't they?"

Blythe nodded. "They should have been our backup. You know as well as I do how pissed off Lake has been over having to stand down and let another unit take the lead in what should be the New York unit's case."

"Actually, I believe it is *my* case. I was brought in on it by the original investigating team."

"The reason why I always forget that is because, to me, you're already a part of our team."

"Thank you for that, and I'm sorry for sounding so territorial." Daryl scrubbed at her face. "Maybe I'm just going stir crazy."

Blythe began tugging Daryl out of her seat. "Then let's go for a walk. I'm still a little nervous about taking the wheel since finding out my non-accident was in fact me being hit by a demon body. Let's blow off our fictional workload, ignore our real caseloads that, even undercover, I'm stuck with having to complete paperwork on." She led an unresisting Daryl out of the office and through the living room. "I'll even treat you to one of those brightly colored smoothies you love so much."

"You had me on the 'ignore our caseload,' but if there's a smoothie in the offering, please, lead the way."

❖

Daryl loved the simple pleasure of being able to hold Blythe's hand in public without anyone taking a second glance at them. Daryl enjoyed feeling the sun on her face and just half listening as Blythe and Mia conversed. The minute they had been heading back to their front door, Mia Connelly had descended upon them, demanding their attention and regaling them with the latest goings-on. Daryl enjoyed watching Blythe speak, whether it was as an agent to her team or as a friendly neighbor catching up on all the gossip. She was enjoying the subtle hand squeezes that were substituting for Blythe rolling her eyes at how outrageous Mia was. Daryl paid attention when Mia let out a squeal.

"Oh my goodness, Claire, you look like the Pied Piper of Hamlin."

Daryl looked up to see what had caused Mia's outburst. Claire Benson was leading ten very small children with the harried look of a mother hen desperate to keep all her chicks in order. The other mothers that were with her were too busy talking to other adults to notice that Claire had way too many toddlers to corral.

"You've got your hands full there," Daryl said as she stepped back to let them all pass by her.

"I thought a play date meant one child. I obviously didn't read the fine print that mentioned toddlers travel in packs!" Claire gently steered a little boy forward after he'd decided to make like a salmon and swim against the toddling tide. Claire just scooped him up and balanced him on her hip. "Hope I get yours in this group real soon." She winked at Daryl and sent a dashing smile Blythe's way.

Daryl was oblivious to her words. She'd felt the insistent press of Virgil as he worked his Impressor magic upon her. Her sight narrowed in on the child in Claire's hold.

Calum Bridges, Daryl realized.

"Gee, I've never seen anyone so excited to deal with dirty diapers and sloppy mealtimes," Mia teased.

Daryl couldn't take her eyes off the little boy as a woman gingerly stepped through the tiny throng and took the child from Claire.

"Thanks, Claire, you'll hurt yourself carrying Eddie here. He's deceptively heavy. I swear Julie feeds him rocks when I'm not looking."

Julie was obviously the bored looking first-grader that was staying as far away from the noisy rabble as she could. "I do not, Mom!" she said, giving her mother a dark frown. "He eats them all on his own!"

Daryl finished watching the procession going by with some amusement. She turned her attention to Mia once the mothers were out of earshot. "Who's the cute kid that eats rocks?"

Mia was eager to impart her knowledge. "That's Caroline Jenkins's son, Eddie. She was in your shoes. She adopted Julie first in another state and then went through it again here to get Eddie." She gave Blythe a considering look. "I believe she went through Miller's Agency this last time so if you two are looking to expand your brood I'd say you went to the right place."

Recalling how Eddie looked just like his adoptive mother, having the same green eyes and smattering of freckles, Daryl had to silently agree. *When it comes to getting the perfect child to suit all needs, I'd say we are exactly with the right people.*

CHAPTER TWENTY-EIGHT

The euphoria of having found another of the missing children was still buzzing through Daryl's brain later that evening.

"Well, that explains why Virgil couldn't sense Calum. He's been out of the country since we've been here. Little Eddie Jenkins, otherwise known as Calum Bridges, was visiting his adoptive grandparents in England."

"You're getting closer, baby, to finding all the children you need to. The DNA results proved it; you found Matthew and Heather just like you said you had."

"But meanwhile more children are being taken. My job is never ending."

"But you have help, so you're not entirely alone in your search."

Daryl nodded. "I wonder how many of my previous cases were linked to demons and I just never had any clue. Do you realize we'd have no idea what was happening with Lailah and her part in this case if it wasn't for Ashley's unique investigative skills?"

"I'm more than aware there's no way the DDU team would have infiltrated the Baby Aid groups like Ashley has been able to. Although, my team was to have joined us here once we'd established who the kidnappers were."

"How do you explain to Lake that he and his team have been usurped by two angels, a shape shifter, and a detective from Chicago who can see demons?" Daryl shook her head. "I fear I'm going to have to have a quiet word with him. He's always been aware I'm a little *different*. Maybe I can distract his anger toward Chicago's DDU for straying on his turf."

"Would you tell him the truth?"

"Can you honestly say you're glad to know the truth about..." She gestured expansively, "*Everything?*"

"I don't honestly know. I'm seesawing between the excitement of knowing something so secret and awesome and then I'm terrified because demons are real and I'll never be able to spot them in a crowd."

"Maybe there are some things we're not meant to see."

"What? Follow by faith and not by sight alone? I don't buy that line of reasoning." Blythe's look of displeasure made Daryl smile.

"My mother would have loved you," she said.

"Your mother would have seen how much I love you and hopefully have approved of me."

"What's to disapprove? You're a top-notch FBI agent, top of her field in the DDU. You're beautiful, compassionate, and *passionate.*" Daryl paused. "But I probably wouldn't have brought that up with my mother right away."

"You flatter me."

"You are amazing and soon to be the mother of my child if Ashley's calculations are on target." Daryl started as her cell phone rang. "Jesus!" She snatched it up and read the number on the screen. *Speak of the devil.* "It's Ashley." She quickly answered the call.

"Better start gathering your money together. A baby has been born and Lailah is circling around it like a vulture over her next meal." Ashley sounded as if she were beginning to run. "I've got to go; she's on the move."

Daryl looked at Blythe when the call ended abruptly. "Start preparing the nursery. It looks like we're going to be mommies."

❖

Two nights later, the unexpected sight of Rafe waiting at the top of the parking garage opposite Miller's Agency made Ashley want to weep.

"Oh, lover, are you a sight for sore eyes." She walked straight into open arms and burrowed into Rafe's chest.

"Hard day at the office, Ash?" Rafe kissed her hair softly.

"I'm just a little sick and tired of following a baby snatching demon around while she plots and plans to steal another's child."

"I know, love, I know." Rafe tightened her grip. "We're coming to the conclusion soon."

"Not soon enough for me. You do realize that if this was my case I'd have shifted into the form of the mother she's now stalking and the second she touched that baby I'd have banished her ass back to hell?"

"I know, but this isn't your case and there's not just a demon involved. She's got a human partner and we need to stop her from continuing this practice too."

"I could just shift and be there when she took the child. It would be that simple."

"Yes, you could, but Daryl has got to see her side of this investigation through too. I'm not incurring the wrath of Blythe just so you and I can pack up and go home." Rafe sighed a little. "As much as I'd really like to do that."

"You miss Trinity."

"I miss my own bed and my own office with my own cases. I need to go home. I'm tired of chasing demons out of my own jurisdiction."

"Want to just banish and run? The bitch is back in her hidey-hole at the agency. We could just creep in and send her on her merry way."

Rafe groaned. "Oh, that sounds so tempting. But no, we're here to see this through properly. We've hijacked enough of this case as it is. We catch all the ones involved and then banish the demon among them. Then we catch a plane, and I buy Trinity the best damn cat toy on the way home."

Ashley drew back in Rafe's arms. "Why are you up here?"

"I brought you something to eat and I wanted to be with you while you demon watch in case she chooses tonight to take the baby. I got you your favorite family-sized bag of chips and a deli sub sandwich. Plus"—she lifted out a large sized drink—"enough caffeine to keep you awake tonight."

"You are truly the love of my life," Ashley said, reaching for the soda and sucking up the cold liquid through the straw greedily. "God, I needed that."

Rafe was looking down at the agency. "Do you think she'll make her move tonight?"

"She's been in the victim's home enough the past two days to warrant the thought it's going to be very soon. Those watching over her say she's been very attentive to the mother, making herself invaluable."

Rafe grimaced. "It's so fucking creepy. I'll be glad to see her banished."

"Any news from Blythe?"

"That Miller woman is a sharp cookie. She called them up to say she had a few positive 'clients' that she was considering for them and she hoped to be in touch very soon. Blythe said it was a very professional call. She got the impression it was a done deal but that Miller was dragging it out a little."

"That's because the baby hasn't been taken yet."

"But it was a heads up to the fact they needed to get their cash ready."

"I wonder what her angle is to all this. Other than the money, of course."

"Maybe that's all it is. Some people make greed a profession. And since when do child takers have any other thought than I want it, I'll take it?"

"When they are teamed up with a demon who has her own agenda to satisfy." Ashley cocked her head to the building below. "I hope she tries something tonight. I've been trailing her all day, and she looked agitated and anxious."

"An agitated demon isn't something I want near a child." Rafe shifted closer to Ashley. "But it may be what we need to have her act sooner rather than later." She pressed a kiss to Ashley's temple. "You'd better eat up. If you're right, you're going to need all your strength tonight."

Ashley took a bite from her meal and hoped all the angelic eyes in surveillance were wide-awake.

❖

The sound of her cell phone vibrating across the bedside table woke Blythe from a deep sleep. She fumbled for it, hearing Daryl murmur beside her as she woke too. Voice husky with sleep, Blythe answered the call. "Hello?"

"Lailah has taken your baby."

Rafe's voice brought Blythe crashing into full wakefulness. "Oh my God. When?" she blurted, shaking Daryl into action beside her. Blythe switched the phone to speaker.

"The child was taken from his nursery at three twenty this morning. Eli watched the abduction and followed her all the way back to the agency where we were watching and taking photographs so you will have your proof. I'll inform Lake your team can surround the house now that they're here on site and do what they can to reassure the mother that we know where her child is. The less local law enforcement knows about tonight, the better."

"Has she hurt the baby?" Daryl asked.

"No. According to Eli, she's got a cot all set up in her lair and she's making sure he's comfortable. She's quite the little mother." Rafe's sarcasm was very clear from her tone.

"So we should expect another call today calling us in to collect," Blythe guessed.

"And we'll be right behind you with angels at the ready. I'll keep you appraised all day with what's happening here. We have an angel in the room watching Lailah's every move and the dumb bitch can't see him. I'll expect a call from you the second you hear anything on your side."

Blythe heard Rafe mutter something out of earshot of the phone. "Got to go. Ashley says we can stand down for a few hours. Thank God, because I'm shattered standing up here on the roof of the parking garage like some fucking sentry."

Blythe was still smiling as she hung up her phone. "Rafe's finally getting some sleep just as she wakes us up." She noticed Daryl's intense look. "You ready to finish this?"

"You bet I am. I want all my hard work concluded and the children safe."

"We should hear from Miller today." Blythe shivered. She could feel her whole body vibrating with a strange excitement and nervous energy. She cupped Daryl's face in her hands. "You and Virgil got us here." She leaned forward and kissed Daryl lightly. "Do you think you can go back to sleep a bit? I want to fall asleep in your arms before all I've grown accustomed to has to change."

Daryl pulled them both back down into bed and cradled Blythe to her tightly as if frightened to let her go.

"Whatever happens, I want us to take this part of us back with us. I don't want to leave it here in the Heights," Blythe said. "Where you go, I go. Even if that means me heading to Vermont."

"You'd do that for me?"

"I love you more than anything else. I think you're my One."

Daryl's brow crinkled. "Your One?"

"Talk to Ashley about it. I'm going back to sleep before we have a baby waking us."

"I'm too excited to sleep now."

"Then run through police procedure, Detective, because I am not getting up this early unless Serena Miller calls us."

The phone began vibrating again.

"You know that's Lake," Daryl said, propping her hands behind her head and looking disgustingly awake.

Blythe sighed and reached for the phone. She read the caller ID. "You're right, as usual," she told Daryl and answered the call. "Yes, sir?" When Lake began, Blythe resigned herself to no more sleep that night and dragged herself out of bed to go put a pot of coffee on.

Chapter Twenty-nine

Daryl couldn't bring herself to move away from the land line phone in their office space. Her eyes moved from it to her cell phone, willing either one to ring. The only calls that had come in were more warning texts telling them to *stay away or else*. Their frequency was disturbing.

"Miller won't call any quicker with you hovering waiting to pounce on the phones," Blythe said. "Besides, it's only ten a.m. She's probably still getting through her legitimate clients before she can call the ones she's kidnapped a baby for."

Agonizingly, the call didn't come through until five that evening. Daryl forced herself not to snatch the phone up on its first ring and schooled her voice to sound normal.

"Daryl? This is Serena Miller. I am very pleased to tell you I have a baby waiting to be placed in your home."

"Oh my God, Ms. Miller, that's fantastic news." Daryl didn't have to fabricate her pleasure.

"Congratulations to you and Blythe, it's a boy," Serena sang.

"A son." Daryl pretended to be surprised. "When can we come get him?"

"Do you have your...donation?" Serena asked.

Daryl shook her head at her choice of wording. Ninety thousand dollars was no donation; it was a pledge to dig themselves deeper into this deception. "Yes, it's all here waiting."

"I need you to come after office hours for obvious reasons. You'll need to park inside the compound too, so I'll make sure the barrier is left raised. The cleaners leave at eleven tonight, so eleven thirty will be perfect. Can you make it?"

"For our son, we'll be there whenever you wish," Daryl said, hoping Serena was buying her sincerity.

"Daryl, I can't wait to hand this little boy over to you. He's going to have Blythe's coloring."

"He sounds just perfect to me. I can't ever thank you enough for what you're doing for us."

"I hate seeing couples childless when they don't deserve to be. You will give this baby the family he needs. I couldn't have found a more deserving couple to match a child to. Just be sure you're here at eleven thirty. Drive into the parking lot, and make sure no one is watching."

Daryl's ears pricked at the sudden edge to Serena's voice. "Oh, believe me, Ms. Miller. I'll be very careful about prying eyes where my family is concerned."

"I knew you'd understand."

Daryl could all but see Serena's self-satisfied smile. "Until later tonight then."

"Yes. And congratulations again to you both."

The line went dead, and only then did Daryl reach over to halt the recording equipment that had captured the whole conversation.

"Gotcha." She looked up at Blythe who was standing in the doorway. "Seems we've got a late night appointment to go pick up our newborn, and I mean *very* newborn, baby son."

"Phone Ashley so they can get set up whatever it is that angels and demon hunters do for this kind of thing."

"I'm guessing it's just like any takedown, only with more wings present and no jail time involved." Daryl called Ashley and gave her the details of the call and the meeting place. Then she called Lake and set up a video conference so they could go through their strategy for the final time. She was aware the team had been camped out at the mother's house all day, keeping the woman informed as to their investigation and assuring her the baby was safe and would soon be back home. Daryl didn't envy them that task. She preferred to be in on the arrest, what there would be of it. She would never have thought it feasible or even believable that she would choose to be surrounded by angels and a demon to bring a case to closure. She rose from her chair, scooped Blythe up in her arms, and swung her around.

"We're going to get our baby!"

Blythe laughed with her. "Then maybe you can finally put these cases to rest."

Daryl hoped with all her heart Blythe was right. It had been a long time coming.

❖

The roads were eerily quiet as Blythe drove them to the agency in the dark. Before setting out, they had received a final call. This time a deep, unearthly voice had told them to stay away or the child would suffer. The threat had unsettled both her and Daryl. Blythe was intrigued as to why they were being so forcefully warned off. Did the demon have an idea who they really were? They had no choice but to go through with their plan.

"These streets are strangely empty," Blythe said.

"The Heights are usually never this silent." Daryl peered out the windshield at the sky. "Do you think something else is going on?"

"What? Like angelic forces at work?" Blythe followed Daryl's line of sight upward before turning her attention back to the road. "Who knows what they can do if necessary." She steered the car under the raised barrier of the Miller's Agency and parked in a space away from the spotlights dotted around the lot. She and Daryl got out and scanned the area. "No sign of anyone watching us," Blythe said, reaching for Daryl's hand and pulling her close.

"No sign of Rafe or Ashley either."

"I'm not surprised. I'd say they are masters of blending in." Blythe led the way to the front door and rang the bell. Serena Miller opened the door and ushered them inside.

"Ladies, I am so happy you're here." She clutched at Blythe's hands and squeezed. "You're going to love this little boy. He's perfect for you."

"We can't wait to meet him," Blythe enthused. "Where is he?"

Serena steered them toward her office. "I'll just go get him. Make yourselves comfortable and we'll seal the deal here." She swung open the door and gestured for them to go inside. "I'll be back in just a moment with your son."

Blythe watched her disappear down the hallway. She could feel Daryl's agitation all but rolling off her in waves. "Calm down, sweetie, we're nearly done here."

"I just want to take the child and go," Daryl said, fidgeting in her seat. She craned her neck to try to look down the hallway where Serena had disappeared.

They both reacted to the loud bang from another part of the building.

"What the hell was that?" Blythe asked, rushing to the door. The familiar weight of her gun at her side made her feel much better and more like her usual self. She unfastened her jacket so that she could reach it easier. Daryl moved to her side, her hand under her own jacket resting on her gun.

"I'm not staying here waiting." Daryl pushed past Blythe and started off down the hall. The sound of raised voices could easily be heard in the silent building. Blythe tugged at Daryl's sleeve and motioned which room it was coming from. They pressed themselves against the wall and listened to the sounds of an argument coming from inside the conference room. Carefully, noiselessly, Blythe turned the doorknob and slipped the door open a sliver.

"No! No! You called them in already? You said the next child would be mine. You promised!"

The high-pitched scream of a female split through the air and set off a baby's frightened cry.

"I said you could have a child of your own soon. But not this one. This one has to go to the women in my office. Mia said they had more than enough wealth that I could raise the asking price. You know she's never let us down finding us the couples who are desperate to spend out to get exactly what they wish for. They have the money I requested. You can have the next child," Serena said.

"You said that the last time and I had to give the child away. I want this one."

"He's not yours. He's already been bought and paid for."

"He could be mine. I *need* him."

"No. What you need is to give him to me and let me go finalize this business deal then you and I can talk this over."

"I'm done talking. I'm done *taking*. I'm having this child and no one is stopping me."

Having heard enough, Blythe pushed open the door and stepped inside. Serena jumped at the intrusion, but Lailah just stared at her. The child was firmly held in her arms.

"Is there a problem, Serena?" Blythe asked. She couldn't take her eyes off Lailah. She tried desperately to see the demon behind the obvious human skin. She wondered what evil was hidden behind the dark lenses.

"No, no problem at all," Serena lied. "I was just thanking Lailah for looking after the baby for me while I was seeing you to my office."

Daryl took a step into the room. "Lailah, it's lovely to meet you again. The last time I was here you were very kind to me."

Lailah's rage lessened a little. "You were upset."

"Yes, I was. I wanted a baby so much for Blythe and I."

"You can't have this one. I need this one. I warned you to stay away. You needed to be frightened off. This child is mine, not yours." Lailah ground out the words between tightly clenched teeth as if she were holding back a fury she could barely control.

"Why do you need him so badly?" Daryl's voice was soft, coaxing, drawing Lailah out. With her quiet voice and the calmness she projected, Daryl posed no threat.

"He fits my purpose."

"He fits ours too. To be a family. To keep him safe, to love him," Daryl said with a gentle smile.

Blythe moved as far into the room as she could without drawing attention to herself.

Lailah's hold on the baby tightened and he squirmed, crying louder.

"Let me hold him please. He's upset. He needs to be calmed." Daryl stepped forward, ignoring Serena completely, all her attention focused on Lailah.

Blythe's attention never wavered from Lailah either. She noted that Lailah's focus was on Daryl. Carefully making good use of the distraction, Blythe took another step closer. Serena, however, wasn't as cautious and bustled forward to confront her partner in crime. Lailah raised the baby over her head.

"No one comes any closer," she warned ominously.

"Don't hurt the baby, Lailah. He's done nothing to you. If you have a problem with those of us in the room then take it out on us. Do not take it out on the child." Blythe had moved closer still in the commotion around Serena and was ready to go for her gun at the slightest provocation.

With a furious unearthly scream, Lailah clutched the child to her chest and ran straight through Blythe blocking her path. The force of the blow flung Blythe aside as if she had been hit by a speeding vehicle. Blythe smashed into the frosted glass paned windows that lined the conference room wall. The force of her hitting it cracked and splintered the reinforced glass into a large spiral pattern. Dazed, Blythe tried to stand up and bit off a scream as the pain in her ribs cut off her breath. She broke my ribs, she realized, almost passing out from the pain. *How the hell did she manage that?*

"Lailah!" Serena yelled after her, hastening to follow, but Daryl grabbed her and swiftly handcuffed her into a chair. "What are you doing?" Serena stared stupidly at her predicament.

"Reneging on our deal but getting that baby anyway. And when I do, you and I are going to have a long talk about your adoption policies."

"You're police?" Serena's was incredulous. "But I checked you both out."

"We're not the only ones you didn't vet properly. Lailah isn't the perfect little child kidnapper she appears to be either." She snapped the handcuffs tighter making Serena wince. "I'll be back for you."

Blythe was still clutching at her side when Daryl came to her aid.

"Are you all right?" Daryl's hands rested lightly on Blythe's arm.

"I feel like I got blitzed by a linebacker. That woman is deceptively strong." She winced as the pain in her ribs intensified with every breath. "I think she broke my ribs."

"You need to stay here. I can't afford for you to be hurt any further." Daryl was already halfway out the door. "I'm sorry, but I have to stop her."

Blythe clutched her side and tried to move without jarring herself. "You're not going alone." She gingerly followed Daryl out into the hallway and watched as she began rattling the door handles, checking for an open room.

"You're hurt," Daryl tossed angrily over her shoulder then halted as the sound of the front door swinging shut echoed down the hallway. "She's outside." Daryl took off in that direction.

"Good," Blythe muttered, trying to hurry her steps. "Now Ashley can deal with her."

Chapter Thirty

Ashley and Rafe were hidden from view under the cover of Eli's wings. They stood at the back of the agency car lot, watching the door they knew held Lailah's lair. Ashley had said that demons always return to their safe place whenever they were near.

"Blythe has been hurt," Eli announced starkly.

"How?" Ashley asked.

"Lailah has broken several of her ribs. The demon refused to give up the child, and Blythe stood in her way of escape."

Ashley shot a look toward Rafe who was unusually silent.

Rafe just shrugged at her. "Fucking demons are nothing if not predictable in their unpredictability."

"Virgil says she's heading our way," Eli said.

Ashley heard the door to the agency slam shut and saw Lailah rushing out with the baby in her arms. "Damn it, she still has the baby. I was hoping they'd had the handover by now and this would be simple."

"It would appear she's not ready to let this child go," Eli said.

"Well, she's not taking it anywhere else." Ashley stepped out from under the invisibility cloak of Eli's wings and positioned herself directly in Lailah's path.

The woman skidded to a halt. "Who are you?"

Ashley heard the demon tenor in her voice. The human façade was slipping; the true nature of this creature was making itself known. "I'm someone who knows exactly what you are."

Lailah's face hardened. "You know nothing, human." She began taking a step backward and spun when she heard the sound of running behind her. Daryl appeared around the corner of the building, her feet slipping on the tiny pebbles of the lot. She stopped abruptly, scattering the gravel around her.

Ashley didn't acknowledge Daryl and wasn't acknowledged in return. They had separate agendas here. Daryl's was to recover the child. Ashley's was to banish the beast.

"You know that baby isn't yours, Lailah. Please let me have him. He was meant for us." Daryl took a few cautious steps forward, and Lailah stepped back only to find Ashley moving in closer behind her.

"Stay back!" Lailah hissed, *literally* hissed, as her true face began to escape its human cover.

"You need to give the baby to that woman," Ashley said kindly, not wanting to provoke the demon while she held the tiny infant in her grasp.

"I will give this child to no one." Lailah tightened her hold even more and the child squirmed in her arms.

More footsteps sounded, and Blythe came into view. She had her right arm tucked in close to her side, cradling her ribs. Ashley let out a sympathetic wince at how much pain Blythe appeared to be in.

"Please, we just want our baby," Blythe pleaded as Daryl reached to help hold her upright.

Ashley wondered why both Blythe and Daryl remained in character as the adoptive parents, but then she saw something in Lailah's response. She reacted to them *sympathetically*. It was like a bodily tick; they begged, she responded. Could the demon actually be torn between giving them the child and keeping it for herself?

"Why do you want the child?" Ashley asked, drawing Lailah's attention back to herself.

"That's no concern of yours. You have no place here. Leave before I make you regret being here."

Ashley saw the glint of red eyes flash behind the dark glasses the demon wore. "I regret a lot of things, Lailah. But sending you *home* won't be one of them." She watched with satisfaction as Lailah recognized the emphasis she'd placed on home. The air began to shift and alter around Lailah. *And here she comes.* Ashley saw Lailah begin to shift and grow taller before her eyes.

"I am making my home here, little girl, and you won't stop me." Lailah's voice changed and growled.

Ashley looked over at Daryl and Blythe. Neither of them showed any signs of witnessing or hearing what she could see. *This could get very dangerous, and they really need to know what they're up against. They're still seeing a small woman holding a baby, while I am witnessing her start to transform into her demon form.* She looked over her shoulder and whispered, knowing full well Eli would hear every word. "Eli, I need you to *reveal.*"

"And your reasoning behind that preposterous request is what exactly?"

"Because I need Daryl and Blythe to realize what we are up against. I need help, Eli. This war against the demons is more than Rafe and I can handle alone. We need their support, and Daryl is already halfway there with Virgil. They need to see what is out there so they can fight it, Eli. They need to *see* as well as *know.*"

"Do you really want to make that decision for them?"

Ashley heard the censure in Eli's tone. She cast a look at Rafe. "No one should face these things alone, Eli. It's too much for one soul to carry. They're like Rafe and me; they have found their One in each other. Reveal the true world to them, please. We need to save that baby and the world against whatever comes next." She waited what seemed an inordinate amount of time before she saw Eli move without disturbing his protective stance over Rafe. He seemed to be everywhere at once. Angelic hands reached out to rest upon the heads of Daryl and Blythe.

"Reveal," Eli intoned as he stared at Ashley. "And on your conscience be it."

CHAPTER THIRTY-ONE

Daryl was aware of a touch resting upon her head. She recognized it wasn't Virgil's crushing press against her shoulders so she stood still until she could process what was happening. She watched in a dawning awareness as her eyes started to see everything clearer. This wasn't her being Impressed upon. This was as if a gray gauze had been lifted from her eyes and she could see the world through a much sharper lens. Something moved behind her, and Daryl looked up into the face of the most beautiful man she had ever seen. He was dressed head to toe in white. His suit had a strange glow to it. His pale hair brushed at his shoulders, almost mirroring her own style.

"Virgil?" Daryl whispered and the man smiled and nodded. Daryl looked to Blythe and realized she had been touched too. Daryl's hope faded as she saw Blythe's revulsion displayed clearly on her face. *If this is her reaction to what surrounds me, I can't expect her to be with me. She deserves not to see the world this way or be with someone who is a part of it.* Daryl gazed at Blythe, trying desperately to commit her beauty to memory. It was only then Daryl realized Blythe wasn't looking at Virgil or her. Her head shot around and she saw the reason for Blythe's fear. Lailah stood just feet away, shedding her human skin before them like someone shrugging off a robe. Her dark glasses slipped from her nose as her face seemed to melt away like molten wax. Fixated on what was being revealed to her, Daryl wasn't certain if the transformation took hours or mere seconds. All she recognized was, with her new sight, she could see what Rafe and Ashley saw on a daily basis. The demon world was revealed to her now. Before her very eyes, Lailah's human form dissolved away and

Daryl could see what Lailah was. She heard Blythe's breath escape in a rough gasp that had nothing to do with her injury.

"Oh my God," Blythe whispered. "Tell me you can see this too?"

Daryl grasped Blythe's hand gently, to both hush and soothe her. Daryl let go and with one look at Virgil, she stepped forward toward the demon. She heard Blythe hiss her name behind her, but she didn't falter. She looked up as, in her natural state, Lailah now towered a good foot in height above her. Her skin was a burnished copper red. Her face was ugly and contorted as huge fangs had erupted through her gums and stretched her mouth cruelly. Her eyes, no longer hidden, were aflame. Daryl was certain she could feel the heat from the furnace burning in them. Squashing down her terror, Daryl moved closer, hyper aware Virgil was right beside her. Her eyes darted to Ashley who had Eli easing closer to her with Rafe now visible to Daryl's newly awakened sight. Daryl could see Rafe held a lethal looking weapon. Eli radiated with a brilliant white light that outshone Virgil's more comforting glow. Daryl had so many questions but knew she had something more important to attend to first.

She had to face her first demon.

Lailah was watching her with a curious gaze. Her breathing was loud and the air she expelled was acrid.

"I understand you want this child," Daryl said.

"This child is mine. I need it." Thick drool slithered from Lailah's now massive tongue that lashed over her fangs as if tasting something sweet.

"I see that now." Daryl stopped right before her, close enough to feel her breath. "But please. Could I just hold the child one time? He was going to be my son, the one who'd grow up to look enough like my love that he'd always be special to me. I understand he's yours now. All I ask is to hold him one time before you keep him." A tear escaped Daryl's eye and tracked its way down her cheek. She didn't think it was Virgil's doing this time.

Lailah cocked her head to study Daryl carefully. Daryl trembled in the face of the demon that held the baby to her naked chest. Her skin resembled snakeskin, mottled and leather looking. Daryl's breath caught in her throat when Lailah held out the baby, cradled in hands tipped with lethal claws that grew out of her fingertips.

"Say good-bye to your son," she hissed.

Daryl gathered the baby up in her arms. She looked him over to make sure he was unhurt. The baby looked up at her with innocent eyes.

What nightmares have you seen already, little one?

"I warned you away, you and your mate," Lailah said, reaching out and resting her massive clawed hand on top of Daryl's head, holding her in place. "You don't listen very well."

"We wanted the child more." Daryl's skull burned with the heat from Lailah's skin touching her. She willed herself not to shake beneath the obvious intimidation.

"Tell the hunter to still her feet," Lailah growled, fixing a stare in Ashley's direction.

"Please, stay back. The child's safety is more important here." Daryl could see Eli and Rafe shifting their positions.

"I could crush your skull with just one hand," Lailah said, flexing her talons and piercing Daryl's skin with her lethal claws. "I know how fragile you are. I blew you away before. I can do it again just as easily and this time I could still that human heart beating in your chest."

"Please, just let the baby live."

"You humans place so much faith in the act of living." She roughly drew Daryl in front of her. Lailah's huge jaws gaped open, venom dripping off every word. "Where I come from, death is a much more sought after commodity." She relaxed her grip and patted Daryl's head condescendingly. She drew back her hand and hissed. "Let me show you."

Daryl cradled the baby to her chest and swiftly turned her back on Lailah. "Virgil, *protect!*" For the first time, Daryl got to see the huge white wings rise to spread above her and start to close around her like a shield. Daryl felt the cruel slash of claws rip through her leather jacket and score into her back. The burning fire from the talons scorched through her skin before the heavy weight of Virgil's wings covered Daryl from Lailah's wrath. The pale wings protecting her did nothing to deaden the screams erupting from Lailah as her following swipes were deflected. Daryl had the child in her arms keeping him safe while Virgil did the same for her.

❖

Ashley watched dispassionately as Lailah's furious ear-piercing screeches turned into ones of terror when Rafe plunged the Spear of Light through her body and pinned her to the ground like a bug in a specimen case.

"Shut the fuck up, bitch," Rafe grumbled, sticking her finger in her ear and shaking her head. "You'll call every demon hunter in Connecticut here for a chance at your hide."

Ashley was thankful that Lailah instantly quieted at the threat. As a reward, Ashley planted a kiss on Rafe's cheek. "Thanks, babe, nice spearing as always."

Rafe frowned at her and pulled her aside. "One question before you banish this thing. Eli touched me so I could stop from being blinded by the bright lights, and I felt like my brain was being electrocuted. But he touches Blythe and Daryl and they just shake it off and carry on. What gives?"

Ashley tried not to grin at how pissed Rafe was. "You'd been touched by a demon first, Rafe. Eli had to battle with that for you so you could see clearly."

Rafe glared at her. "Sure, it's never fucking simple where I'm concerned."

"You're an original, my love. Now let me see what Lailah has to say." She carefully stood before the trapped demon, well out of reach of the flailing claws.

"Give me the child back," Lailah demanded as she tried to free herself from the spear.

"You're not going anywhere, Lailah, so quit trying." Ashley shoved her hands in her jeans pockets and rocked on her heels. "So tell me, why would you need a child so much? It's not usually something a demon has on top of their want list when they escape from hell."

"He was promised to me."

"So it's Serena's fault because she what? Told you if you kidnapped enough babies for her business you could keep one for yourself?"

"It was a lucrative deal. I could take the babies easily and I got well paid for it. Those women weren't sure they wanted to keep their babies. They didn't want them as much as the people Serena and her lover found for them. The outcasts of society, wanting their own chance at a 'normal' family. A niche market Serena could easily exploit. Desperate women like those two over there." She nodded her head toward Daryl and Blythe who stood well back huddled over the baby in Daryl's arms. Virgil had his wings spread out over both of them like a canopy. "So I took them away and had Serena give them to the ones who wanted the most."

"How did you and Serena start this business?" It wasn't like a demon to do anything for anyone else out of the goodness of its heart.

"She found me not long after I arrived here. She has a good heart under the greed. She took me in, gave me a job, let me live in the building."

Ashley snorted derisively. "How sweet. And the kidnapping started how exactly? When you couldn't pay the first month's rent?"

"She wanted a child, so I got her one. A girl. I took her right from under the noses of the nurses in the hospital, just hours after her birth."

Ashley spun around to check this information with Daryl.

"That's got to be Tanya Pope. She was the one I deduced as being the first to be taken. No wonder we couldn't find her. She's been with one of the kidnappers all along." Daryl let out a satisfied grin. "That's the last child I needed to find."

"How many have you taken, Lailah?" Ashley wanted to make certain there were no other children to add.

"Six, if you count my own child there." Lailah struggled again against the spear trapping her.

Daryl's smile at that news said it all. Ashley nodded to herself, pleased that part of the interrogation was done. "I'll ask this one last time. Why do you need a child? And remember, you are held in place by the Spear of Light. You can't lie to me now."

"I don't have to tell you."

"True, but I think you want to. You did so well for so long taking these children and no one ever realized how or who until now. You're amazing." Ashley wasn't surprised to witness Lailah preen at her praise. Demons were all the same, vanity and ego above all else. "So why do you need a baby?"

"The Preacher told me that a sacrifice had to be made for me to keep my human flesh."

"A preacher? What kind of preacher?"

"One who ministers only to demons."

Ashley digested this information. Based on what she knew of many of the religions around that world, that didn't exactly narrow it down. She looked to Eli who shook his head. *Oh, that's just great. This is new information to all of us then.* "A sacrifice had to be made? And you took that to mean a child?"

"What else could it possibly mean?" Lailah asked.

"Did you not think maybe sacrificing your own selfish desires?"

Lailah considered this. "He said all goodness springs from the purest sacrifice. What do humans consider more pure than a newborn child, untouched by life?" She shrugged as best she could for one speared. "It sounded simple enough to me. But every time I took a child, Serena had someone to sell the child to. Though the money was good, I grew tired of waiting." She stared at the baby in Daryl's arms. "He is mine."

Ashley looked into the night sky and watched as two lights descended. They looked like stars falling from the sky. "Where's the Preacher, Lailah? Above or below?"

"He walks the earth. He talks of a day when all demons will walk among the flesh and never need to shed their disguises again. And ones like you will never know the difference. We'll be hidden from your eyes by our perfection."

"Where is he?" She needed to know where to start searching for something else to banish back where he belonged.

"He is everywhere and anywhere." Lailah chuckled then sneered evilly. "He is hidden from your eyes, human."

Ashley laughed at her, causing the demon's eyes to narrow at her. "Oh, honey, you'd be surprised what these eyes can see." She stepped back as the two angels descended and secured Lailah between them.

"No! No! I haven't made the sacrifice! I earned it! The child needs to die so I can be reborn!" Lailah struggled against her heavenly hosts. Finally realizing her dreams of staying above were being destroyed, Lailah let out a piercing wail as she was ceremoniously yanked free of the Spear and taken away to be banished.

Ashley watched her go. Her mind was already working on the next puzzle. Who was this Preacher who had a demon flock at his disposal? Ashley had the foreboding feeling Lailah hadn't been his only disciple.

CHAPTER THIRTY-TWO

"Oh my God," Blythe said. She couldn't believe what she had just witnessed.

Rafe went to her side. "Neat trick, eh? It never gets old banishing demons back from where they came from." She gently slipped a hand over Blythe's side and winced when Blythe did. "You need these fixed." She curled a beckoning finger to Eli. "I wouldn't usually ask, but there's no way we can explain this to her team."

Eli nudged Rafe aside and laid his hand on Blythe's ribs. She looked up at him, in awe that she was seeing an angel and amazed as she felt the agony in her ribs ease. She took a deep breath and felt no more of the excruciating pain.

"Wow!" she exclaimed. "Did you just heal me?" Blythe ran her hand over her side. "It doesn't hurt as much."

"I mended your ribs, yes," Eli answered. "I've left the bruising though and some tenderness because you'll need that for your cover story."

"Thank you," Blythe said sincerely. "I can't believe I'm thanking an angel for healing me. Let alone seeing an angel in the first place." She looked to her left. "*Two* angels."

"You'll get used to it." Rafe gestured to Virgil who was peering over Daryl's shoulder, his attention fixed on the baby she held. "You'll have your own angelic third wheel now." She grinned at Eli's very obvious clearing of his throat. "You know I'm joking, Eli. After all, you're Trinity's favorite big bird."

Ashley dug Rafe in the side with her elbow. "Stop antagonizing my guardian angel, sweetheart, or he'll rescind your being my One status."

Daryl looked up at that. "I'm told I need to talk to you about that 'One' thing."

"Sure thing, Daryl. We'll chat once we've got this scene squared away and all our stories in line." She looked at the baby now asleep in Daryl's care. "I think you need to take that baby home too."

Daryl shifted the child in her arms and handed him over to Blythe. Startled, Blythe hastily accepted him and felt his solid warmth cuddled in her arms.

"I think you should be the one who hands this baby back to his mother," Daryl said softly. "You didn't get the chance before. This time you can get closure."

Tears pooled in Blythe's eyes at Daryl's sweet gesture. She looked down at the baby, remembering the last child she had held and how he had begged for her not to leave him. This time, she could hand this boy back safe and sound and know she could step away with the job done right. She smiled as Daryl wiped the escaping tears gently from her cheeks. Behind her stood Virgil, and together, he and Daryl made for a striking pair. It only reinforced what Blythe had always suspected. Daryl had a pure heart. She was someone who was blessed with infinite kindness and a protective spirit. Blythe knew she couldn't have found a more loving heart to keep safe and know that her own was equally loved. But for now, she was royally pissed.

"You put yourself in danger, Daryl, facing up to Lailah alone."

"But I wasn't alone," Daryl argued, "I had all of you behind me."

"She was going to rip your head off." Blythe tried not to let her anger wake the baby in her arms.

"But she didn't get that opportunity." Daryl edged closer. "I was doing my job. I'll always put the children first, Blythe. It's what I've grown up doing."

Blythe stared at her stonily. "Well, the next time you go head to head with a demon I'm going to be right by your side, okay? We're partners, Daryl Chandler, and you're not alone anymore." She calmed a little as Daryl moved closer still to lay a protective arm about Blythe's shoulder.

"He's got no idea what's transpired around him," Daryl marveled, looking at the child.

"That's okay. I'm going to be having enough nightmares for all of us from this." Blythe watched as Rafe was busily looking around the remains of the human form of Lailah. Ashley, however, had spotted something else.

"Hey, Virgil. You might want to sort Daryl out. Her back is ripped to shreds where Lailah caught her. She can't afford an infection. Demons aren't exactly renowned for their *next to godliness*."

Daryl stood motionless while Virgil set to healing her back. "I wondered why it was hurting so much. I guess in the excitement it seemed the last thing to think about." She peered over her shoulder to watch Virgil at work. "I might have to swing by our home to change clothes. I can't think of how to explain what's left of my jacket to Agent Lake."

"Some things are best left out of the reports," Ashley said. "Before we go anywhere, we have to get our stories straight."

"We'll defer to you on that," Blythe said, rocking the baby in her arms. "After all, I'm sure you've had more practice."

Daryl held up a hand as if raising a question. "I need something clarified, please. How come one minute we're seeing Lailah as a human and the next we're seeing the world through totally different eyes? One that brought angels and demons front and center?"

Ashley squirmed a little under Blythe's and Daryl's scrutiny. "I asked for it to be revealed to you," she admitted sheepishly. "But if you don't want to keep this knowledge, it can be taken away again. Just give me the word and I'll have Eli remove it from you."

Blythe and Daryl shared a look.

"I'd rather know what I'm up against," Daryl said. "Don't take it back, please. I've been blind long enough to the world and Virgil beside me." Daryl's attention turned to Blythe. "This is your last chance. If you don't want to be a part of this world, you don't have to be. I'll try to let you go, let you find someone ordinary to love."

Blythe's throat tightened at the obvious pain in Daryl's voice. "I'm already in love with someone *extra*ordinary, and she is my One and only. I don't want to lose this sight, and I will not lose you either, Daryl Chandler. We're in this together. But why reveal all this to me too, Ashley? After all, I don't share the abilities Daryl obviously has."

"I didn't want Daryl to be alone with this knowledge. You'll be there for each other in this, like it should be." Ashley gave Daryl a pointed stare harkening back to their previous conversation then reached for Rafe's hand as she returned to Ashley's side. "You have no idea how grateful I am to have Rafe's support in this fight against the demonic forces. You two need to be prepared and both need to know what is happening before your very eyes."

Everyone was quiet for a moment until the baby in Blythe's arms cooed in its sleep.

"We'll set the scene here while you guys go gather your team to come back."

"What about Serena?" Blythe asked, only now remembering the woman cuffed to the chair in the agency.

"We'll keep an eye on her too. It won't hurt her to wait while you return the child she had stolen for you." Ashley waved them off then said to Eli, "Time for you to work your crime scene magic once again."

Rafe walked beside Blythe as she and Daryl headed back to their car. "You need to tell Lake only your side of the night. You came, Lailah refused to give up the baby, she and Serena fought, Lailah ran off, knocking you sixty ways sideways, and by the time you had Serena contained, it was all over out here."

"Lake's not stupid," Blythe said.

"That's why you bring him here and we tell him what happened outside. It all happened so fast. She was going to hurt the child and I shot her."

"You *shot* her?"

"I haven't yet." Rafe grinned. "But I will once you guys have left and we can stage the scene. Believe me, when you come back here, you'll be hard-pressed to argue away the evidence."

"You stage the scene?"

"It's what we do best to cover demon tracks."

Blythe shook her head. "What kind of world have we been ushered into, Rafe?"

"The kind where shades of gray are the new normal. It's the greatest cover-up the world has happening every second of every day. Congratulations, you've just gotten ringside seats to the madness."

Blythe looked at the baby in her arms. She thought of all they'd been through, all she'd seen, and what was to come. She searched his face, marveled at the dark hair that covered his head in tiny spikes. *Had it been worth opening this world's Pandora's Box for her to see all the evils unleashed?* The little boy woke up and stared up at her, his face crinkling as he yawned.

Yes.

CHAPTER THIRTY-THREE

Still riding on the euphoria of handing over the baby to his mother and her grateful delight, Blythe had to forcibly switch gears in her head to get her mind focused on what lay back at the crime scene. She was grateful Lake, Caldow, and Browning had taken their own SUV to the scene. It had saved her and Daryl having to report anything without Rafe and Ashley ready to corroborate their stories. Lake hadn't wanted to question them too much in front of the grateful mother and the local police who had gathered at her home at Lake's instigation. One of the local police department cars was following behind them and a coroner's van had been called to the scene. Police had been sent to arrest Mia Connelly for her involvement.

Ashley met them all as they entered the agency's parking lot. Blythe introduced her to Lake. Ashley walked him and the other police officer through the scene. Rafe joined her, and Blythe was impressed at how their professionalism disarmed Lake. Blythe knew he was still fuming over having the case taken out of his hands and being told to step back. Blythe could hear Rafe explaining why to him.

"Ashley had information that Lailah had tried to set up this adoption scam in Chicago originally but had skipped town when she couldn't find the right partner. There'd been a few aborted attempts at child snatching, so when Ashley got the call that something was actually happening here we had to come check it out to see if it was related." Rafe paused at the edge of the crime scene. The local Crime Scene Investigators were setting up their equipment to gather their evidence. "When we heard she had a healthy distrust of men, we felt we had to make this a women-only worked case. The damn woman seemed to have a strange sixth sense when it came to males, and I reckon had your team been here she would have bolted and we'd have been left with nothing." Rafe nodded her head in deference to Lake. "So thank you for letting us take the lead. We owe you one. You've got my number. Call it in anytime."

Blythe was mesmerized by Rafe's performance. Rafe spun such a convincing tale that Daryl, standing beside Blythe, nudged her.

"Did you know any of that?" she whispered.

"It's all made up," Blythe whispered back. "Rafe told me she'd have to fabricate something believable to cover the fact they had to stop my team from being here tonight for the hand over."

"Do you think he'll swallow it?"

Blythe looked over at the dead body of Lailah lying on the gravel. A bullet hole was neatly drilled into her skull. She couldn't help wonder how Rafe had pulled that off to fool the crime scene team who were taking their measurements and photographing the scene. She had a feeling Rafe had played this game before. She feared she was going to have to learn the rules to it now.

"He has no reason not to. Our part of the story of what happened is entirely true. Rafe says that the more truth told, the more the untruths get to slip by."

"I have a feeling life for us altered irrevocably tonight." Daryl was looking to where Virgil was standing beside Eli as they watched Ashley and Rafe walk Lake and his team around.

"I hate knowing Rafe and Ashley have been dealing with this knowledge alone for so long without being able to talk about it." Blythe couldn't imagine the stress that must have caused Rafe. She thought of how bad she had felt keeping what she had learned from Daryl, and her chest ached in remembrance.

"Do you really feel comfortable knowing there are real demons running around?" Daryl asked quietly.

Blythe leaned into her, seeking her warmth and her solid presence. "I feel comfortable knowing we have angels that protect us. Virgil saved you and the baby tonight." Blythe's hand slipped to touch Daryl's back. She had watched Daryl removing the ruined jacket and peeling off her shredded shirt. All that marred her back were the faint lines of where the demon's talons had scored through her flesh. They would fade in time. The presence of demons would not.

"Would you really have let me go if I couldn't have understood your true calling?" Blythe was astonished by how strongly Daryl had wanted to keep her safe, no matter what it had cost them.

"Yes," Daryl said softly, capturing Blythe's eyes. "And I would have died a thousand times if I'd had to watch you walk away from me."

"The only walking I'll be doing is right by your side, my love," Blythe said, wanting desperately to take Daryl into her arms and reassure her everything was going to be fine now. She spotted Lake heading in their direction. "It's show time, Detective. Hope you've remembered your lines."

❖

The flight back to New York was oddly subdued given the successful outcome of the case. Daryl and Blythe had given their account of what had happened at the agency. Serena Miller had been led away from her business and placed into the back of a police van. Daryl had seen her catch sight of the body of her business partner left in place while forensics worked their magic. When Daryl and Blythe had joined Serena in an interrogation room, Serena obviously had decided to lay all the blame at the dead woman's feet and at her lover, Mia. She'd at first pretended to have no knowledge of the truth behind each child's abduction. Daryl let her spin a tale of how every woman had agreed to give up her child and watched her play the concerned adoption agency manager who wouldn't deal with such a crime.

It wasn't until Daryl brought up the existence of her daughter, whom they knew had been stolen, that Daryl finally saw realization dawn on Serena's face. She knew Serena finally got it; the truth was out. She wasn't going home to her child anytime soon and now that they knew the little girl was yet another kidnapped child there was little possibility Serena would ever lay eyes on her daughter again. One by one, Serena gave up the new names of the children Lailah had stolen. She furnished them with the names of the couples that had wanted a baby so badly they had been prepared to pay anything they could to have a family.

She spoke in detail about the deals she had brokered with each one, using Mia's knowledge of the Heights and its people, and how they had been matched with the child just perfect for them. It had been a perfect setup. Lailah had stolen the necessary children to make a family whole, and Serena had made sure no one would ever find out about the lack of legality. Daryl had been amazed by how little feeling Serena had for the birth mothers. She'd seen a need in the marketplace, one she could use to her advantage, and grow wealthy in the process. The lesbians were a means to an end, they wanted the children, Serena wanted their money. By the end of the interview, Daryl didn't know which was worse, the demon that had taken the children, or the human who felt perfectly justified in selling the stolen children as she saw fit. She found both equally abhorrent and evil.

Serena Miller was left in the custody of the Connecticut police. Mia had already spilled her side of the story in another interrogation room. Ashley had stepped back to let Lake take over the case again, as she didn't want to be too involved with the legal side. Her part was done. It fell back onto Daryl's investigation, and Daryl was immensely gratified to see it brought to a close. Serena Miller wouldn't escape a harsh sentencing. As for Lailah, she was dead to this world and banished in another. Daryl felt those were fitting punishments for both sides of Lailah's character. She'd had a chance to see the body in the morgue and had been amazed by how human Lailah looked when she had seen what had stepped out from the human flesh. Virgil had stayed silently by her side as she examined the face of the woman who had shown her both kindness and then the depths of pure evil. She couldn't help but wonder how many more demons were out there hiding behind human eyes. Daryl was eternally thankful for Virgil's presence.

The return to their house at Cranston Heights had been swift and under cover of darkness. Lake had ordered them to gather their personal belongings and leave the rest to the clean up team that would remove all traces of their operation from the house. Daryl had felt bad that they couldn't say good-bye to the neighbors they had spent so much time getting to know, but she understood the necessity of leaving without a word. Because of Daryl's investigation, families were going to have their children removed from their houses and returned to their biological parent. It also pained her to leave the house that had become hers and Blythe's. She had loved living there, sharing a life with Blythe, fitting into society, and falling in love. It had been very hard closing the front door behind them and walking away without a backward glance.

"You do realize that when the story gets out, everyone will think we got caught up in the baby buying sting?" Blythe said from her seat beside Daryl. "We're going to be the talk of the Heights, the couple that skipped town in the dead of night."

"Our role wasn't exactly something we could have explained to the neighbors. Especially given what is now going to happen because of it. I don't think I could have stood seeing Niki's reaction to what her wife was involved with behind her back."

"I feel so sorry for Liz and Claire," Blythe said as if reading Daryl's thoughts.

"I do too. But this is where I have to step back. I found Matthew Malone. Their son Justin doesn't really exist."

"It's going to be a horrible ordeal having to part these children from the parents who wanted them so desperately."

"Just as awful as for those mothers who had their children stolen from them at the time when the mother and baby bond grows."

"It's a no-win situation, isn't it?" Blythe closed her file and placed it on the table before her. She checked her watch. "We should be landing soon."

"We go back to the DDU and then what?"

"We make sure Lake has all he needs from us and then hopefully we get a few days off to decompress before it's back to work as normal. New cases are piling up. We need to move on to the next case in the stack." Blythe leaned over and squeezed Daryl's hand. "But you are coming home with me and we're going to talk."

"That sounds serious, Agent Kent."

"It is." Blythe ran her thumb over the wedding ring Daryl still wore. "I like seeing this on you."

"I love wearing it."

"Then we need to talk about you thinking that leaving me because you have an angel by your side was the only way we could continue."

Daryl looked suitably chastised. "I didn't want you hurt by the world I was going to be a part of."

"I was more hurt by you thinking I wouldn't choose to be by your side no matter what the world throws at us."

"I told you I had no experience in relationships."

"Then aren't you lucky I know enough to keep you by my side so we can learn together?" Blythe leaned closer. "I love you, Daryl, and I'd love you if your talent for finding kids was pure luck and wishful thinking. But it isn't, and I'm still staying right by your side where I belong."

Daryl grasped Blythe's hand and pressed a firm kiss upon her knuckles. "I'm sorry. I just love you too much to want you dragged into a world where demons live."

"I wasn't dragged. I walked in freely holding your hand. You'll learn soon enough it's you and me, babe, against the world."

Daryl smiled, finally at peace. "Do you think Lake would even consider taking me on now? Seeing as the first case we work on together had two other women muscling in on the investigation and resulted in a suspect being both dead *and* banished."

Blythe smiled. "I'd wager you salacious sexual favors that he has a desk cleared for you in the office just in case you ask for a job on our team."

"Sexual favors, eh?" She bit her lip in thought and caught the flame of desire spark in Blythe's dark eyes. "We'll talk about how salacious when we get back to your apartment."

"I love your way of thinking, Detective Chandler."

Daryl brought Blythe's hand up to her lips again and kissed where the wedding band sat on her finger. "And I love you. We'll sort this out to both our satisfactions, I promise you."

Chapter Thirty-four

The office was silent save for the flipping of pages as Nathan Lake read Daryl's report. She sat the other side of his desk, her attention drawn to the view from Lake's window. The sight of row upon row of glassed skyscrapers was still daunting to a detective more used to a rural setting to conduct her business. She turned her head away from the grand architecture and looked out the other window the office afforded. Daryl focused in on Blythe. She sat at her desk and was laughing at something Trace was telling her. Daryl couldn't help but stare as the pleasure lit up Blythe's face. She had never seen anyone more beautiful.

"Judging by the look on your face, Detective, I'm guessing I stand a better chance of offering you a job here in New York City now."

Busted, Daryl swung back around to face Lake. "Would I still be welcome on your team seeing as I will be actively dating one of your agents?"

"I'm well aware of Blythe's views on that matter. My best agent is ready to pack and move to Vermont if you turn down anything I offer."

Daryl shook her head. "I'm going to have my hands full with that woman." She noticed Lake didn't disagree with her. She let out a small sigh. "My dad is going to kill me for leaving behind my own desk and nameplate on the door to become what is essentially a foot soldier in someone else's army."

"You'll be more than just another body, Daryl. We all have our own strengths here. You'll be adding your unique talents to a much wider system of investigations. You'll have the whole of the United States caseload at your fingertips. I'd say you working with us this time proved to be very beneficial. The feds had to acknowledge their screw-up and do an about-face at your results. I've heard tell of a certain head getting ready to roll concerning that screw-up. Though I'm still disgruntled that some of us were consigned to the bench by the unexpected arrival of the Chicago contingent."

Daryl chewed at her lip as she considered the best way to broach her next question. "How would you feel if that particular scenario raised its ugly head again in the course of an investigation?"

"Is there an actual chance of that occurrence?"

Daryl shrugged. "Who knows?" She knew better though. Her world, along with Rafe and Ashley's, were now inexplicably linked.

"I remember Ashley Scott from an old case Blythe was in on years ago. She's an unusual private investigator. She does the job but doesn't seem to stick around much after the dust has settled."

"I don't think she's the stay in one place kind of girl. Although, now that she's settled with Rafe, that may have changed."

"Ah yes, Detective Douglas. The same one who just happens to be Blythe's best friend. How curious was that?"

"Pretty damn strange." Daryl knew the irony of it all was lost on him. "Douglas is a detective, Blythe's an agent, both work in the Deviant Data Unit. I guess their paths had to cross eventually."

"And they crossed right into your investigation. How did that make you feel?"

Daryl tried not to grin at his blatant attempt to interrogate her. She'd lived long enough with Blythe to recognize that tactic when it was employed. "I'm glad they were there to assist at the end. They had their own leads to follow up on. They got as much closure to the case as I did. It was a win/win situation. I have no regrets whatsoever about working with them. I'd do it again in a heartbeat."

Lake appraised her silently for a moment. "Your mother once told me that if I ever got you to work with me I was never to question how you did what you can do."

Daryl tensed at his quiet revelation.

"If that's all it takes to get you on my team so I finally have your considerable expertise in the DDU, then I won't question your methods. Be it your hunches, your amazing knowledge of locations out of the blue, or your steadfast belief that you know exactly where someone is and can lead us to them. I won't even question your acceptance of two interlopers who shut me out of my part in your investigation."

Daryl couldn't help herself. She laughed at his unshakable irritation at being pushed aside by Rafe and Ashley. "With all due respect, sir, you might want to suck that up and move past it. You might have to get used to those interlopers interfering again."

Lake rolled his eyes heavenward. "Damn it. That's pretty much what Douglas said to me." He looked out his office window at his people. "Is Blythe all right with all this?"

Daryl nodded. "She's willing to give it a try, sir."

"I asked your mother when you were younger if you were psychic. She laughed and said you were so much more than I would ever understand. She said you were your father's daughter and that meant, some day, you'd make a mighty fine detective."

Daryl smiled at his comment. She could all but hear her mother's soft voice getting her point across. "I'm not psychic, Nathan. I'm just able to find lost children among all the other investigations I get placed before me."

"I've said I won't ask. But I do want you to bring your talents to the DDU." He walked over to the window facing the city. "I don't have any special powers myself, but I'd be a fool not to recognize that there's something more than usual happening on the streets. I can sense it, feel it almost."

"And you think I can help with that?" Daryl joined him at the window. When she looked out, all she could see was their reflections. Lake was watching the city below and Daryl stood with Virgil beside her. The angel was silently imitating Lake's perusal of the busy world below.

"I think you're the kind of woman I need on my team and by my side for whatever we're to face. That's why I've always fought to get you. I think you're needed here." He cocked his head toward the office behind him. "And I think you've found your reason to be here."

Daryl silently agreed. She brushed her finger across the wedding band that she still hadn't removed. "I need to talk to someone about acquiring these rings for real."

"I'll take it out of your first month's salary." Lake looked immensely pleased with himself now that he finally had what he'd always wanted.

Daryl decided she wasn't going to make it that easy for him. "So do you want to tell my father or should I?"

EPILOGUE

Blythe thought there was nothing prettier than Central Park in summer. She clutched Daryl's hand a little tighter, strangely excited at their rare moment of free time to be together without the cases of the DDU calling their attentions away.

Daryl finished the last of her hot dog and wiped at her mouth with the napkin. She tossed the rolled up paper into the nearest trash can.

"I don't know how you can eat those things," Blythe said, wrinkling her nose as Daryl brushed away the crumbs on her shirt.

"Trace said they're only a true hot dog when they are bought from a street vendor. I'm merely testing her hypothesis."

"You're going to eat from every hot dog vendor in the city to prove her right?"

"I might just do that. I'm a detective; investigating is all part of my job." She lifted Blythe's hand to brush her lips across Blythe's knuckles. "After all, I did all the doughnut testing back in Vermont. I'm up for new challenges here in the Big Apple."

Laughing, Blythe knew she was beat. "Well, Detective, I'm taking you to a proper restaurant tonight, where the napkins are made of linen and there are more condiments than just ketchup and mustard."

"I'll look forward to that. I can think of no better way to celebrate our first wedding anniversary. Can you believe it's been a whole year since we had our fake wedding pictures taken?"

"I like the fact we're celebrating it even if it wasn't real." Blythe leaned into Daryl's side, snuggling closer. "But I'll enjoy celebrating our real wedding date a whole lot more."

Daryl agreed. "We'll make it a day to remember once we can decide on a date. Dad says he has dreamed of the day he can give me away to the person I love. Once he knew I was a lesbian, he just hoped I'd find the right woman." She planted a soft kiss on Blythe's temple. "He's told me numerous times of how you're perfect for me."

Blythe had adored Daryl's father on sight when Daryl had taken her back home to introduce them. She loved spending time with Linus Chandler. He knew so many stories about Daryl growing up that Blythe couldn't hear enough of, much to Daryl's embarrassment. He'd also helped her see what a marvelous woman he'd been married to and had seen through his eyes just how much she had championed Daryl's being *different*. She sincerely regretted never having the chance to meet such a special woman.

"Remind me, we need to pick up peanuts on the way home."

Blythe turned to where Daryl's attention was drawn. Virgil was seated under a tree, his wings at rest around him, sharing peanuts and birdseed for the park's resident wildlife. If anyone looked up from their busy pace as they bustled through the park it would just seem that the squirrels and birds had found something of interest at the base of the tree. To Blythe's eyes, the animals and birds were having a picnic with an angel as their host.

"Why doesn't he get grass stains on his white suit?" Blythe asked.

"I've no clue. You know, I really think he likes the squirrels best of all. I'd have thought he'd feel more of an affinity with the birds, him having wings and such."

"He loves all God's creatures and they love him." Blythe drew Daryl down to sit with her on a nearby bench. She enjoyed a moment in the warm sun watching Daryl's angelic partner playing in the park with the wildlife. It made for a very surreal moment. Blythe was getting used to them.

"I'm really looking forward to marrying you again," Daryl said. "Some days, when I think about it, I just want to run to the roof of the DDU building and shout my damn fool head off up there about how lucky I am."

Blythe couldn't think her heart could contain just how much she loved Daryl. She took Daryl's face in her hands and kissed her soundly. "I love you so much. You are just too sweet for words."

"Oh, honey, I ain't sweet," Daryl drawled, mimicking the tone that Blythe usually reserved for when she had naughty, sex-filled intentions.

Blythe kissed her again. "You're my sweetheart and I love you, Daryl Chandler-Kent."

"I do like the sound of that. Have since the first time I heard it too." She captured Blythe's lips and didn't pull back until both of them needed to breathe. "I love—" Her words stilled as her attention was captured by something somewhere over Blythe's shoulder.

Blythe stayed still, watching Daryl's pale eyes focus intently.

"There's a demon glittering behind us."

Nonchalantly, Blythe turned around enough to look over her shoulder. "Ooh, a sparkly yellow demon at one o'clock." She could see the shimmer around a man who was furtively picking his way around the park. He was purposely avoiding any contact with the *real* humans in his path.

Daryl spoke Virgil's name just above a whisper. He finished his impromptu picnic with the critters and appeared by Daryl's side. "You need to check in with whoever is on demon watch today. Tell them there's a Class C demon in Central Park. He's easy to spot. He's the idiot who decided that to blend in he needed to badly resemble George Clooney."

"That's why he's a Class C. It obviously stands for clueless in his case," Blythe murmured. She watched Virgil disappear from sight and then just as quickly there was an angel presence following in Clooney's footsteps, marking him for banishment.

Virgil reappeared, nodded toward Daryl and Blythe, and headed back toward his party guests.

Blythe rested her head on Daryl's shoulder and smiled as Daryl hugged her close. "So this is how it's going to be, is it? Constant interruptions to our daily lives by demons, banishments, and paperwork for our real cases?"

Daryl nodded, her chin brushing the top of Blythe's head. "It wasn't the life I expected for us."

"But it will never be boring," Blythe replied. "And we'll be in it together. It's what couples do; they share."

"Not everyone shares demon knowledge or has angels who pop in for friendly visits."

"I know neither of us exactly signed up for this. But you live among angels, my love. It's a part of what makes you the woman I adore."

Daryl sighed and pulled Blythe even closer to her. "I'm forever grateful you came in on my case with me. I can't imagine my life without you now."

"And you won't have to. We're going to get married one day and live happily ever after, solving cases with the DDU, and setting up demons to be banished back to hell."

"Gee, when you put it like that it just sounds so romantic."

Blythe reached for Daryl's hand and played with the wedding band on her finger, just like the one still on Blythe's. Neither had wanted them removed until they exchanged their vows for real. "Just think how fantastic our wedding is going to be. I'm going to wow you with a beautiful wedding dress that I haven't picked out yet. You are going to look so handsome in a new suit that you'll no doubt wait until the last minute to get. And then there's your best man who will truly outshine the whole wedding party!"

Daryl's laughter warmed Blythe's heart.

"But yours will be the only heavenly body I'll have my eyes on." Blythe stood, tugging Daryl up after her. "Gather your angel, darling. We're going home to practice the honeymoon before Lake calls us back to the office."

Daryl let out a soft whoop and waved to signal Virgil that they were leaving. "Lead the way, Agent Kent."

"Or maybe *you* could lead. I'm always open to suggestions." Blythe waggled her eyebrows suggestively at her, enjoying the familiar flush of redness that colored Daryl's face.

"Best decision of my life to bring my case to the DDU," Daryl said, hurrying her step, pulling Blythe along with her out of the park.

"You're a sweet talker, Chandler, but I need that tongue of yours put to a better use. So employ that famed finding skill of yours to get us a cab home. Unlike your angel here, you and I aren't blessed with wings to spirit us back faster to celebrate our anniversary in style."

As soon as Daryl's feet hit the sidewalk, she whistled for a cab. "Let's go home, Blythe."

Blythe grinned at her, giddy in the moment of being madly in love and being able to act on it. "Yes, home and straight to bed. After all, you and I do all our best work together undercover."

The End

About the Author

Lesley Davis lives in the West Midlands of England. She is a die-hard science fiction/fantasy fan in all its forms and an extremely passionate gamer. When her Nintendo 3DS is out of her grasp, Lesley is to be found on her laptop writing.

Her book, *Dark Wings Descending*, was a finalist in the Lambda Literary Awards for Best Lesbian Romance 2013

Visit her online at www.lesleydavisauthor.co.uk.

Books Available from Bold Strokes Books

First Love by CJ Harte. Finding true love is hard enough, but for Jordan Thompson, daughter of a conservative president, it's challenging, especially when that love is a female rodeo cowgirl. (978-1-60282-949-7)

Pale Wings Protecting by Lesley Davis. Posing as a couple to investigate the abduction of infants, Special Agent Blythe Kent and Detective Daryl Chandler find themselves drawn into a battle over the innocents, with demons on one side and the unlikeliest of protectors on the other. (978-1-60282-964-0)

Mounting Danger by Karis Walsh. Sergeant Rachel Bryce, an outcast on the police force, is put in charge of the department's newly formed mounted division. Can she and polo champion Callan Lanford resist their growing attraction as they struggle to safeguard the disaster-prone unit? (978-1-60282-951-0)

Meeting Chance by Jennifer Lavoie. When man's best friend turns on Aaron Cassidy, the teen keeps his distance until fate puts Chance in his hands. (978-1-60282-952-7)

At Her Feet by Rebekah Weatherspoon. Digital marketing producer Suzanne Kim knows she has found the perfect love in her new mistress Pilar, but before they can make the ultimate commitment, Suzanne's professional life threatens to disrupt their perfectly balanced bliss. (978-1-60282-948-0)

Show of Force by AJ Quinn. A chance meeting between navy pilot Evan Kane and correspondent Tate McKenna takes them on a roller-coaster ride where the stakes are high, but the reward is higher: a chance at love. (978-1-60282-942-8)

Clean Slate by Andrea Bramhall. Can Erin and Morgan work through their individual demons to rediscover their love for each other, or are the unexplainable wounds too deep to heal? (978-1-60282-943-5)

Hold Me Forever by D. Jackson Leigh. An investigation into illegal cloning in the quarter horse racing industry threatens to destroy the growing attraction between Georgia debutante Mae St. John and Louisiana horse trainer Whit Casey. (978-1-60282-944-2)

Trusting Tomorrow by PJ Trebelhorn. Funeral director Logan Swift thinks she's perfectly happy with her solitary life devoted to helping others cope with loss until Brooke Collier moves in next door to care for her elderly grandparents. (978-1-60282-891-9)

Forsaking All Others by Kathleen Knowles. What if what you think you want is the opposite of what makes you happy? (978-1-60282-892-6)

Exit Wounds by VK Powell. When Officer Loane Landry falls in love with ATF informant Abigail Mancuso, she realizes that nothing is as it seems—not the case, not her lover, not even the dead. (978-1-60282-893-3)

Dirty Power by Ashley Bartlett. Cooper's been through hell and back, and she's still broke and on the run. But at least she found the twins. They'll keep her alive. Right? (978-1-60282-896-4)

The Rarest Rose by I. Beacham. After a decade of living in her beloved house, Ele disturbs its past and finds her life being haunted by the presence of a ghost who will show her that true love never dies. (978-1-60282-884-1)

Code of Honor by Radclyffe. The face of terror is hard to recognize—especially when it's homegrown. The next book in the Honor series. (978-1-60282-885-8)

Does She Love You? by Rachel Spangler. When Annabelle and Davis find out they are both in a relationship with the same woman, it leaves them facing life-altering questions about trust, redemption, and the possibility of finding love in the wake of betrayal. (978-1-60282-886-5)

The Road to Her by KE Payne. Sparks fly when actress Holly Croft, star of UK soap Portobello Road, meets her new on-screen love interest, the enigmatic and sexy Elise Manford. (978-1-60282-887-2)

Shadows of Something Real by Sophia Kell Hagin. Trying to escape flashbacks and nightmares, ex-POW Jamie Gwynmorgan stumbles into the heart of former Red Cross worker Adele Sabellius and uncovers a deadly conspiracy against everything and everyone she loves. (978-1-60282-889-6)

Date with Destiny by Mason Dixon. When sophisticated bank executive Rashida Ivey meets unemployed blue collar worker Destiny Jackson, will her life ever be the same? (978-1-60282-878-0)

The Devil's Orchard by Ali Vali. Cain and Emma plan a wedding before the birth of their third child while Juan Luis is still lurking, and as Cain plans for his death, an unexpected visitor arrives and challenges her belief in her father, Dalton Casey. (978-1-60282-879-7)

Secrets and Shadows by L.T. Marie. A bodyguard and the woman she protects run from a madman and into each other's arms. (978-1-60282-880-3)

Change Horizons: Three Novellas by Gun Brooke. Three stories of courageous women who dare to love as they fight to claim a future in a hostile universe. (978-1-60282-881-0)

Scarlet Thirst by Crin Claxton. When hot, feisty Rani meets cool, vampire Rob, one lifetime isn't enough, and the road from human to vampire is shorter than you think... (978-1-60282-856-8)

Battle Axe by Carsen Taite. How close is too close? Bounty hunter Luca Bennett will soon find out. (978-1-60282-871-1)

Improvisation by Karis Walsh. High school geometry teacher Jan Carroll thinks she's figured out the shape of her life and her future, until graphic artist and fiddle player Tina Nelson comes along and teaches her to improvise. (978-1-60282-872-8)

For Want of a Fiend by Barbara Ann Wright. Without her Fiendish power, can Princess Katya and her consort Starbride stop a magic-wielding madman from sparking an uprising in the kingdom of Farraday? (978-1-60282-873-5)

Broken in Soft Places by Fiona Zedde. The instant Sara Chambers meets the seductive and sinful Merille Thompson, she falls hard, but knowing the difference between love and a dangerous, all-consuming desire is just one of the lessons Sara must learn before it's too late. (978-1-60282-876-6)

Healing Hearts by Donna K. Ford. Running from tragedy, the women of Willow Springs find that with friendship, there is hope, and with love, there is everything. (978-1-60282-877-3)

Desolation Point by Cari Hunter. When a storm strands Sarah Kent in the North Cascades, Alex Pascal is determined to find her. Neither imagines the dangers they will face when a ruthless criminal begins to hunt them down. (978-1-60282-865-0)

I Remember by Julie Cannon. What happens when you can never forget the first kiss, the first touch, the first taste of lips on skin? What happens when you know you will remember every single detail of a mysterious woman? (978-1-60282-866-7)

The Gemini Deception by Kim Baldwin and Xenia Alexiou. The truth, the whole truth, and nothing but lies. Book six in the Elite Operatives series. (978-1-60282-867-4)

Scarlet Revenge by Sheri Lewis Wohl. When faith alone isn't enough, will the love of one woman be strong enough to save a vampire from damnation? (978-1-60282-868-1)

Ghost Trio by Lillian Q. Irwin. When Lee Howe hears the voice of her dead lover singing to her, is it a hallucination, a ghost, or something more sinister? (978-1-60282-869-8)

The Princess Affair by Nell Stark. Rhodes Scholar Kerry Donovan arrives at Oxford ready to focus on her studies, but her life and her priorities are thrown into chaos when she catches the eye of Her Royal Highness Princess Sasha. (978-1-60282-858-2)

The Chase by Jesse J. Thoma. When Isabelle Rochat's life is threatened, she receives the unwelcome protection and attention of bounty hunter Holt Lasher who vows to keep Isabelle safe at all costs. (978-1-60282-859-9)

The Lone Hunt by L.L. Raand. In a world where humans and praeterns conspire for the ultimate power, violence is a way of life... and death. A Midnight Hunters novel. (978-1-60282-860-5)